SHADOW OF SPAIN

SHADOW OF SPAIN

Fiona Buckley

SEVERN
HOUSE

First world edition published in Great Britain in 2021 and the USA in 2022
by Severn House, an imprint of Canongate Books Ltd,
14 High Street, Edinburgh EH1 1TE.

Trade paperback edition first published in Great Britain and the USA in 2023
by Severn House, an imprint of Canongate Books Ltd.

severnhouse.com

British Library Cataloguing-in-Publication Data
A CIP catalogue record for this title is available from the British Library.

ISBN-13: 978-0-7278-5086-7 (cased)
ISBN-13: 978-1-4483-0627-5 (trade paper)
ISBN-13: 978-1-4483-0626-8 (e-book)

All Severn House titles are printed on acid-free paper.

Typeset by Palimpsest Book Production Ltd.,
Falkirk, Stirlingshire, Scotland.
Printed and bound in Great Britain by
TJ Books, Padstow, Cornwall.

For Susan and Jean,
my friends for more than half a century
and also
for my cousin Godfrey,
experienced seaman and historian of the Norfolk coastline

PROLOGUE

Hertfordshire, March 1588

'Where's Watkin got to?' said Will Thomson breathlessly, dodging aside as the elm tree that he and his son were felling creaked and began to fall. 'Did ought to be here as well . . . steady . . . out of the way, young Tom!'

They both stepped back quickly as the tree crashed into the grass of the field behind them. The fall of the elm sent a flock of rooks cawing into the skies, spelling ruin to several nests and the first eggs of the season. Will, indifferent to the plight of the rooks, which regularly followed the wheat-sowers and gobbled up half the strewn seed, stepped round the great tree where it lay awaiting the mammoth business of chopping it up to provide fuel for their employer's hearth, and peered into the narrow belt of trees beyond. 'Where *is* Watkin? Thought he went into the trees for a pee but it don't take that long!'

'Here he is!' said Tom, as their missing colleague burst out of the trees. ''Bout time, too . . . Christ, what's up with him? *Watkin!* What is it?'

'Easy, boy,' said Will, as Watkin arrived beside them, ashen-faced and almost speechless. 'Watkin, lad, what's happened?'

'Murder's happened!' gasped Watkin, almost in tears. He was only eighteen, and had seen nothing worse in his life than the slaughter of a sheep, and that had been done with speed and efficiency. 'On the road! I saw it!'

Will and his son, two sturdy figures with identical flaxen heads and identical sleeveless leather jerkins, finally persuaded a shaken and reluctant Watkin to lead them back through the trees and show them what had happened.

'I were just here,' Watkin said nervously, coming to a halt in the middle of the tree belt, halfway between the field and the road that ran past the further edge of the trees. He was thinner than the other two, a skinny brown-haired youth in patched breeches and a calfskin jerkin too big for him, both of them handed down from an elder brother. He was trembling, shocked, glad to be in the company of the others. 'Just here I were, and I heard voices and one of them sounded frightened, pleading, and I didn't like it so I crept toward the road and peeped from behind that tree there, that great old oak' – he pointed – 'and there was a fellow standing holding a horse and another one on foot, facing him, with a crossbow . . .!'

His voice at that point shot up several points. 'Take your time,' said Will.

'The one with the horse . . . he was doing the shouting and pleading. I couldn't make out no words but he was pulling at his belt pouch, as if he wanted to offer money . . . but the other one was saying something but I couldn't make him out either and then . . . then . . .' Poor Watkin gulped. 'He used the crossbow. Got the fellow in the chest. He's there lying in the road. Him with the bow, he just vanished into the trees on t'other side of the track. Had a horse hidden there, maybe. I dunno what he looked like; I weren't near enough for that. The . . . the dead man's horse he just left. It's loose somewhere . . .'

He led the way. They emerged from the trees at the side of the track and halted. 'There,' said Watkin.

He had no need to point. The dead man lay on his back in the middle of the track and the bolt that had killed him jutted from his chest. Will went forward and knelt beside him. He was quite dead; the bolt had clearly struck him in the heart. Will stared at him, wondering what sort of man he was. He didn't look that young for there was some grey in his beard and there were a few lines on his face. He was dark, in a way that was not quite English. His belt pouch was open and a purse had been half-pulled from it but when Will felt the pouch, his fingers at once discovered coins, and something crackled, too, like paper.

He stood up. The others were watching him fearfully from the side of the track. A little further along, a horse with a saddle and trailing reins was grazing on the verge.

'We got to tell the master,' Will said. 'Catch that horse if you can, Tom; if you can't, get a cap full of oats from the stable store and see if that will tempt him. Watkin, come with me. We'll see the steward, and explain and he'll surely let us see Master Harman, and meantime we'll ask him to send some men out with a bier of some sort. Dear God! What a thing to happen!'

ONE

Disturbance at an Unofficial Council

It was early in 1588 that an intimate and shockingly disturbed gathering took place in the palace of St James'. It was almost exactly four years after the time when my royal half-sister Queen Elizabeth nearly lost her life at the hands of a demented Catholic called Dr William Parry. He hid in the gardens of Richmond Palace with a knife in his sleeve and when Elizabeth came out to take the air was for a few moments close enough to her to kill. And might well have killed her except that, according to Parry when he was arrested, he was so daunted by her majestic presence, which had reminded him powerfully of her father King Henry the Eighth, that he lost his nerve.

I could believe it, for in public, Elizabeth always was majestic. Of late years, she had acquired a liking for economy but it didn't apply to her gowns. Her farthingales were immense, often spanning the full width of the paths she walked on; her ruffs stood out behind her head as though they were there to shield it. Ropes of pearls, emerald or ruby pendants, diamond earrings set her glittering in even the cloudiest light. Elizabeth in her majesty was a daunting sight. If she was coming towards you, you felt as though you stood in the path of an oncoming and possibly vengeful goddess.

But even Elizabeth couldn't maintain such a presence for every hour of every day. Alone with her ladies, she would put off her mighty farthingales and ruffs, don loose robes and velvet slippers, and become like any other rather tired woman in middle years. When I attended at court, which I did once or twice a year, I was among her bedchamber ladies and I saw her like that many times.

There were other occasions, though, when she would don a dignified but less intimidating mode of dress, with moderate farthingales and ruffs, in order to talk informally with her closest associates in the business of ruling the realm. These little gatherings usually took place at times when there was much business on hand. They were unofficial and informal in style but they were recognized as useful. For one thing, they were a way of helping Sir Francis Walsingham, who was Elizabeth's Secretary of State, and Sir William Cecil, otherwise Lord Burghley, the Lord Treasurer, to assemble the agenda for the next full Council meeting.

The gathering at St James' Palace in the March of 1588 was just such an event. I had rarely seen St James' before, although Elizabeth was fond of it. It was small as palaces go and it was away from the Thames and the noisy shouts of bargees and ferrymen and the river smells. Its gatehouse was imposing enough, flanked by tall towers, but the slender proportions of the towers and the warm red brick of their walls had a friendly air. King Henry the Eighth, Elizabeth's and my mutual father, had had it built as a retreat from the formalities of the court, a private home where he could as it were take off his crown, put on his slippers and play with his spaniels. Elizabeth too used it as a retreat. It was a natural place for the kind of informal meeting I attended on that March day.

It wasn't, of course, informal to the point of having no guards on duty. There were guards at the door of Elizabeth's innermost suite, where we were gathered, and entrance was forbidden to anyone else. Two of her ladies were quietly sewing in a corner of the room, but they were there for propriety since so many men were present. The true members of the gathering consisted of the queen herself, Sir William Cecil, Sir Francis Walsingham, Sir Robert Dudley, otherwise the Earl of Leicester (also known as the queen's Sweet Robin), and me, Mistress Ursula Stannard. I did not know why my presence had been requested, for it was hardly usual. True, I was half-sister to Elizabeth, the result of an adventure on the part of King Henry during Queen Anne Boleyn's decline. I was also one of Her Majesty's secret agents. Elizabeth sometimes did ask my opinion on this or that. We were of one blood; we had a rapport. But she usually did that in private. I was female, not a candidate for a seat on the Council. Now, I was nervous.

Elizabeth had a throne-like seat, of course, set upon a dais. She was still the queen and the hands that lay in the lap of her semi-formal gown were clasped over a small jewelled gavel. The rest of us were seated in ordinary settles or in my case on one of the steps up to her dais. Like the queen, I was in semi-formal dress and I remember that my stays were sticking into me. With the years, my midriff had thickened somewhat. I was no longer the lithe being that I used to be, though there was no grey as yet in my dark hair, and no dullness in my eyes, which remained their own clear hazel.

In a way, we were an ill-assorted company. Robin Dudley wasn't much liked by the others. He had been Elizabeth's favourite for too long and at one time had tainted her with scandal. He was still handsome, though of late years he had put on weight and had his doublets cut to conceal his bulging stomach. Walsingham and Cecil were eyeing him askance, just as they always had, and of us all, he was probably the least well informed about the subject in hand.

Walsingham, so dark of hair, eye and skin that the queen called him her Old Moor, was as usual dressed in black from head to foot. Unlike Robin, he was far from being a favourite. In fact, Elizabeth disliked him so much that she had at times thrown things at him. But she also trusted him, as much as anything because her gravest enemies were the Catholics, who regarded her as illegitimate and therefore a usurper on the throne, while Walsingham was a Puritan who detested the Catholics and what he called their flamboyant Popish rites. He saw them as a threat not only to Elizabeth but to all England. What he really thought of Elizabeth herself, no one knew.

I knew what he thought of me, though. He disapproved of me because he didn't consider that a woman ought to be a secret agent. He had however often found me useful and being both ruthless and pragmatic he hadn't scrupled to use me, even if it meant sending me into danger. Though on these occasions, he usually implored me not to take risks. I think I annoyed him as much as anything because he couldn't help worrying about me. When I came into the room behind the queen, and he realized that I was not there just to play propriety, he positively glowered at me.

I think Cecil had been told beforehand that I would be there, for he smiled as I came in. It was Cecil, I am sure, who was the rampart at Elizabeth's back. She did not love him, nor did she dislike him. But she relied on him always to be there, with her best interests at heart, and he had never failed her.

We were here because the next Council agenda would have to deal with alarming matters and there was a curious reluctance to begin. I think we all shared a feeling that to talk openly about certain things was to make them real – as though they weren't in fact entirely real and desperately dangerous. I know I felt like that, anyway, and I had few responsibilities compared to the others.

The proceedings therefore began in a mannerly fashion, with refreshments. There were small tables dotted about, laden with goblets, jugs of Canary wine, dishes of raisins dusted with nutmeg and cinnamon, platters of small almond cakes, gingerbread biscuits and slices of cold meat pie. But on the table nearest to Cecil there was a businesslike leather folder, and on top of it lay a pair of eyeglasses. Cecil, like all of us, was growing older. While we nibbled the refreshments, sipped the wine and talked of anodyne things, we all kept stealing glances at the folder and the eyeglasses.

It was a beautiful day. Beyond the windows, birds were winging across a blue sky and though the trees were still bare, the leaf buds were bulging, subtly changing the shapes of their parent twigs. So we began by enjoying the pie and the biscuits, licking cinnamon and nutmeg dust off our fingers and talking about the warmth of the sun, the fine display of crocuses in the grounds and the like.

What lay behind these platitudes was the unspoken knowledge that it was little more than a year since the queen's cousin, Mary Stuart, formerly queen of Scotland, had been beheaded in the great hall of Fotheringhay Castle. It had been necessary, but we all knew that under Elizabeth's dignified surface lay both guilt and anger. The final decision had been taken without her knowledge or consent. Walsingham had decided to act without them. It was another reason for being careful what we said.

The queen eventually called us to order. Abruptly, just as

Cecil finished making a harmless comment about spring flowers, she lifted her gavel and rapped on the arm of her chair. We all turned towards her.

'Enough pleasantries,' she said. 'We are an informal meeting but we are a meeting just the same.' She was using the royal *we* which indicated that she meant business. She said: 'We have no doubt that there is an unwritten agenda in Sir Francis' head. However, before we begin, there is something that we wish to know, that Mistress Stannard here can perhaps tell us. That is why she is present. Ursula, of all of us here, you are closest to the common people. You are the mistress of two good houses, Hawkswood and Withysham, and you are also the owner and leaseholder of a third, by name Evergreens. You personally employ or dismiss your servants; you personally inspect their work; you regard your two closest servants, Roger and Frances Brockley, as friends and they dine at your table.

'You visit markets in person; you decide what is to be bought for your household and what produce of your farms should be sold. Everyone in the land must of course know by now that we are threatened with an invasion from Spain. They could hardly not know, with the hammers ringing like tolling bells in every shipyard, with commanders seeking volunteers for our army and our navy, with every seagoing merchant coming home full of foreign gossip and spreading it about in every market he attends. So we have had the danger proclaimed publicly and warned our people to prepare themselves, to be ready to fight. Ursula, tell us, what do our people feel? Are most of them afraid or are most of them angry? When they gather in taverns what do they say to each other about this situation? Are many of them planning to abandon their homes and flee to the hills of Wales or Scotland? No, don't stand up. Stay where you are, and say what you know.'

I quaked. It was a huge, all-encompassing question to which I could only offer limited answers. I cleared my throat but then, because she – and indeed all the others – were waiting expectantly, I did my best.

'Majesty, I know only what I have seen and heard in Surrey

and Sussex, where my houses are,' I said. 'I haven't heard of anyone wanting to run away from their homes. I think . . . my own households are awaiting instructions from me. They know about the danger from Spain, of course. They have heard the criers in Guildford and Woking and Chichester. Those who serve me are good, honest English folk, ma'am. Already, a number of the younger men from the villages near to my three houses have gone to volunteer as soldiers or sailors. People are angry, I think – angry that the king of Spain should so outrageously plan to attack us and destroy our peace. But there is fear too – fear for our religion, fear of what would happen to it if the Spaniards got into England, fear of a marauding army, especially among the women. There is talk of beacons being built on the hilltops and they know what it will mean if those beacons are lit. They can see their whole world being torn apart. What more can I say?' I asked. 'If it comes to it, I am sure our people will fight, ma'am, and fight well. They know they have reason!'

Walsingham said: 'Have you sensed any sympathy with the Catholic cause?'

'Not here in the south,' I said. 'In the north, it may be different but I know little of northern England. I have only one Catholic in my employment and he has no more wish to see his world turned topsy-turvy than anyone else.'

'You have one in your *employment*?' Walsingham exuded disapproval.

'He serves me well, Sir Francis. He is my assistant cook. He is good at his job. You have visited my home and you have eaten his dishes.'

'She means that he didn't put belladonna in your fruit pie,' said Dudley, and thereby raised a laugh from them all.

'Enough,' said Elizabeth. 'Ursula, you have done your best. Be easy, now. Sir Francis, what is the first item in your informal agenda?'

Walsingham gave me one final, fulminating glance and then said: 'The first item is to report on and discuss the negotiations with the Duke of Parma. At the moment . . . yes. My lord of Leicester?'

'Which negotiations?' asked Dudley. 'The official ones or

the real ones? I am aware that both exist, but as yet I don't know many details.'

'The official ones aren't proceeding at all; nor are they meant to,' said Cecil. He had a long face, with a thin fair beard that he stroked when he was worried, and a deep crease between his brows. He was worried very often and rarely smiled. But when he did smile, it often had a disconcerting touch of mischief or even wickedness about it. He was smiling like that now.

'The full details of our dealings with Parma are known only to a few,' he said. 'Though you should of course have been one of those who knew and I am sorry that by chance you have not been informed, my lord. They have never been discussed in a full council.' He was clearly pleased that the queen's Sweet Robin had been put at a disadvantage.

Elizabeth gave him a sharp glance and then intervened. 'The decisions about negotiations with the Netherlands were taken by us. We took care that they were known to as few people as possible. We first began to consider them while you, Robin, were still in the Netherlands, trying to help the Protestant rebellion there.'

'It was and is vital,' said Cecil, 'that the details should have no chance to leak out and get to Philip's ears. However, we need to speak of them here. I will fill in the gaps for you, Leicester. The talks that are taking place in Ostend are the standard peace talks that Philip will expect us to hold with Parma's representatives. He will expect us to be alarmed by his preparations and worried because just across the North Sea lie the Netherlands, which are under Spanish control. In all probability, he will take it for granted that we will make panicky attempts to persuade his nephew the Duke of Parma, who is at the moment running the Netherlands for him, not to assist any Spanish invasion. He will be amused at the thought of us offering inducements and Parma, perhaps, continually asking for just one concession more while smiling within his beard and staying on his uncle's side all the time.'

'Our negotiators,' said Walsingham, taking up the tale with an air of satisfaction, 'will probably still be in Ostend in March next year. Old Sir James Croft is our principal delegate. He is doddery with age and has instructions to dodder to the point of idiocy if necessary, while my Lord Burghley here has selected the two most pompous learned doctors he could find, and has instructed them to waste as much time as they can by lecturing all the negotiators in Latin. We are offering certain inducements, of course. But meanwhile, the secret negotiations, which are the real ones and the ones we intend to talk about here and now, include different inducements and Parma seems to be genuinely interested. It's a delicate business. We have our fish on the line and hope to keep him there.' With feeling, he added: 'It is maddening, *maddening*, to have the Netherlands, only just across the North Sea from us, still in Spanish hands. If only that Dutch rebellion had succeeded!'

At this point, he glared at Dudley, who looked appropriately grave and observed: 'I got a bloody nose in the Netherlands and I regretfully admit it. The rebellion has now faltered and faded. Leaving Philip, as he supposes, with a good second string in the Low Countries. That Scottish queen,' he added vindictively, 'is as much trouble dead as she was when she was alive.'

'Unfortunately true,' said Walsingham. 'When she was alive she tried her utmost to get in touch with Philip, hoping to coax him into mounting a campaign to put her on the English throne. Now she is dead and he wants to avenge her. Mercifully, the Duke of Parma seems to be a man of common sense, even if he is King Philip's nephew. He has stopped Philip's original policy of trying to convert the Dutch Protestants by force and the indications are that he has no stomach for war with us. Though according to the agents who work in the Netherlands, the rebellion caused him to raise a large and well-trained army. Therefore, we have no stomach for war with him, either! Hence our clandestine approaches to him.'

'But just what are we offering?' Dudley enquired.

'Final decisions about that have not yet been taken,' said Elizabeth. 'They will have to be discussed in a full Council meeting. They are likely to involve sums of money that will deplete our treasury, trade concessions that will irritate our merchants, and of course, promises not to intervene on the side of any future Protestant rebellions in his territory. As yet, no details have been spelt out to Parma. We have merely hinted. Bait for our big fish,' said Elizabeth. 'However, our first approach did indeed meet with cautious interest. We are now waiting to hear what Parma has to offer on his side. Walsingham, what is the matter with you?'

Walsingham was moving uneasily in the corner of his settle. He had a long-standing bowel problem and very often had to interrupt council meetings while he fled to the privy. He now begged the queen's pardon and left the room, trying to walk with dignity though I could see that he found it difficult.

I bridged the embarrassing moment by remarking: 'I knew nothing of the secret correspondence till now but I am impressed. It sounds as though it's proceeding quite fast.'

'We foresaw the need for it,' said Elizabeth. 'We sent Magpie to Brussels to make the initial approach back in October.'

'And it was a wise move,' Cecil agreed. 'It was Magpie, in fact, who brought back the first news that Philip really is assembling an invasion fleet. He picked that up in Brussels. Sir Francis Drake is now on his way to try and wreck the Spanish fleet while it's still in port. I believe that that is item two on our unwritten agenda. The announcement that he has sailed.'

He mentioned the name of Sir Francis Drake with some respect. Drake was an eminent seaman and explorer, with a reputation both for competence and ruthlessness. He had always protected Elizabeth's interests but I knew that he had taken many innocent lives in the process and from what I had heard, he had never even tried to do otherwise. I hadn't met him and from what I had heard of him, I didn't particularly want to. But in our present circumstances, I could see that he might well be the man for the hour.

Dudley was frowning. 'Why are there all these codenames? I can never see the point of calling our agents things like Magpie, or – what's that other one, Pigeon. It's an absurdity. What is amusing you, Ursula?'

'I used to own a horse called Magpie,' I said. 'A weight carrier, for the benefit of my very large chief cook John Hawthorn. But Hawthorn has given up riding now, and I sold Magpie a year ago. He went to a good home.'

Everyone smiled at me indulgently. I was known for my sentimental attitudes towards my horses. It was my habit, whenever it was possible, to go to the stable and say goodnight to my fine bay gelding, Jaunty. Dudley's smile was friendly, though. He had once been the queen's Master of Horse and he understood.

I was wondering who Pigeon might be but had no opportunity to ask. Cecil had turned to Dudley and was somewhat irritably explaining the codenames.

'We use those names because if we want to mention them anywhere where we might be overheard by the wrong people, we can do so without giving away any identities. Here in private we can use their real names if we like. Magpie is called that because he has a real gift for picking up useful odds and ends. He was the one who warned us that Spain was shipping weaponry from Hamburg and other places, and taking it round the north of England and down through the Irish Sea, because the North Sea is too well watched. It was clear evidence that Philip of Spain was laying plans against us. It was through finding out about that, that he realized that Philip was probably preparing an invasion fleet. Then he confirmed his suspicions by, as I said, picking up odds and ends.'

'We were able to intercept the whole consignment,' said Elizabeth. 'Most satisfactory.'

'Magpie's real name,' said Cecil, 'is Juan Smith. Spanish mother, English father. Catholic. Born in England but his mother took him to Spain when his father died. He trained as a priest in that wretched seminary in Rheims where they spawn the Jesuits and he came over as a Jesuit to look for converts. We caught him and turned him. I think he was glad to be turned; he spent his early childhood in England and I believe his heart was with us all the time.'

With sudden savagery, Elizabeth said: 'Philip is obsessed with religion. He doesn't only want to conquer England because of Mary; he wants to conquer it in the name of God. His God.'

Walsingham re-joined us, with a visible air of relief about him, and did so in time to catch Elizabeth's remark about obsession. Resuming his place on the settle, he said: 'Some of Philip's more imaginative spies have been telling him that the English Catholics are in the majority and ready to rise and support him if he invaded. Mad enthusiasts!' He was contemptuous. 'Our agents have been trying to inform him of the opposite. It's a piquant situation. They usually have the task of giving him inaccurate information. But that, for once, is the truth.'

'And it's true because I have never allowed you to persecute them as you wanted me to,' Elizabeth said. Her tone now was mild, but her words were pointed. 'If they keep quiet and pay their fines for not attending our church services, I am content to let them be, and in return I think most of them, like Ursula's Catholic cook, would rather stay quiet and safe than risk the perils of treason, in spite of Pope Pius' disgraceful instruction to them to disobey my laws and assassinate me if they get the chance. Except for wantwits like William Parry, of course.'

There was a little laughter and a pause, while we all once more reached for the refreshments. I wondered, not for the first time, at the twists of fate that had brought me here, eating chicken pie and drinking wine in this exalted company.

My young mother, Cecily Faldene, had been a lady-in-waiting to Queen Anne Boleyn and had left the court in disgrace, carrying a child whose father she would not name. She took refuge with her brother, my uncle Herbert Faldene, and his wife, whom I knew as Aunt Tabitha. They sheltered her, mainly, I think because Thomas Faldene, my kind grandfather, was still alive, and living with them. He insisted. And so they took her in, disapprovingly and none too kindly, but still, she had a home and in due time so had I. I was often harshly treated but nevertheless I was clothed and fed and – because my grandfather insisted – allowed to share my cousins' tutor. When I was ten years old, my grandfather died, but he had left his wishes concerning me in writing and they were respected. My uncle and aunt continued to shelter us.

When I was sixteen, my mother also died. And when I was twenty, I eloped with Gerald Blanchard, who was supposed to be betrothed to my cousin Mary.

We were happy. Gerald was employed by Sir Thomas Gresham, who worked in Antwerp, raising funds for Elizabeth's coffers. We had security and position. Our daughter Meg was born. Then Gerald died of smallpox. He had been good at finding sources of money, but not at saving his own. I found myself poorly provided for, except that Gresham stepped in. It was through him that I was able to get a post as a lady-in-waiting to the young queen. But my stipend wasn't enough, not to dress as a lady-in-waiting was supposed to dress, or to support my daughter and her nurse. To earn extra money, I undertook my first secret mission.

Others followed. There came a time when I didn't want to go on with such a way of life but then I found out who my father was. I was Elizabeth's half-sister. From then on, there was a bond between us, and when asked to undertake any mission, I always knew that although Walsingham or Cecil might have given the orders, they really came from her and were for her, and I could not say no.

Elizabeth had allowed the pause and had been sipping wine herself, but now she set down her goblet and wiped her lips with a napkin. As she moved, there was a flicker of reflected sunlight from her gown. Today she was not dressed to intimidate, but nevertheless, her black velvet gown was scattered with silver embroidery and its open front revealed a kirtle of silver satin. She had a silver ornament in her elaborately arranged red hair, and she wore a rope of pearls and matching earrings. She glittered, intentionally, with the trappings of power.

But as she cleared her throat, about to resume the business of the gathering, I found myself seeing through the armour of velvet and silver, to the woman within. Perhaps because we were related, I had experienced this even before I knew that we were sisters. Such moments came to me as easily when she was in her full regalia of huge skirts and wagon-wheel ruffs as when she was in her night-rail. This time, I knew that within that sparkling carapace, her body was tired, because the years were piling up, and so were her burdens. Not just the weight of her regret for Mary's death, but the greater burden of reigning, of being responsible for keeping England safe and solvent, of keeping Philip of Spain at bay.

But Elizabeth wouldn't thank me for my compassion. I must

keep it unspoken. She was now saying, in tones both clear and precise, that if Drake should fail to crush the fleet that Philip, we understood, was calling his Armada, while it was still in its lair, the Lord High Admiral, Charles Howard, Earl of Nottingham, was laying detailed plans for resisting an attempt at invasion.

'The Lord High Admiral is determined,' said Elizabeth, 'that an attempt at an invasion is all it will amount to. He proposes . . . Master Cecil? You have the latest details. This, I think, is item three and will be a major item on the agenda for the full Council. It is our wish that we should all know of his suggestions.'

Cecil reached for his eyeglasses, put them on his nose, and picked up the folder. He drew out a sheet of paper. 'He proposes to have a strong force at Plymouth, preferably under Sir Francis Drake. Drake will be back in England fast enough if his efforts in Spanish waters fail and our coasts are threatened. Lord Howard is equipping an additional force and will add it to the Plymouth fleet. Plymouth is a likely first target for Philip; it's the first principal port that his Armada will come to. But Sir Henry Palmer will have a squadron of ships at Dover, to guard the strait and the sea to the north, in case Parma lets us down and really does send shiploads of soldiers from the Netherlands in the hope of linking up with the Spanish shiploads. We'll do our best to make sure that if he does try, he can't. There will also be sixteen big and well-armed vessels in the Thames, to prevent any attempt either by Philip or Parma to attack London that way. Every effort is being made to ensure that we shall have enough ships.'

'Ah,' said Elizabeth. 'Things have moved on since the last Council meeting. I hadn't heard about Lord Howard's extra ships before.' She had dropped the royal *we*, I noticed. The formality was slackening a little. This often happened on these occasions. They would warm, gradually, into an awareness that all those present were friends.

Walsingham said: 'It would be useful to know what Philip's plan of battle is. How many vessels is he planning to launch, of what types, and how does he intend to deploy them? We ought to brief one of our agents to discover these details if he can. Do you agree, your majesty?'

'Yes, I do. Who do you suggest we should send?'

Inside myself, I froze. *Not me!* I begged, in a silent plea to Elizabeth, Cecil, Walsingham, Fate and Almighty God. *Is this the real reason why I was invited to join this meeting? But I don't want to go to the Netherlands, into enemy territory to do the impossible! Does Walsingham want to suggest me? My sister, please not, please . . .!*

And Walsingham *was* looking at me. There was no doubt about it. I felt my heart turn to a lump of lead and sink into my shoes. I saw Elizabeth glancing at him and then at me. He turned to her in a questioning manner and then, thankfully, I saw her shake her head at him. I muffled a gasp of relief as she said: 'It will need an agent of considerable experience. It could be a difficult task. Magpie might be the man.'

Again, I spoke inside my head, this time saying, *God be thanked.* Elizabeth was saying: 'We should certainly try to find out. That's precisely the kind of information . . . God's teeth! I said there were to be no interruptions! What's *that*?'

Someone was knocking, quite forcefully, on the door. 'Oh, open it!' barked the queen and as I was nearest to it, I obeyed the order. I found a dishevelled individual outside, smelling so strongly of horse that I almost reeled back. He must have got out of the saddle only minutes before.

He said: 'I have a letter for my Lord Burghley, from Master Browning, steward of Theobalds, his Hertfordshire estate.' He sounded breathless. 'I was told it was of great import. Master Browning said I was to give a password, Full Moon, and it would bring me to my Lord Burghley's presence no matter where he was, no matter what hour of the day or night. Please . . .!'

'Admit him!' Elizabeth snapped.

I stood back and the messenger ran in. He wavered, looking from face to face, bowing to the queen but clearly not knowing which one was Burghley, until Cecil beckoned to him. Then he ran to kneel at Cecil's feet, pulled a little scroll out of his belt pouch, and held it out.

Cecil took it, broke the seal and unrolled the scroll. It seemed to be two scrolls, one inside the other. He read the outer one first and then looked up, gathering our eyes. His face was hard. 'That melodramatic password was only for use in case of dire need. Browning clearly thought that this was such a case and I agree with him. Magpie was on his way with Parma's latest response to us. Mercifully, the letter he carried has reached us but not by Magpie's hand. He was stopped on the way. Whoever stopped him fortunately had no opportunity to search him; that is why Parma's letter has come to us unharmed. Magpie himself is dead. He was murdered.'

TWO

The Last Resort

'What happened?' Elizabeth demanded. 'And how did it happen?'

'Juan Smith travels to and fro between us and the Netherlands,' said Cecil. 'When he was coming to us, he didn't always use the same route. Sometimes he came straight to the court or to my London house, or else he might avoid them both and go instead to Theobalds and hand whatever message he was carrying to my steward, Browning. Browning is in my confidence. He would see that it reached me, wherever I chanced to be. For Smith, varying the route was meant to confuse anyone who was following him, perhaps make them think that he was an innocent traveller after all. In England, if anyone asked him his business, he would pretend to be a clerk, carrying letters about Church affairs.'

He paused to consult one of the two scrolls again. Then he said: 'This time he evidently intended to pass his message on to Browning, for he was apparently stopped when he was on the right road for Theobalds. He was on a road leading past Longwood Farm, which belongs to Theobalds. There, he was accosted and shot dead with a crossbow.'

'Who found him?' said Dudley.

'It seems that a man working for Longwood's tenant, Master Harman, became aware of some kind of argument going on, on the road bordering the farm. He went to see what was happening. He actually witnessed the shooting and ran away to fetch the other men he was working with. It seems that he was only a lad and was very frightened. Two other farmhands went with him and found our man lying in the road with the crossbow bolt through his chest. They had the body brought to the farmhouse. Master Harman recognized him as Juan Smith, a man who had stopped at Longwood twice in the past, once because his horse was lame and he wanted to borrow a fresh mount, which the Harmans were able to provide, and a second time, because Mistress Harman had given him such pleasant refreshments the first time! Harman knows nothing of Smith's – that is, Magpie's – business but he realized that Smith was very likely going to Theobalds and sent word accordingly. Browning has taken charge of the body and the letters he was carrying, and despatched this man' – he nodded at the kneeling messenger – 'equipped with my password, to find me.'

'What's in that other scroll?' Walsingham asked sharply.

Cecil, clearly shaken, was still holding it but seemed to have forgotten it. He scanned it quickly, and then looked up and with obvious pleasure said: 'This is the report we've been waiting for. It's from Parma – it has details of the way he proposes to appear to make a seagoing fleet ready without actually doing so. I fancy that whoever killed Magpie must have heard the farmhand coming and so he lost his chance to search his victim. On your feet, man!' Cecil held out a hand to help the messenger up. 'You've done well; so has Browning. The message Juan was bringing hasn't been lost. We've lost Magpie. But it could have been worse.'

'Very much worse,' Elizabeth agreed. 'Give the man some wine, Cecil. Ursula, give orders about his accommodation and food until he and his horse are fit for the ride home. We will adjourn this meeting. We have clarified matters sufficiently, I think. My Lord Cecil, kindly prepare an agenda for the next full Council and bring it to me for my approval. Walsingham, we will need a replacement for Magpie. That is urgent.'

'Pigeon,' said Walsingham shortly. 'He's been trotting to and fro, feeding inaccurate information to Parma, so that Parma can repeat it to Philip. He can take this on as well.'

'Who *is* Pigeon?' Dudley asked.

'Another spy that we turned,' said Walsingham. 'He loves his English homeland more than he loves his religion. Torn between them, just as Smith was; an unhappy state of affairs for them but useful for us. That's all you need to know. Ursula . . .'

I was already on my feet. I left at once to carry out my orders.

A fortnight later, my term of duty at court came to an end and I made ready to leave for Hawkswood, my Surrey home. The day before I was to set out, Elizabeth spent the morning as she often did, practising dances with her ladies. Every court lady needed to be skilled at the latest dances. But when it was over, she beckoned to me and said commandingly: 'Follow me, Ursula.'

As always on such occasions, I received sharp looks from some of the other ladies. They all knew that I was the queen's sister but that didn't stop them from being jealous whenever she marked me out in any way. Once, this state of affairs had hurt me, but not now. I was used to it. It was just part of my awkward position in the court. The fact was that because of our kinship Elizabeth often liked to have me near her even when I served no special purpose there. I think that was essentially why I had been one of that intimate group two weeks before, for I had had precious little to contribute. Indeed, I had almost fainted with fright when, for that one dreadful moment, I thought I actually had been asked there for a purpose.

Now, Elizabeth led me away through the room where we had had that disturbed meeting, and on into a room that she used as a study, and sometimes as a private parlour. There, she took a seat, and when I hesitated, gestured me impatiently to another. 'This is no formal interview, my Ursula. So, you are going home tomorrow.'

'Yes, ma'am.' I sincerely hoped that she wasn't going to refuse to let me go.

But no. 'I shall miss you,' Elizabeth said, 'but you have your responsibilities at home. You are a widow, with no man to help you, and you have a ward to care for, I believe.' She wasn't using her royal *we*. But it was an intimacy on which I wouldn't presume.

'Mildred isn't exactly a ward,' I said carefully. 'She too is a widow now. Until her marriage, she was my companion but as she was so young – she is still only twenty – yes, I suppose that she was virtually my ward then. Her marriage ended tragically, as you know. Now, as Mistress Atbrigge, she has returned to my care. At the moment she is in charge of Hawkswood in my stead but I ought not to leave her alone too long with such a taxing task.'

'I dare say. But Ursula, if and when the Spanish Armada approaches our shores, and there is truly danger to this realm, you will be in danger too.'

'Everyone in the country will be that, surely, ma'am.'

'Call me sister. Ursula, you *are* my sister. It means much to me, as you know. But it could also mean much to others. You must understand that I have spies in Spain, including a particularly good one, Sir Anthony Standen, who has wormed his way right into the Spanish court. According to him, if Philip invades, it won't be for the purpose of throwing me off my throne and taking it himself; he has enough on his hands, ruling Spain and trying to hold on to the Netherlands. But in return for leaving me on my throne, he will try to make me accept his peace terms and I now know what they will – would – be.'

Her face was drawn. I looked at her, with love and also with concern. Elizabeth had a shield-shaped face, and a shield is precisely what it was. Behind that still, pale, pointed countenance, and the golden-brown eyes that were so inexpressive, she hid her thoughts, her feelings and her fears. But once more, I found myself able to see beyond it. Elizabeth was weary and afraid and dared not reveal it to any.

She must not guess that I had seen it. I waited, as inexpressive as Elizabeth herself, and at length, she said dryly: 'One of the terms he wants would be easy enough. He would want me to stop interfering in the Netherlands. After my Robin's sorry debacle there, I won't be able to afford to go on supporting the Dutch Protestants anyway. If they rebel again, they will be on their own. In fact, that's one of the inducements I am offering to the Duke of Parma! Even my imitation delegates at Ostend will have to discuss it. It is a demand that Philip and Parma alike are bound to insist on. Well, I could meet it. I am already meeting it, in fact, whether I like it or not. But there would be another. To cease what he calls the persecution of Catholics in England. Walsingham complains because he doesn't consider that it is persecution but Philip thinks otherwise. He would want me to allow them to follow their religion without paying fines and to let Jesuit priests roam the country, seeking converts. I know what that would mean. So do you, I fancy.'

'It means,' I said, 'that after a while, when he felt that the Catholic faith had become widespread enough in England, had become, well, normal enough, the Inquisition would be brought in.'

'Yes.' Elizabeth's voice was that of someone controlling pain. 'It's the same gradual policy that Parma is now using in the Netherlands. Philip's original policy there was too heavy-handed and caused the rebellion. Philip apparently learned lessons from that. However, his ambitions remain the same. He wishes to return my Protestant state, and that of the Netherlands, to what he believes to be the one true faith. And *then* to clamp down on what he calls heresy. He means, in time, one way or another, to make us both Catholic. To make us afraid to be anything else.

'And that,' said Elizabeth, 'is something I could *not* accept. Not ever. It is something from which my people, the majority of my people, look to me to protect them. But what will happen if – when – I refuse to co-operate? I can't run away, Ursula. I can't put my own safety first. My business is to be in the forefront of the defence, heartening my commanders, my soldiers, my countrymen. If despite all our efforts, the Spanish forces overcome my defences, I must still be here, representing my country, speaking for my people. There are proprieties in these things, of course. I don't suppose I would be thrown into a dungeon. The terms would be discussed at the highest level, which means with me and with my council.

'I think what Philip would actually want would be England as a province of Spain, me allowed to rule as a puppet queen. There would probably be a Spanish presence, to make sure that I kept to the terms. But the terms I have just mentioned are unthinkable. To agree to any such thing would be to betray the entire English nation. Yet, if terms couldn't be agreed, what then? I could I suppose be controlled by having one or more of my councillors taken to Spain and kept in honourable – I hope it would be honourable – captivity as I kept Mary Stuart – as a hostage for my compliant behaviour. Or I might just be done away with.'

'No!' It burst out of me, a horrified cry.

'Who knows? I would be in Philip's hands. I executed Mary Stuart, the Catholic queen he once hoped to place on my throne. He regards himself as the defender of the Catholic faith. If his troops had landed here as part of one of Mary's plots, and managed to overthrow me, and put Mary in my place, what fate would then have been mine? To execute a queen is a terrible thing. But when I let Mary go to the block, I did exactly that. I set a deadly precedent. Philip might follow my example. But . . .'

The golden-brown eyes under their faint, fair brows looked straight into mine. 'It would probably be more convenient for him, if he could control me through a hostage who is not a great name. Kidnapping one of my foremost men, Cecil for example, would be a tiresome business. As I said, there are proprieties. He would be expected to feed and house his hostage in a style appropriate to his rank. I did that for Mary, right up to her death! But you are another matter.'

'Me?' I said, stupefied.

'He no doubt knows of your existence. But you are no great name. You are not a countess, nor are you a councillor. You are base-born, and you have been a spy, working against him in hidden ways. You are my sister and I love you. What a magnificent hostage you would make, and he wouldn't need to house you in any expensive fashion.'

I had begun to tremble. Philip had a long history of burning heretics to death. If he threatened me in that way . . .

'I see you understand,' said Elizabeth. 'You are or could be the ruin of my country except that I wouldn't allow it. Not even for you could I expose England to the slow erosion of the new religion that my people have embraced, free of the Pope's commands. Don't look so frightened, Ursula. I have thought long about this. When the sails of a Spanish

Armada are sighted, I will send an escort to bring you to
me. I shall know all the news at the earliest possible moment
and if . . . God forbid! – our defeat seems inevitable then
you must run. An armed escort will ride with you to
Scotland. Any of your own people that you wish to take
with you can accompany you or follow you. I believe that
your maid Dale cannot ride far or fast but she and her
husband could follow, as I said, more slowly, if you want
them. I have already sent word of my plans to young King
James and you will be well received. Above all, you will be
safe. I don't think Philip will try to conquer Scotland as well.
You must do this, Ursula, for your own sake and mine, and
for the future of England. I will brook no argument. *We* will
brook no argument.' The royal *we* struck me with the force
of a cannonball. 'Do you understand?'

'Yes, ma'am.' I did. My heart was a cold lump of misery
in my chest, but I understood all too well. I would have to
do as I was bidden and not just *because* I was bidden.
Elizabeth might talk of England but my motives would be
simpler. I wanted to live. Above all, I didn't want to die a
heretic's death.

'You may call me sister,' Elizabeth repeated. Then, grimly,
she said: 'For my people, I must remain staunch, the indomit-
able queen, a woman with the heart of a man, or a lion. I must
be the leader they can trust to the end; ready to die for my
people. Day after day, I meet the eyes of my court, and
my calm face is my shield. They don't know what lies behind
that calm. At night, alone in the dark, I sweat with terror. You
will go to Scotland as I command?'

'Yes, sister,' I said. 'Unless,' I added thoughtfully, 'we
were to surrender gracefully, and invite Philip to come to
England to negotiate in person, and spread a fine table to feast
your conqueror, and then poison him.'

'What . . .? Oh, Ursula . . .' The tautness went out of her
pale face and she burst out laughing. 'Oh, my Ursula, I shall
miss you so much, because always you bring a brightness
with you. Something you did *not* get from our mutual father.
You make me laugh even when I am confessing to fears and
nightmares! The Spanish aren't here yet and may they never

be! What I have told you concerns only the last resort. For now, go home to Hawkswood and may you find everything there in good order and just as you would wish so that you can take comfort in your own home and the company of your people.'

THREE

A Bowl of Ink

The day I left the court was dull, cold and rainy, and much as I wished to go home, my heart was heavy, and not just because of the shadow of war. I did indeed wish to relieve my young friend Mildred of the task of running Hawkswood, but I also knew I would have to comfort her. When I brought her, newly widowed, back to Hawkswood with me, she was pregnant but a letter had now reached me, saying that the child had been born two months prematurely and had only lived a day.

It was over quickly, so ran the letter, from Mildred herself, though it wasn't easy to read, for her writing was straggly and spotted, I think, with tears. *I am getting better. The bleeding has almost stopped. But I am in great sorrow. It was a son, and I had only one day to hold him in my arms. We tried to save him but he was too weak to suckle. The birth came on so suddenly that there was no time to fetch a midwife but our little maidservant Bess Hethercott delivered me; she comes from a big family and has knowledge of such things. My maid Hannah Durley has cared for me with great kindness but I long for your return. Your sorrowful servant, Mildred.*

I had another letter, from my steward Adam Wilder, and this too was a poignant cause of grief. He wrote that he was very sorry to tell me that two of my oldest horses, Bronze and Rusty, had died during the winter. They were favourites of mine and my stable would be strange without them. Bronze had been accidentally injured a few months before and never, it seemed, quite got over it. He had become hopelessly lame and had to be put down. My head groom Arthur Watts had seen to it and Bronze hadn't suffered. Rusty had simply died one night in his stall.

At court, I had my own horse with me and my manservant

Roger Brockley and his wife Frances also had theirs. But Fran, who was my personal woman (usually addressed as Dale because that had been her maiden name and habit dies hard), could not endure too long in the saddle even though her little blue roan mare was an ambler. Therefore, as we needed transport for our luggage in any case, especially my court dresses, which had to be packed as tenderly as though they were made of gold leaf, we had travelled with a little carriage that I had had built for me.

I had no need of the carriage while I was at court so Eddie Hale, the groom who had driven it, took it home again but knew the date on which he should return to take us home. He had arrived on time and it was he who brought me the letters from Mildred and Wilder. I had expected either Rusty or Bronze to be in the shafts and instead there was a sprightly chestnut trotter, named Pharoah because he was by a stallion called Egypt. He had in fact been bred at the stud of trotters I had established to increase the inheritance of my young son Harry. Pharoah had a noble head and tail carriage and rather too much of a noble spirit. While Eddie and Brockley were loading the luggage, I eyed his impatiently stamping hooves and his tossing golden mane with some anxiety and said I hoped he wouldn't overturn us.

'He's fast, madam,' protested Eddie. Eddie had a cheerful grin, wiry dark hair that always stuck up in spikes that no amount of water or combing could apparently flatten, and he had a ready tongue. I had once or twice found him useful in tight places but always had the feeling that he needed suppressing. It was a feeling shared by Brockley. Steady Brockley with the calm grey-blue eyes and the high forehead with its scattering of gold freckles was now in his sixties, and he had been with me in far more tight places than Eddie had.

'We're not in a race,' said Brockley sternly, also surveying Pharoah with misgiving. 'A quiet, even-paced trot is all we'll need.'

Silently, I yearned for Bronze or Rusty and wondered if it was permissible to pray for the souls of departed horses and did so anyway. *May you forever have lush fields to graze in and gallop over, and the company of many kind and gentle angels to bring you apples and oats and caress you. Amen.*

I was in this pensive mood all the way home. Eddie was actually a very good driver and Pharoah didn't overturn the carriage, though Brockley and I, he on his beautiful dark chestnut Firefly and I on my bay Jaunty, were concerned at the times when Dale was inside, and were watchful, just in case.

The track leading to the gate of Hawkswood House led through woods, but the house itself was on a rise and approaching riders could be seen from the upper windows. When I returned from a journey, I usually found a good many people gathered in the courtyard to welcome me. It was the same this time, but the smiles of greeting seemed tempered. My tall, grey-haired steward Wilder wasn't smiling at all, but was subdued and grave. I noticed that he was now completely grey, that not a single brown hair remained, and also, he was beginning to stoop. Soon I would need to find him an assistant who could one day replace him and I knew he would hate it.

I felt rather the same about my cook, big, hefty John Hawthorn. I knew that his assistant Ben Flood, though he was considerably younger than John, would never be able to take over from him. Short, bald Ben was in many ways a gifted cook but he was also a born second in command. Both Hawthorn and Flood were there to receive me, but Mildred was not and the first words I spoke as I dismounted, were: 'Mistress Atbrigge, how is she?'

'Mistress Atbrigge isn't here, madam,' Wilder said. 'She is quite well now and she has gone to West Leys, as there was trouble there and Master Spelton wasn't home.'

'What?' I put my hand to my head, confused by this turn of events. West Leys was a farm about two hours away, on an average horse. It belonged to an old friend of mine, Christopher Spelton, who had married Kate Lake, once a ward of mine. He was her second husband and I was fairly sure that she had married him more because he loved her than because she loved him. She had adored Eric Lake. Nevertheless, Christopher had made her happy and she now had two small daughters, one by each of them. The last I had heard was that after an infant son had died, like Mildred's baby, Kate was once more expecting.

'Is it something to do with Kate?' I asked sharply. But at that moment, my sixteen-year-old son came running from the house, and instead of coming to a halt in front of me and bowing, as his tutor had taught him to do, he threw himself into my arms and said: 'Oh, Mother, I am so glad you're home; it's been so awful, all hushed voices and telling me and Benjamin to keep out of the way. Well, Master Dickson and Wilder have explained things, but I'm so glad to see you back again.'

'I'm here now; I'll put it all to rights. Where's Benjamin?'

Benjamin Atbrigge was Harry's playmate and Mildred's stepson. He was a tight-lipped boy, who had come to us after a dreadful experience and was still recovering from it. I hoped that my home would be quiet and friendly enough, in time, to heal him, and the companionship of Harry was part of the healing process. Harry for his part was pleased to have a companion of his own age. The two of them were usually together. Harry said: 'He's still upstairs; Mr Dickson said I must greet you first.'

'Poor Ben. I'll talk to him soon. Come, let's go inside and Wilder, perhaps you would do some explaining! I want to know what has happened at West Leys.'

Inside the great hall we found Peter Dickson, Harry's elderly tutor, waiting to detach Harry from me and lead him away, saying that I would talk to him soon but Wilder must first speak privately to his mother. There was a good fire in the hearth and I paused there, taking in its warmth. I looked at Wilder with eyebrows raised.

He said: 'Madam, I am sorry to greet you with this. It concerns your former ward, Mistress Kate Spelton. Mistress Spelton's sister-in-law, Mistress Ferguson, sent word, thinking to find you here and knowing that you would want to know, and indeed seeking your help . . .'

'Get on with it, Wilder.'

'Mistress Kate was with child . . .'

'Yes, I know.'

'She was brought to bed too soon.'

'Like Mildred!'

'Not quite so, madam. Mistress Kate caught the measles. There has been an outbreak in Guildford, and she had been there, at a market, shortly before she fell ill. Her illness caused her child to be born prematurely and she didn't recover.'

'Good God!'

'No one else in the house fell ill,' Wilder said. 'They had all had the disease already. Her sister-in-law came to be with her and is still there. She did her best, that we know. A midwife who has attended Mistress Kate before was fetched from Brentvale, and Joan Janes, who is married to one of the farmhands and has skill in matters of childbirth . . .'

'I have met her. She ought to know all about it,' I said. 'She's had ten of her own, and two of her daughters are maidservants at the farmhouse. She was there too?'

'It seems so. Mistress Spelton was surrounded by skilled women but it was all in vain. She hadn't the strength to battle with the measles and childbirth all at once. The child survived. It's another girl. She is feeble but continues to live. They've found a wet-nurse. But Mistress Spelton . . . they lost her.'

'I see.'

It was hard to take in. So Kate was gone, at thirty. Dear Kate. Poor Kate, who had been through some very hard times, but had come at last into a safe harbour, or so I thought. But life was always perilous for married women. I was myself lucky to be still alive. I had a daughter and a son but in between them I had had a disastrous childbed which had killed the baby and come within inches of killing me. I couldn't imagine what it had felt like, struggling with measles and a premature birth at the same time.

Wilder was saying: 'The message that the sister-in-law, Mistress Ferguson, sent was so frantic that Mistress Atbrigge went at once to do what she could. I suppose that the sister-in-law found it hard to assume authority in another woman's household. Mistress Atbrigge took her maid Hannah with her. Master Harry lent Hannah his cob because Mealy is quiet and Hannah is still such a nervous rider. The house for orphans where you found her, madam, never instructed the orphans in riding.'

He looked round as Brockley and Dale went by, carrying a big baggage hamper between them. 'That is the news, madam, and I am sorry to burden you with it the moment you step through the door. As you see, your belongings are being brought in. Dinner will be ready in an hour but meanwhile, will you take some refreshment?'

'Thank you. I will, and so must the Brockleys. After dinner, I shall rest. I expect I shall ride over to West Leys tomorrow.'

In the crowd that had gathered to greet me, another face had been absent. As Wilder was turning away to fetch my refreshments, I said: 'Where is Gladys?'

I felt anxious, for if anyone was eager to be there when anything of the slightest importance was happening, it was Gladys Morgan. She was an aged Welshwoman whom Brockley and I had rescued from a charge of witchcraft, long ago, and who had thereafter attached herself to me and become one of my household. She was not at all an attractive character, being not only ugly, with her brown fangs and her small, dark, knowing eyes, but also averse both to washing and to combing her iron-grey hair. She was horribly inquisitive, and frequently rude. In fact, she had a real gift for cursing people. I had no idea how old she was. She had been well on in years when Brockley and I first met her and now she was shrunken and lame and stooped and in the nature of things, one of these days . . .

I would never have said I loved her; I wouldn't even have claimed to be mildly fond of her, but she was part of my home, just like any other piece of furniture. Wilder, however, was looking vaguely around as though he expected her to emerge from under the table or out of a sideboard cupboard. 'I don't know, madam. Perhaps in her quarters?'

My welcome home had been somewhat overwhelming. A wave of exhaustion suddenly struck me. I called for a glass of cider and a honeycake to be brought to my little parlour and went to sit there for a while. I had two parlours; the other, which was bigger, was known as the East Room because it caught the morning light so well. It was a good place to greet formal callers or to sit down with account books. The little parlour, however, was where I took close friends and where I sat when I wanted to be private and quiet. Just now, privacy and quietness were something that I needed.

I drank the cider, which was pleasantly sour and more refreshing than the heavy Malmsey wine that was its alternative. My head housemaid Phoebe made the cider and she was teaching the skill to Mildred. I then ate the honeycake, and rested, thinking. Thinking about Scotland mainly and hoping to heaven that I wouldn't have to abandon my home and go into exile there and wondering how, from such a distance, I could possibly keep in touch with Hawkswood. Perhaps it wouldn't be possible and I would have to let go of Hawkswood, and my other properties – and their people. Thinking of that made me feel that I was bleeding inside. Better *not* to think about it, I decided, and went in search of Gladys.

She didn't have a bedchamber and nor did she actually share the big attic room at the western end of the house, where the maidservants slept. Most of the maidservants would have refused to tolerate her. However, there was a small adjacent attic, opening off the bigger one. In bygone days when my husband Hugh's parents had had far more servants than I had, their crowd of maidservants had slept in the larger attic and the senior maidservant who was supposed to keep them in order but considered herself too superior to share a room with them had slept in the little one. Gladys had a truckle bed there now.

I found her there. She was sitting on the side of her bed with her back to the doorway and seemed to be hunched over something. Whatever it was, she was so intent on it that she wasn't aware of me until my shadow fell upon her. Then she turned sharply, and the bowl that she was holding between her hands slopped a little.

'What are you doing, Gladys?'

'Naught that matters. You're home safe; God be thanked. Thought you'd likely be toppled out on to the highway, with that high-stepping colt in the shafts.'

'I made the journey on Jaunty. After the first three miles or so, Dale didn't want to ride any further, so we hitched Blue Gentle behind the carriage and put Dale inside. She was the one in danger, though as it happened there wasn't any.' I moved nearer, and saw that the small bowl in Gladys' hands was full of some dark liquid, which had splashed over her fingers and made a blot on the floor. Beside it, next to Gladys' feet, was one of my ink bottles. 'That's my ink! What in the world are you about . . . are you scrying?'

I didn't even know if she would recognize the word, since I couldn't recall ever mentioning it to her or to anyone else, either. I hadn't heard it myself since I was a child and one of Aunt Tabitha's maidservants had been caught at it. She had been thrashed and dismissed, with a severe warning about the dangers of getting a reputation as a witch.

But Gladys was clearly familiar with it. 'Aye, that's what I'm at. Don't do it often. My grandma taught me the way of it, long, long since.'

'Did you really ever have a grandma? I can hardly imagine it.' I found it impossible to visualize Gladys as young. I couldn't think how she would have looked as a girl, let alone a girl child, learning dubious arts at the knee of a grandmother – who probably looked and sounded exactly as Gladys did now. 'I never knew you did scrying!' I barked at her. 'I'd have put a stop to it if I had! Come to think of it I can remember times when my ink seemed to be used up faster than it should. Gladys, get rid of that at once. Throw it out of the window, and I'll take the bowl away to be washed and call someone to mop the floor. I won't have occult practices in this house.'

There had been a previous occasion when, because she feared I was in danger, Gladys had performed a spell involving the sacrifice of a cockerel at dawn. That she had done it in my interests, and I had actually escaped the danger I was in, had made it impossible to be angry with her. Though I was, and afraid for her too. Since joining my household, she had been taken up for witchcraft a second time and once more, we had had to rescue her. It seemed that she couldn't learn.

'I'd finished anyhow.' Gladys turned round to sit facing me. Gladys was not in the habit of standing up before her betters. 'And I saw enough, so I did. You can look into the ink yourself if you want; I reckon you've got something of the Sight, like

I have. I can tell. You're unhappy, Mistress Ursula, indeed you are, I can tell that, too. The ink might bring you comfort.'

'I wouldn't dream of doing such a thing! I said, get rid of that . . . that . . . Did you see something comforting in it? If so, tell me. If not, don't.'

'I saw trouble,' said Gladys, eyeing me slyly.

'You always do, you croaking old raven, and just at the moment, no one needs to go scrying into a bowlful of ink to know there's trouble coming. We're in danger of a Spanish invasion.'

'I saw the ships. And a darkness overhead like a thundercloud . . .'

'I dare say!'

'Sky wasn't *all* dark. Line of light, there was, far away beyond the masts of the ships, like the bright edge of a storm cloud, when there's a wind behind it. Whatever's coming, it'll be all right in the end. Only I saw you as well. There was another ship, pulling away from a place with white cliffs. You was on that. And I saw Mistress Mildred, looking at someone I couldn't see, face all adoring. Reckon she's going to fall in love again.' The idea caused Gladys to laugh, or rather, to cackle.

'Stop that!' I said. 'You sound like a hen laying an egg!'

'I was a croaking raven a minute ago.'

'Don't talk nonsense. And throw out that ink . . . Oh, give it to me.' I seized it from her, marched to the window and emptied it out, to land in a clump of bushes below. 'I shall see Mistress Mildred tomorrow,' I said. 'I hear she has gone to West Leys.'

'Aye. Life's dangerous for women.'

'It will certainly be dangerous for you, if you keep on playing with magic!' I snapped.

FOUR
West Leys

For the rest of the day, I was occupied with the affairs of Hawkswood, some of which took me by surprise. One of the first things I learned, much to my horror, was that like poor Kate at West Leys, my son Harry had had the measles and was now suffering from contrition because he had ridden over one day to call at West Leys and feared that he had given it to Kate. I reassured him about that. He had visited the market in Guildford at about the same time that she had, wanting a new bridle for his cob Mealy. It was likely that he and Kate had both picked it up there.

I then rounded on Wilder and demanded to know why no one had sent to tell me when Harry fell ill.

'He had it lightly,' said Wilder, and Phoebe joined in to say: 'Little Bess Hethercott, that you brought back from Devon to be a maid here, she knows all about everything in families, it seems, more than any of us. She comes of a big family, and she said she'd had measles along with all the rest of her brothers and sisters and she knew what was done for her, and how she'd had to help look after the others when she was getting better and they were still ill.'

'Oh?' I said. It was true enough that Bess was the eldest of an enormous brood and that although she was not yet sixteen, she was a very capable lass indeed.

'She was splendid,' Wilder said. 'She fairly took over, said she'd seen it all before. She had the lad laid in a dark room and sent Ben Flood off to Woking, hell for leather, on Master Harry's cob, to buy red cloth for Master Harry's bedcurtains. *And mind you get it fast, no dithering!* she shouts at him, the minute he's astride. When he got back she was all ready with scissors and threaded needles and she had the other maidservants joining in and she had Master Harry's bed hung with

red curtains before you could say *guard his eyes* because that
was what it was all about, it seems. Like with smallpox. Red
light makes the rash come out and protects the eyesight.
Anyway, Master Harry is safe from measles now for the rest
of his life and he was never that ill, madam. We'd have sent
for you at once if he'd taken a bad turn but he never did, and
we all know not to disturb you when you're attending the
queen, not unless there's no alternative.'

Nervously, Phoebe said: 'We didn't know if you'd had it
yourself and it wouldn't have been right to call you back here
if there was any risk to you.'

'I had it as a child,' I said. 'But I understand. Phoebe, don't
look so scared. I don't dismiss servants except for really
desperate reasons. Such as being caught plotting against the
queen or committing murder or stealing my one set of silver
dishes. Harry is clearly now in the best of health, and Bess is
to be commended.'

Next, I needed to talk to Peter Dickson, the boys' tutor. He
had kept Benjamin, Mildred's stepson, from running down
with Harry to greet me saying that Harry should greet his
mother first. I agreed with this at first but Dickson said ruefully
that Benjamin had been upset about it and I changed my mind.
The boys must in future be treated like brothers, I said. I then
had to talk to Benjamin and reassure him about his place in
the household.

I also had to hear Dickson's report on their studies. Harry,
despite the interruption caused by the measles, was nevertheless doing well in most subjects including Greek and Latin.
He would never be gifted with accounts but was at least taking
an interest, especially with the accounts to do with the stud
of trotters.

'Just as well, since he will one day be the stud's proprietor,'
I said to Dickson. Benjamin was also very forward in Latin
and Greek, having been taught them by his father, but he was
backward in history, completely uninformed in the countries
of the world and had no knowledge of music. Dickson, himself
very skilled on the lute, had begun to introduce him to it.

After all that, I had to interview the stud groom, Laurence
Miller. I reproved him for having put Pharoah between the

shafts of my baggage vehicle. 'There are other horses here, Splash or Blaze, that could have pulled it. Why Pharoah? Dale travelled part of the way in the carriage; she could have been tossed out onto her head!'

'I didn't fear that, madam. Pharoah was in want of some practice on the highway, and needed a good long journey to settle him down. He is spirited but he has never overturned anything, I assure you. He will be all the more saleable now. His full brother, Caesar, one year older, is well trained too and identical to look at. They can be sold as a matched pair.'

'Oh well, let it go for the moment. But never do anything like that again, Miller. Genuine journeys shouldn't be used as training exercises.'

Miller bowed, politely, even contritely, but without much humility. He was more than just a stud groom. Because of my relationship to her majesty, Cecil considered that I should be watched over. Whenever I was at Hawkswood, Miller made regular reports to him on all that concerned me. I sometimes longed to dismiss him, just to prove to myself that I could, and to enjoy giving Cecil a little trouble over finding a replacement. He had never sought my consent to this constant watchfulness.

After that, there were a myriad other things that Wilder and John Hawthorn wanted to discuss. Salt was running low; how much should we buy? There were extra people in the household now, Bess Hethercott, Jenny the new young maidservant, Ben Atbrigge, Etheldreda the new poultry maid. It would make a difference to the size of our usual order. The merchant from whom we bought spices had put his prices up; should we find another source of supply? Should we order this, not order that; regrettably the roof had had to be repaired after the storm in January; young Jenny worked hard but had the weirdest ideas about how to clean woodwork.

'I caught her using silver sand, madam,' Wilder said in horror, 'it almost took the varnish off the panelling in the hall except that I stopped her in time.'

I was late to bed and feared I would sleep badly, but did not because Dale, who understood me so well, gave me a potion. It was one of Gladys' inventions but I had used it before and knew it wouldn't harm me. In fact, it did me good. In the morning, I rode off to West Leys.

I went alone. It wasn't far and I felt no need of an escort. Dale was tired after the journey from St James' and didn't want a two-hour ride, and she never liked it if Brockley and I rode out without her. Once, long ago, Brockley and I had very nearly become lovers. It hadn't happened and it never would but there was a silent bond between us and Dale knew it.

The farmhouse at West Leys, where my former ward Kate and my friend Christopher Spelton had lived so pleasantly, bringing up their family, was a farmhouse at the top of a gentle slope where cornfields and meadows were draped like a patchwork coverlet. There were labourers' cottages dotted about on the edges, including one extraordinary, rambling place, covered in shaggy thatch that nearly swept the ground. It was longer than it was high and resembled some low-level growth that was gradually expanding and would one day swallow up the meadow beside it.

It housed a family so large that Christopher called it a clan, like the clans of Ireland and Scotland. It was ruled by the Joan Janes who had tried to help when Kate was brought to bed. She had borne six sons and four daughters. She had married her daughters off, and although from what I had heard she was now living in the farmhouse to help Bessie Ferguson, she usually dwelt in her own sprawling home, along with her sons, her daughters-in-law, many grandchildren, and some of the offspring of her brothers, whom she had outlived. Several of the farmhands were her sons, and two of the maids in the house were her daughters.

The farmhouse itself had two storeys plus attics under the thatched roof, and it was one of the warmest, friendliest houses I have ever known. It stood upon a kind of shelf above its sloping fields and behind it, on level ground, there were more fields and a patch of woodland and then there was another upward slope, steeper than the one below. This was not farmland. It was a common, with grass and herbage, where sheep wandered, and there was a path leading up to the summit, disappearing over a saddle in the crest.

I knew that Kate and her first husband, Eric Lake, had often walked up that path in the early morning, towards the rising sun as it lifted above the saddle. I also knew that she and Christopher had taken to doing the same thing. Now, there would only be Christopher.

Though at the moment, apparently, he wasn't there. Christopher had once been a Queen's Messenger and not just that. He had also, like me, undertaken secret missions from time to time. When he married Kate and took over West Leys, he gave all that up, but there came a bad year when a harvest was lost, and he took to accepting secret work again, because it was well paid. It was ill luck that Kate should be brought to bed too soon, when he was absent.

Even before I reached the house, I could have told that something was very wrong. There were a couple of farmhands in one of the meadows, inspecting a cow and a tiny newborn calf. I recognized them, Hal Pursell and young Timothy Janes (the prolific Joan Janes' last son), and they recognized me. They called greetings to me, but they didn't smile. Their faces were sombre. Then, as I drew near to the house, I saw that some of the windows were shuttered. As usual, a couple of dogs greeted my arrival by barking and leaping to the end of their chains, and there was a great cackling from a flock of geese in a nearby pen, but even the dogs and the geese sounded as if their hearts weren't in it. I supposed that I was imagining that, but perhaps not, for animals are sensitive to atmosphere.

My arrival had been noted, however. As I dismounted, the front door opened and there was Bessie Ferguson, Kate's sister-in-law, on the threshold. A lad appeared round the side of the house, and took Jaunty's bridle. I relinquished it to him and hurried forward. 'I came at once. They told me as soon as I got home. Oh, Mistress Ferguson . . .'

'You're Mistress Stannard, aren't you? I remember; we last met when Eric died. And now it's Kate herself, oh, dear God, poor Kate. She suffered so much; it wasn't fair; how can God let such things happen? I'm thankful to see you. Come in, come in. We're all in disarray . . . Oh, be quiet, you dogs! Hush! *Hush*, geese! I swear those geese could outdo a band of trumpeters!'

The last time I had seen Bessie she was buxom and rosy, and in a way she still was, but the buxomness now had run to fat and her kind blue eyes were tired. She took my cloak and led me inside, into a house shadowy because of all the closed shutters. The big warm kitchen was as usual, however, with a good fire and a simmering stockpot, and Mildred was there, sleeves rolled up, making pastry. She had a greased pie dish at hand and a pile of chopped meats on a wooden tray. She turned to me with an exclamation of delight and relief mingled.

'Ursula! You're home! We are so glad to see you. Oh, I would embrace you but I am all over flour. Oh, Ursula, it has been so awful! I got here just before Kate died; I was there when . . . Oh, I can't talk about it!'

'I know. Dear Mildred. I am so sorry for your sad loss, quite apart from this dreadful news about Kate.'

'I try not to think about it. Poor little thing. He survived just one day. I saw him and held him . . . I like to think that he had that much of life, the memory of his mother's arms, to take . . . to take into the darkness with him . . .'

Tears were threatening. I put my arms round her and for a few moments, she stood in them, her face hidden against my shoulder. A warm tear or two found its way through my sleeve on to my skin. Then she drew herself away, brushing a hand across her eyes, and gave me a shaky smile. 'I am recovering. I know I must put it behind me and I will. Bessie and I are so thankful to see you. With Christopher not here, we've been at our wits' end. The funeral is over, did you know? Two days ago now.'

Bessie, as though surrendering to tiredness, had deposited herself in a battered basketwork chair. 'My husband was here for that,' she said. 'But he couldn't stay. There was some trouble at Whitefields . . .'

Whitefields was the big house near Dover, which Kate's brother Duncan had inherited the previous year, on his father's death. I wished he could have stayed longer. Bessie and Mildred looked so harassed. At the very moment when the word shaped itself in my mind, Bessie said it out loud.

'I feel hopelessly harassed. Distraught, even! I want to go

home and of course Mildred is here and oh, how I thank her for coming to the rescue, but neither of us is fit to look after things even together, never mind alone. The maidservants are dear good souls; they're about the house somewhere . . .'

'Hannah's with them. She's so willing, bless her,' Mildred put in.

'. . . but neither Mildred nor I can give orders to the farm-hands, though there is a good bailiff and he's managing for the moment. But there are decisions to take, when to sow this, dig that, sell something else. The bailiff doesn't decide those things. Christopher and Kate did; they both understood the work. We can manage the maidservants, but there are things to buy, things to sell, accounts to keep – we can't make head or tail of the account books . . .'

'And there's the children,' said Mildred. 'They're upstairs; the baby's with the wet-nurse, and Bessie and I, taking it in turns, are trying to teach little Susanna and Christina their letters, getting them to learn how to read. Every day, one of us tries to spend time reading with them. They're darlings; I really love them. I'm also doing most of the cooking because I'm good at it. Kate used to do all that, you see, that's how the house was organized.'

'The baby's such a little scrap of a thing,' said Bessie mournfully. 'We feared she wouldn't live. We had her baptized at once; the vicar came from St Peter's in Brentvale, and we called her Elizabeth, after the queen and after me as well, I suppose, but we had to call her something . . .'

Poor Bessie stopped for breath.

'I'm sure you've been doing your best,' I said, 'and Elizabeth is a very good name; I'll be amazed if Master Spelton doesn't approve.'

I was thinking fast and with a sinking heart. Someone must deal with the account books and the more important orders about the farm and it looked as though that person would have to be me. I had hoped for a peaceful time at home but that delightful dream was rapidly vanishing. 'I'd better talk to your bailiff at once. I am used to running Hawkswood; I expect I can understand how West Leys works. I'll look at the accounts, too.'

Bessie heaved herself up. 'Mildred, we have forgotten our manners. What about some refreshment for Mistress Stannard? No doubt Jimmy has given her horse a drink of water and a feed, but his rider has had nothing!'

'There's cider in the pantry,' said Mildred, pressing pastry into the pie dish. 'And wine in the cellar. Just let me get this pie into the oven.'

'I'll fetch the refreshments. What will you have, Mistress Stannard? We've cider, wine, some mincemeat patties . . .'

'I don't need anything to eat,' I said hastily. 'Though I am thirsty after the ride. Could I have a glass of cider?' The cider barrel was there in the kitchen, but if I asked for wine, Bessie would have to lever her bulk down the cellar stairs and then up them again with a big flagon in her hands. She was, however, already opening the cellar door.

'I know Mistress Stannard likes good wine. I remember that from the last unhappy occasion here and . . .'

In order to address Mildred, Bessie had paused at the cellar door and turned her head to look towards both Mildred and the window. She stopped in mid-sentence and stood there, apparently struck silent and motionless. I too turned towards the window.

Two riders were approaching and I recognized one of them. Relief poured through me. It was Christopher Spelton.

FIVE
One of our Own

Christopher was home. He could now take the reins of West Leys into his capable hands. None of us need worry any more about account books and instructions to the bailiff. I could go back to Hawkswood whenever I liked. 'But who's that with him?' I asked.

'I don't know.' Mildred had just toppled the chopped meat into a pan and had been scooping liquid out of the stockpot to add to it. She glanced briefly out of the window and then turned back and began stirring the mixture with a hard, indignant hand. 'Oh, really!' Mildred was only twenty but now she looked and sounded like an irritated housewife aged forty. 'A guest! At such a time!'

Bessie opened the back door, shouted for Jimmy and then went round to the front of the house with him to greet the new arrivals. I went out after them and as I stood behind Bessie watching the riders approach, I heard her muttering: 'Dear God, what a muddle; he doesn't know, he has no idea and now he's bringing us a stranger to look after . . .'

And then Christopher and his companion were with us, dismounting and handing their horses to Jimmy and they were turning towards us, smiling, and Christopher was saying: 'Well, I'm home. May I introduce Master Berend Gomez, an old acquaintance I met on the road? I suggested that he should break his journey and spend a night here. We haven't met in years; we'll have so much to say to each other . . . What is it? *You're* here, Bessie? Has Kate already had the baby? Surely not; it shouldn't have been due yet . . .'

'Please come inside,' said Bessie, and sounded almost steely. The two men at once doffed their caps and followed her without any further words. But once in the kitchen, Christopher stopped

short and said: 'There's been trouble. I can tell. What is it,
Bessie? And you're here as well, Ursula?' The blood drained
out of his face, and Master Gomez, glancing around at us,
hung back. 'Please,' said Christopher, 'tell me it's not what I
fear!'

Bessie gave me a pleading look. 'Mistress Stannard, as you
were once my sister-in-law's guardian . . .'

'Come in here,' I said to Christopher, and led him away
into the rarely used parlour, leaving Bessie and Mildred to
cope with the oddly named Berend Gomez. I shut the door
behind us, steered Christopher into a settle, and said, as gently
as I could: 'I am sorry, Christopher, so very sorry. Kate fell
ill with measles. She went into labour too early and I think it
was all too much for her.'

He stared at me in silence for a moment and then burst out:
'Are you telling me that she . . . Yes, you are. I can see it in
your face. I've lost her. Oh no! Not my Katie . . . Oh, poor
Katie! How she must have suffered . . .'

I waited, while he struggled with tears. At last, steadying
himself, he said: 'Go on. Tell me everything.'

'When Kate fell ill, I was at court, but Mildred came over
to help. She and Bessie were here. I understand that everything
possible was done to save Kate. When I got home, I heard the
news and came myself, as soon as I could. I have only just
arrived, in fact. I have been told that the . . . the . . . funeral
was yesterday.'

'So I can't even see her one last time, to say goodbye.'

'Christopher, I'm so *very* sorry!'

He looked dreadful. Christopher Spelton was a stocky, sturdy
man, by now in his forties. He was bald except for a ring of
brown hair like that around a tonsure, and his brown eyes were
the kindest eyes anyone could imagine. But now they
were full of tears, and his pleasant, tanned face was drawn as
if by physical pain. I turned away, saying: 'I will get you some
wine.'

'Thank you,' said Christopher's voice behind me. 'But,
Ursula, what of the child?'

'The baby lived. You have a new daughter,' I said. I reached
the door, called to Bessie to fetch the wine, and came back

to him. 'I haven't yet seen her. I understand that as she was premature, she is very small but she is alive and Bessie has found a wet-nurse. The baby has been christened Elizabeth. It had to be done quickly, as at first it was feared she wouldn't live.'

'I see. Well, Elizabeth is a fine name; I am pleased with it.' He sat up a little straighter as Bessie came in with the wine. 'I hear I have a new little lass, Bessie. Named for you?'

'For her majesty the queen, sir, only that does mean named for me,' said Bessie, trying to smile.

'I like the name. Can I see her?'

'I'll get the wet-nurse to bring her to you, sir. I got Mary Bright from Greenways Farm just beyond Brentvale. Just lost her first, but willing enough to take on Elizabeth for a while and earn at the same time. Her mother's managing the Greenways kitchen for the time being.'

I too welcomed the chance to see the new baby. She was brought to us by Mildred's maid Hannah who had apparently been sharing the work of caring for the child, and Mary Bright, who turned out to be young and clean, if plump. The baby, swaddled in knitted blankets, was so tiny that I could hardly believe she was real, until she opened her eyes and looked at me, and pulled a minute hand out of her covers, to wave it in the air.

'Give her to me,' said Christopher, and took the bundle into his arms. He looked into his daughter's little face. His own was taut and bloodless under the tan, but his voice was kind. 'Hallo, Elizabeth. I am your father. I will try to make up for your lack of a mother. Welcome to West Leys, my pet.' He put a forefinger into the little pink wavering fist and the baby's fingers closed round it.

He looked at me. 'I have heard of fathers who rejected babies because they lived when their mothers did not. I don't propose to be among them. Oh, how I wish I had come home sooner! If I had been here, Kate might have . . .'

'No one can know that,' I said. My eyes were prickling. Christopher was a good man and in the course of my life I had learned to value such men. There are plenty of the other kind.

'That's true,' Christopher said with a sigh. He gave the baby back to Mary and she and Hannah bore her away, back to the nursery upstairs. Christopher turned to me. 'I think,' he said, 'that now I had better explain Berend Gomez. I would never have brought him if I had known what had happened. Perhaps I should send him on to Brentvale, to the inn there.'

'It's up to you to decide,' I said. 'But if he is an old friend of yours, perhaps his company would help you. Who is he? You have only told us his name so far.'

Christopher paused, drumming his fingers on the arm of his seat. Then he said: 'He's not really an old friend, just an acquaintance, as I said at first, someone I've once or twice stayed in the same inn with, enjoyed a pint of ale with.' He blinked his nice brown eyes free of tears and looked at me very straitly. 'He's one of our own. You know what I mean, Ursula. We met on the road an hour before we arrived here. We are both bound for London, to see Sir Francis Walsingham. We both have to lodge reports with him. Berend was using a roundabout route to get there . . .'

'Many agents do that,' I said, thinking of Juan Smith.

'Yes. I've done it myself in my time. So I suggested that he stayed the night with me, and tomorrow, we would ride on to London together. I wanted to call here first to see how Kate was . . .' His voice faltered for a moment. Then he said: 'I shall only be gone for a few days. Then I'll be back for good and able to see to things here.'

'What more can you tell me about Gomez?' I asked.

'He's a double agent. The Duke of Parma, in the Netherlands, sends him here now and then. He pretends to be seeking customers for a Dutch maker of earthenware goods. Rather attractive ones, blue and white tableware and vases and floor tiles. I've even bought some dishes through him; Kate loved them.'

His voice wavered again. Once more, he steadied it. 'The maker of the earthenware, Johannes Jansen, is real and Berend really does find English customers for him. At the same time, as far as Parma is concerned, he is finding out all he can about how much support there is among English Catholics for a Spanish invasion. I've been in the north, doing the same thing for the queen. Parma regards Berend Gomez as a useful spy and also a competent messenger who has the gravitas to do some negotiating as well.'

I nodded. Christopher was similarly regarded by Walsingham. Walsingham had once told me that it was his policy that messengers who were entrusted with documents that could bring them into danger should know what they were carrying and therefore might as well be negotiators too. 'Trustworthy messengers and good negotiators both cost money,' he added. 'Why hire two men when one can quite well undertake both tasks? The queen prefers economy, anyway.'

Christopher said: 'Berend is half-English and speaks our language, which makes him extra-valuable. He reports to Parma and anything of importance is passed to Parma's uncle Philip in Spain. Only, as it happens, we turned Gomez years ago. He was caught in the act of snooping in Walsingham's office! He wasn't too hard to turn and not just because he feared execution, either. As I said, he is half-English. He lived here for many years in his youth and he has genuine feelings for England. He had already been feeling torn. We pay him, of course, so he is paid twice, once by Parma and once by us, and I believe he is saving up to leave the spying business, buy some land in England and look for a wife. He gives us news of Parma, and takes inaccurate information back – or accurate information, sometimes!'

'How do you mean?' I was puzzled.

'He'll be reporting that the Catholics in the northern counties aren't at all eager and willing to rise in support of a Spanish invasion. No more they are! There is no such eagerness; alarm would be more like it. Berend is now on a journey back to Walsingham, and once there, he will learn what Walsingham wants him to pass on to Parma next. The lack of enthusiasm for an invasion will certainly be included and there's nothing inaccurate about that! Thank God. We don't want King Philip believing that anyone in England will welcome his army with open arms. Foolish churchmen in Spain, the kind who think that what they want to be so, actually is so, have been telling him all sorts of nonsense.'

He stopped, looking embarrassed. 'I talk about my work

and just for a moment, I'm not thinking about Kate. Ursula, I shall grieve for her for the rest of my life, believe me.'

'I do believe you. I also think that the company of a friend may be a blessed distraction for you,' I said. 'Anyway, it's your house and if you wish Señor Gomez to spend the night here, then of course we'll all make him welcome.'

I smiled at him. Many years ago, Christopher had wanted to marry me and I had refused but between him and me there was still a warmth. I had regretted that refusal later, but by then, he had seen Kate. He had loved her very much. I knew Christopher well enough to know that he wasn't shallow. He wouldn't easily forget her. I said: 'When you get back from London, you'll find distraction in being busy. Mildred and Bessie have been bewildered by the account books and don't know how to give orders about the farm.'

'Before I leave for the court, I had better look at the books and talk to my bailiff,' Christopher said. 'And Berend's company won't be unwelcome; you're right about that. He's a cheery soul. Yes, I will ask Berend to stay. Have you dined yet?'

'No. But when I arrived, Mildred was preparing a good-sized meat pie. Chicken and rabbit, I should say. There'll be enough for us all.' A thought drifted into my mind. 'Christopher, you may not have heard the latest news. Does the name Juan Smith mean anything to you?'

'Yes. We weren't acquaintances as Berend and I are, but I have met him. I know him slightly. He's another turned agent. Half-Spanish – Spanish mother, English father. Opposite way round to Berend. Berend had a Spanish father and an English mother. He was born in Spain and they lived there until Berend was eight; then the father died and his mother brought him home to live with her parents. He's Catholic but like Juan, he has a love for England. Why did you ask?'

'Juan is dead. He was murdered, stopped on the road and killed by a crossbow bolt.'

'*What?*'

'You'll hear all about it when you get to the court. He was codenamed Magpie. Walsingham is insisting on codenames a great deal these days. Magpie was carrying secret correspondence between Elizabeth and Parma. Christopher, are you by any chance codenamed Pigeon?'

He looked startled. 'No. My codename is Sparrow. Berend is Pigeon. And I wouldn't have told you that except that you are the queen's sister – and, of course, one of us.'

I said: 'I think Walsingham may have an interesting – I mean confidential – errand for him, on his next visit to the Netherlands.'

'Indeed? Well, it could be a good thing for Berend to be used for something confidential. He is worried. He has a feeling that Parma has realized that he has at times been fed inaccurate information. There was a tale about a shipyard on our west coast that was supposed to be building warships. It doesn't exist. Berend says that Parma seems to have ways of checking up on his spies and his last interview with the duke was uncomfortable. There was a hint that he should be careful not to make mistakes. Oh well,' said Christopher cheerfully, 'if he tells Parma that the English Catholics mostly don't want Philip to invade, *that's* true enough!'

In the kitchen, the atmosphere had become rather more lively than it should have done in a house of mourning. Bessie was beating eggs and had a row of assorted ingredients in front of her, including preserved plums, some separated eggs and whites, and a little dish of sugar. Mildred, more floury than ever, was rolling pastry again and had a pile of filling ready for another pie. Mutton, ham, chicken and parsnips this time, by the look of it.

Gomez was relaxing in the basket chair which Bessie had vacated. He was stretching long legs towards the warmth of the hearth and it was clear that everyone had now been introduced to everyone else and they were getting on well. In faultless English, Gomez was telling a tale about an incident on the road. He had been riding a hired horse that had once belonged to a party of travelling actors and they had taught it to hold up a front hoof to beg for an apple.

'Believe it or not, that animal, that should have been accustomed to just about everything you could meet on any road, shied like a silly colt because the wind blew what looked like an old floor cloth across the track and I came off. I just came off, as if I'd been a learner who'd never straddled a horse before. So there I was, sitting on the wayside like a fool and that confounded animal looked down at me and held up a hoof, begging for a titbit, as if it had done something clever! Oh well, at least I'd had the sense to hang on to the reins with one hand while I felt myself for bruises with the other. I got up and got back on, and thenceforth kept a sharp eye out for flying floor cloths, believe me.'

When he arrived, I hadn't taken in his appearance or his voice, but now I realized that he had a good speaking voice and a great deal of charm. He was a handsome man, tall, I thought from the length of his legs, dark of hair and eye, dressed plainly but not cheaply, in a quilted brown doublet with a small ruff, stout dun-coloured breeches and good leather riding boots. The cloak he had tossed over the back of the basket chair was of thick black felt. His saddlebags had been brought in along with a pack that he had had on his back and were lying by the wall. A leather sleeve dangling out of one of the saddlebags suggested that he had a waterproof cloak as well, for wet weather. Cloaks like that cost money.

Bessie had moved round the table so that she could face him while she worked and Mildred, who had also moved to give herself a better view of him, was flushed and smiling. Gomez gave me and Christopher a grin as he ended his story and then Gomez, speaking directly to Mildred, said: 'You never know what you're going to get when you hire a horse. They lead hard lives with all manner of riders and they show it. If they're not slugs that don't want to go anywhere, they're brutes that pull your arms out of their sockets and have mouths of *steel*, never mind iron, or else they bite, or they have shoulders as straight as ships' masts. Do you like horseback travel, Mistress Atbrigge?'

'Yes, yes, I do,' said Mildred. 'I have my own horse, Grey Cob.'

'Just Grey Cob? I take that he or she is a grey cob?'

'My parents didn't approve of giving horses what they called fancy names. My father had a chestnut horse and just called him Chestnut.'

'Was it a Puritan home?'

'Yes, well, yes it was, though I think a little differently these days, since I've been a companion to Mistress Stannard, and then married. I'm a widow now.'

'I am sorry. You're young for that, Mistress Atbrigge.'

Pink and a little flustered, Mildred said: 'Oh, do please call me Mildred.'

I knew Mildred's propensity for falling in love at five minutes' notice, all too well. Thank goodness Gomez was on his way to the court. We'd be rid of him the next day.

SIX

The Deepening Shadow

When Christopher first appeared, I had at once thought, *Well, now I can go home,* but when I realized that he intended to leave again almost at once, to make a report to Walsingham, I felt doubtful. He said that he would soon be back but there was never any telling how long these court attendances might be. If Christopher actually wanted to see Walsingham, rather than just depositing a report with a clerk, he might be kept waiting for days. Walsingham was a busy man. Perhaps I ought to wait until Christopher came home to stay. However, while we were eating dinner, I changed my mind again. If I stayed, so would Mildred and that now struck me as a bad thing. I didn't at all like the way that she and Gomez were talking and laughing together so easily.

No. Bessie could surely manage until Christopher's final return. He had said that before he left, he would see his bailiff and glance at the accounts. Gomez would leave with him, of course, but if Mildred were to remain here, I could well believe that Gomez might come back along with Christopher to visit her! Mildred, confound her, really did seem to be taken with him. I knew the signs. I would get her out of the way, and at once. Once dinner was finished and cleared, I told her and Hannah to put their things together. We could set off for Hawkswood and get there before dark. Thank goodness the evenings were lighter now, I thought.

Mildred protested but I was insistent. I think she had expected to go on chattering and laughing with Gomez all the rest of the day. Naturally, I was glad to see that she was no longer brooding on her loss, but I still felt responsible for her. When I first met her, she had been a serious-minded Puritan daughter, and after that she had in rapid succession been the wife of a vicar, then his widow, and in addition had lost the child she was carrying. But she was still only twenty and now it looked to me as though, through it all, the giddy young girl she should have been when she was at home with her parents, the girl they had never allowed to appear, had survived in secret and today had suddenly emerged into the light, like a hatching chick.

Cutting her protests short, I said: 'There are things I must attend to at home, and you should be there; the plans I am making will concern you. Hannah, go and pack for yourself and your mistress. I'll tell Jimmy to saddle our horses.'

Mildred and Hannah (who had also been looking at Gomez with admiration) went reluctantly upstairs and they were hardly out of sight, before Gomez remarked: 'Your friend Mistress Atbrigge is very beautiful, Mistress Stannard. What a misfortune to be widowed so young.'

'Her marriage was a misfortune as well,' I said. 'She has returned to me to be my companion, as she was before. I am glad to shelter and safeguard her again. She is indeed very young.'

'I think she is delightful,' said Berend irritatingly. 'Such pretty hair.'

The pretty hair was my doing. When she lived with her Puritan parents, they were anxious for her to marry but did nothing to help her to become attractive. She wasn't plain but her features were unremarkable. They needed enhancement. Her hair, which then was no more than mousy, was in any case hidden most of the time under a concealing white cap. I had taught her how to wash it in brightening herbs and urged her to brush it well, and I had provided her with some attractive hoods, covered in light brown velvet and studded with various semi-precious beads – amber, topaz, fresh-water pearls and the like. I had taught her how to make sure that a few waves of her hair were visible in front of them. The result had been highly satisfactory.

I had also taught her to choose flattering gowns. Her parents had insisted on either grey or black. But because her eyes were somewhere between blue and green, I had encouraged her to wear gowns of light blue or fresh green or amethyst.

And so, intending simply to improve Mildred's appearance, I had accidentally turned her into something of a beauty, and the experience of marriage had matured her in some ways, defining the shape of her face, giving dignity to the way she sat or moved. She was very different from the Mildred Gresham who had left her home to be my companion. The sooner she was well away from Berend Gomez, the better.

Besides, I really did have plans to discuss with everyone who lived at Hawkswood. The times were growing perilous.

Bessie, Christopher and Berend all parted from us with great regret and pleas for us to remain overnight but I remained resolute. On the ride home, to my irritation, Hannah twice remarked to Mildred that that Master Gomez was a fine-looking gentleman, wasn't he? She'd never seen a Spanish gentleman before and he was handsomer to her eyes than most Englishmen, and Mildred, instead of quelling her, agreed in wistful tones.

In stern tones, I reminded them of how dangerous was the work that such men as Berend did, and I told them about the murder of Juan Smith, otherwise known as Magpie. While they were absorbing that, I changed the subject and remarked to Mildred that it had been very kind of her to go to the rescue of the beleaguered household at West Leys; had she grown accustomed to such things when she was a vicar's wife? I supposed she had had to visit the sick and the elderly.

'Yes, I did,' Mildred said, accepting the new topic without apparent reluctance. 'I miss it,' she said. 'I became quite fond of some of them. The village was very small but it wasn't as small as it seemed. Some of the cottages were full to bursting with big families and three or four of those crowded households had built shacks or little cottages out on their land, for elderly aunts and grandparents. Poor things; I was sorry for them. If they were strong enough, they would keep chickens and grow beans and peas and help to feed themselves but if they relied on their families to bring them food, well, several of them were only just kept alive. Some of those villagers weren't nice people.'

'No,' I agreed. I remembered them well enough myself.

'There were a couple of poor old women,' Mildred said,

'who could hardly walk, and hardly wash themselves, either. One-roomed shacks, that's what they had; fire in the middle of the floor, straw mattresses, none too clean. There was an old man, too. He'd been thrown out of the family cottage because he'd gone deaf and they were all tired of shouting at him.

He used to understand me, though. He used to look at me while I talked and he could make out what I was saying by watching how my lips moved – he told me that. We had quite long conversations and he said it was a blessing to him; he did so want to talk to people. I am glad to be away from that village and yet I wish I could have stayed because I think I really was a help to some of those old men and women.'

This was a healthier way of talking. I kept Mildred on the subject of her reminiscences all the rest of the way home.

We were back at Hawkswood in good time for supper. I hope that Mildred and Hannah slept well; I can't say that I did. I was thinking seriously, and went on thinking for most of the night.

Ever since that private conference at St James' my sense of foreboding had been increasing. The threat from Spain was real. There was no doubt that Philip was preparing an invasion fleet. Sir Francis Drake was in their waters now, doing his best to wreck the fleet before it could sail or even be assembled but he couldn't go on snapping at their flanks in that way for ever. The best he could hope to achieve was delay, during which the English could build up more of our own defences. No one had actually said that but I had worked it out for myself.

One of our defences, of course, was the fact that there was no friendly welcome awaiting them in the north of England, something that must somehow be hammered into the heads of both Philip and the Duke of Parma. Juan Smith was no longer available for the purpose but Berend presumably was. Christopher, I thought, would probably be reluctant to leave his home again and I certainly hoped he wouldn't have to.

Elizabeth was doing her best but she needed time to mature her secret negotiations with Parma, which were intended to discourage or bribe him out of what our agents reported was a scheme for him to gather an army in the Netherlands and join with the Spanish fleet as it came into English waters. The intention after that, or so we understood from the man Anthony Standen, who was doing such good work in Spain, was to make a combined landing of soldiers from both Spain and the Netherlands on the east coast and also send a force up the Thames to attack London that way.

Elizabeth's commanders and her councillors had worked out that since Philip's ships would have to sail past Portsmouth in order to reach any rendezvous with Parma, he might as well land a separate force to take Portsmouth so that a land force could march on London from the west, pincering London between two advancing armies. Cecil and Walsingham had guessed at that possibility long ago and had prepared for it. I had myself recruited agents to seek out Spanish sympathizers in the West Country. There weren't many now. It must be made clear to Philip that he would find few friends along the coast of south-west England.

The longer Drake could keep Philip from getting his Armada constructed, let alone launched, the better our chances of fending him off altogether. But Philip might be very difficult to fend off. We all knew it. He was said to be blinded by the desire to lead – or drag – England back into what he called the light of the true religion. No matter what Drake did, the invasion would in all likelihood be attempted in the end.

And now the messenger who was carrying the secret correspondence between Elizabeth and Parma had been murdered. I didn't like the look of that at all. More and more, I had been wondering what to do if the worst happened and coming to some grim conclusions. As had Elizabeth herself.

And so, after a restless night, during which I had slowly brought myself to a most unhappy decision, I called my household together in the great hall. It was time they knew, in detail, what kind of danger we all faced, and how both I and they would have to deal with it.

Hawkswood House had been built well in the past, and it actually did have a great hall, though the word *great* was hardly accurate because the room in question wasn't so very large. When my entire household was packed into it, it looked very crowded indeed. As well as the boys and their tutor, the

Brockleys and Mildred and all my indoor servants, I had
included the grooms, Arthur, Joseph, Eddie and two brothers,
Jack and Abel Parsons, whom I had hired before I left for the
court.

In addition, I had sent Brockley off early to summon
Laurence Miller, Jerome Billington, who was my chief
forester and also an unofficial bailiff for my gardeners and
farmhands, and rubicund, bouncy Dr Joynings, the Hawkswood
vicar. He wasn't very bouncy this morning. No one was. Such
gathering as this was plainly serious, and I had signalled as
much by placing myself in a high-backed chair and dressing
formally: farthingale, big ruff, jewelled hood. As far as I could
see, every face was grave. Anxiety filled the air like a mist.

It was another dull grey morning. I had had all the candles
in the hall lit. Two sizeable candle rings hung from the ceiling
beams and there were several many-branched candelabra in
sconces round the walls; candles were one of our biggest
expenses. But candlelight is no substitute for daylight. It flick-
ered back and forth across those many faces, blurring their
features.

I had supposed, after all the thinking I had done, that I truly
understood the situation I must deal with, but I was wrong.
Only now, as I seated myself in my chair, did it fully come
home to me how very real was the menace from Spain. Only
then, at that moment, did I fully realize that this happy household might in truth be overwhelmed, that Spanish soldiers
might be billeted here; that my bewildered people might be
forced to abandon their familiar religion and take up the one
ordered by Spain or face dying dreadful deaths. That they
might one day have to live in a world dominated by the
Inquisition.

I sat looking at those candlelit faces, and painfully grasping
the awful size of my responsibility. All these people depended
on me; looked to me for guidance in this time of danger.
Elizabeth, the leader of the nation, had the same responsibility
on a far greater scale, but in the hall of Hawkswood, as I
shouldered my own burden, I learned how weighty such
burdens could be. I saw Harry staring at me, and saw that he
was beginning to understand and that he was frightened.

Dickson had his hand on the boy's shoulder as if to steady him. Dickson had realized the situation too.

For a moment, I almost buckled under the weight. All that held me up, was anger. I could somehow *feel* Philip and the Spanish forces, sense them as though they were an approaching thunderstorm, a growing darkness in the mind. Which made me very angry indeed. What right had Philip, damn him, because of his ingrained belief in a certain kind of worship, to be ready – and he had been ready – to conspire with Mary Stuart to overthrow our queen and our way of life? What right had he to complain if England defended herself by executing Mary? He had executed enough people himself, for far weaker reasons. Why couldn't people who happened to think differently from him be left alone? My home was a happy place. My people were contented. What right had he to make plans to burst in upon us, destroying our peace, trying to force his will on us?

So I stiffened my back, and drew in a deep breath, and started to speak.

'My friends,' I said, 'for I regard you all as friends, these are dark times. Philip of Spain wants to invade England, to conquer us, to turn us into a Spanish possession. We have some reason to hope that he may change his mind for he is faced with an extremely difficult enterprise. We also have reason to hope that if he does attack, he will be repelled. We have better ships than he has, and skilled seamen to man them. Other plans, that I am not free to reveal, are also being made.

'But if the worst should happen, I have to tell you that I shall not be here. I shall be with my sister the queen. She has ordered me to go to her because, if . . . I hate to say these words, but if the Spanish land, she wishes to send me off at once to take shelter in Scotland. I could be used by the Spanish to force her to . . . accept certain demands. I understand her reasons. So, little as it pleases me, and believe me, it does not, I would have to ride for the Scottish border at once.

'Harry, you are my son, and young as you are, you must try in my absence to behave as the master of Hawkswood should. The queen didn't mention you and I think that in her eyes, you are not a potential hostage. You are not near enough to her heart. Your life would be a featherweight against the needs of an entire realm and if there really is a Spanish invasion' – there were gasps at this point but I raised my voice to overcome them – 'then you would be useless to them. Therefore, I wish you to remain here, in the place that you will one day inherit. Though, if the Spaniards actually come to this house then it might be wiser, for a while at least, to pretend to be the son of Wilder here, and Wilder the steward left in charge of my house until my return. We would have to see how matters shape themselves.

'If the Spanish army lands, it may pillage as it marches, and may well plant soldiers in big houses like this or in the homes of villagers like those in our own Hawkswood village. In that case, Dr Joynings, you must lead our villagers.

'You, Dr Joynings, and Wilder, and all the rest of you, will have to welcome invaders, if they come, with courtesy. Give them no excuse for hurting you. And if changes to your religion are ordered, then obey . . .'

This caused a fresh outcry. Several voices cried, *No, never!* And Dr Joynings, now bouncing very heartily, with rage, was exclaiming that he would put his head on the block first.

'But will you go gladly to the stake?' I asked him, and then called Ben Flood, Hawthorn's assistant cook, to stand forth. Ben Flood was the only member of my household who was a Catholic. He made no show of it and on my part, though I knew there was a house somewhere in Woking or Guildford, where he heard secret Masses from time to time, I never asked any questions and he never forced any inconvenient knowledge on me.

I said: 'Until you are commanded otherwise, you will do best to go on living as you have always lived but quietly. There's only one God, as our good queen has said. She says that the rest is a dispute about trifles and I think she is right. But if you are ordered to change your manner of worship – be quiet, Dr Joynings! – then grumble and argue a little, because they'll expect that, but give in. You don't have to believe in any of the changes. What you think and believe inside your own heads, is your affair. No law can see inside anyone's skull. Ben can advise you in any new outward observances. I trust, Ben, that you are prepared to do this – for the sake of your colleagues here. Not merely for the sake of your faith. Are you?'

Ben had once been found scheming on behalf of his faith and I could have dismissed him. I could have turned him out without a character. I hadn't done so. He and his wife, who was then still alive, had been allowed to stay and they had been grateful. Now, when he said: 'Yes, madam,' I thought I could probably believe him. I said: 'Thank you, Ben,' and then said: 'Gladys!'

'I'm here,' said Gladys from somewhere amid the crowd. She was short of stature and I couldn't see her.

'I will ask you for a deadly potion,' I said. 'I wish to carry it. If I should fall into Spanish hands, I may need to put myself beyond their reach, for my own sake, or for the sake of the queen. As I said, through me, she could be coerced.'

There was another outcry, a babble of horror. Many people fell to their knees. Cries of, *No, it can't be going to happen* and *That's mortal sin, that is* and *You won't say that, you blithering fool, if you find yourself facing the stake* and *Oh dear God, protect us from the Spaniards!* burst from several. I could hear Mildred crying and Hannah trying to soothe her. Both were white with terror. My two youngest maidservants, Jennet and Bess, were sheltering in each other's arms. Dale was crying too and beside her Brockley was standing straight, his face grim, his arms folded, whether in determination to defy the Spaniards or determination to make sure that my orders were obeyed, I couldn't tell. Wilder was staring at me and with a stab of pity, I realized that his face had suddenly grown older; that extra years had fallen on him even in the last few minutes.

'*Listen to me!*' I raised my voice to command their attention. 'It may not happen! I tell you again that wise plans have been laid to deal with any attempts by the Spaniards to land. London will be well protected. I have told you once and now tell you again: we have good ships and good seamen and we have brave soldiers! But you have to know, you have to have time to think, to prepare your minds! For the moment, all is as usual. Go now and go about your daily work, and pray. Dr

Joynings, please hold a service to ask God to keep us safe. Do so weekly, until this time of trouble ends!'

Gladys suddenly spoke up. 'Don't think I ain't thought about all this, 'cos I have, indeed I have. Got little phials of hemlock ready, I have. Quite a few. They're on my shelf in the stillroom, with big ink letters H on them.' Gladys couldn't read or write but I had taught her how to mark her potions with certain letters and she knew their shapes. I had also provided her with a shelf of her own in my stillroom, where her potions could be stored and wouldn't become accidentally mixed with the bottles of toothwash or rose water.

'Settled on hemlock, I did,' Gladys now added. 'Better'n belladonna. That makes folk see things and go mad and be sick like they're shooting it out of a cannon. Hemlock's the one. Useful for pain, too – just a sip or two. Worth having handy in any case.'

Someone said: 'Bloody dangerous if you ask me,' but I gave Gladys a smile and said: 'Thank you.' There were more murmurs about the sin of suicide and Dr Joynings was protesting that he hoped none of us would ever be so lost to God's word as to resort to such a thing and adding that I must destroy Gladys' phials of hemlock at once. I said nothing, but looked away from him. He started towards me but Brockley caught his arm and shook a *not now* head at him and pulled him away.

Much of the crowd was seeping away by now. Soon, only Wilder, the Brockleys, Harry, Benjamin and Dickson, Mildred and Hannah remained with me. I had glimpsed Gladys making off in a hurry. Probably bent on enlarging her supply of hemlock doses.

No fire had been lit in the hall, but one was laid and now I plucked a candle out of its socket and used it to light the tinder myself. The blaze rose up, and we clustered round it. Harry was pale and I thought he was trembling. 'As yet,' I said to him, 'Philip hasn't even got a fleet, and Drake is busily trying to set fire to whatever ships he does have in his ports. There's no need to panic yet. Wilder, I think we should all have some wine. Will you . . .?'

'At once, madam,' said Wilder and went at once to see to

it. The wine warmed and comforted. Then Dickson told the boys to come with him; they would study some maps showing the ports that Sir Francis Drake was currently attacking. They let him lead them away. Dale had dried her tears and murmuring something, Brockley took her away as well. Wilder also withdrew. I was left with Mildred and Hannah and then with just Mildred, because Hannah had excused herself on the grounds that she ought to brush the hats and dresses in which the two of them had ridden home yesterday.

Mildred said: 'Before I went off to help at West Leys, when I was still so weak and miserable after losing the baby, I kept saying that everything was so wretched, that I felt so wretched, that I didn't think the sun would ever shine for me again. So Gladys said she would scry for me. Did you know that she does scrying?'

'I do now,' I said. 'She kept it well hidden before. I have forbidden her to do it again. All right, what did she say?'

'She said that a heavy cloud hung over me and not just over me but over the world, but there was light beyond the cloud, and it was moving towards us, and for me especially, something bright, a gold circle like a wedding ring, was shining, just for me.'

'I hope that in due course it will,' I told her. I spoke gently. This was no time for censure. Then, but still gently, I said: 'If this danger passes away and I can stay in peace at Hawkswood, I will try to help it to happen. But leave it to me to choose the man. I shan't fail you, I promise.'

SEVEN
Turning One's Back

During the days that followed, Dr Joynings called on me several times, to bounce and fume and insist that his first duty was to God and to the religion to which he had bound himself, but I kept on repeating that his first duty was to protect the Hawkswood villagers and indeed, those from outside Hawkswood who also liked to attend his services. To do that he must protect himself. Where he led, they would probably follow.

'Do you think that God is so blind that He wouldn't understand?' I said, not once but several times. I ruthlessly cut short Joynings' protests about our duty to be martyrs if it came to it.

'Most people don't want to be martyrs and some that were martyred probably wished they'd chosen otherwise, when it was too late.'

'But madam, Mistress Stannard . . .!'

'Do as I bid!' I thundered at him, and as I did so, I heard my voice echoing in my ears and thought wryly that King Henry, the father who never acknowledged me, who probably never even knew that I was coming into existence, might well have been proud of me. I sounded, I thought, very much like him. I never met him but I knew a great deal about him, from my mother and from Elizabeth.

Having, I hoped, convinced Joynings that he should do as he was told and stop hankering after martyrdom, I then had further duties to attend to, things that I usually did after returning from my regular attendances at court. I had a second house, Withysham, in Sussex, in the care of a steward, Robert Hanley. It was on the northern edge of the downs and was quite close to the village and house of Faldene where my uncle Herbert and my aunt Tabitha lived. Usually, after coming back from court, I travelled into Sussex to visit Withysham and sometimes Faldene as well.

This time, I planned two weeks for the task. Before I left, though, there was word from West Leys that Christopher was home again, this time to stay. I was invited to a Sunday dinner there, along with Mildred and the Brockleys.

I made sure that Gomez wouldn't be there and then accepted the invitation and it was a pleasant occasion, even though West Leys was a house of mourning. Once or twice, when Christopher spoke of Kate, I saw his face stiffen and a glint of tears appeared in his eyes, but for the most part, he was a good host, amusing us with tales of his travels, telling us how well his new daughter was thriving. He had now installed the redoubtable Joan Janes to run the house and kitchen for him and make sure that the children were looked after.

I remarked to Christopher that Janes was an unusual surname whereupon he grinned and said that as far as he had been able to learn, Joan's grandmother had been called Jane, and had died unmarried.

Joan was a massively built woman, with a voice like a bull, a hearty laugh and a quick temper. 'On her first day,' Christopher said, 'she clouted one of her maidservant daughters for being too slow over bringing her a mixing bowl. But she's a good cook.'

He was right. We all enjoyed the dinner. Mildred asked where Gomez was and we learned that he was still with the court, presumably waiting for Walsingham and Cecil to decide whether to send him back to the Netherlands on a new errand, and if so, what it should involve. Recalling the private gathering at St James', I thought it very likely that he would have to take over Juan Smith's duties and might well be the one sent to discover Philip's battle plan for his fleet. Christopher said that he was glad that these days he was only being given assignments within England. I remarked that I was thankful, these days, not to have any assignments at all. I had other things to do.

On the following Wednesday, I started for Sussex. I took Dale and Brockley with me but not Harry. To Dickson, I said: 'Let Harry practise being the head of the house. If the Spanish come, he will have to pretend to be Wilder's son – or grandson – to keep himself safe. He might be used as a hostage if the Spaniards realize who he is. But one day, there will be a time beyond that, when he will have to take his proper place as the master of Hawkswood.'

'He's only sixteen,' said Dickson, looking harassed.

'I have heard,' I said, 'that Richard the Third, as a boy of thirteen, was riding round the country, charged with some sort of commission from his brother King Edward who was raising an army. Sixteen is more than old enough. He will have your support and guidance. You will remain the tutor for Harry and for Ben, just as you are now. I entrust them to you.'

'I will do my best for them both,' said Dickson gravely. I looked at him with sympathy. He was the best tutor Harry had ever had, but he too was growing older and I had just given him a task for which his past experience hadn't well prepared him.

But that was true of us all. None of us had ever before faced a situation like this. I found myself thinking about the long road north to Scotland, leaving my home, being forced to leave all that was beloved and familiar to me far behind, perhaps for the rest of my life. My stomach turned cold. I did have friends in Edinburgh and the Brockleys would join me there; I need not be too lonely. But I would grieve for Hawkswood and Harry and I would worry endlessly: for them, for Elizabeth, for England. I wanted Harry to come into his inheritance and for that reason I didn't think he should come to Scotland with me. Better if he stayed at home, disguised if necessary as the steward's son or grandson, until it became safe for him to resume his proper place in the household. But was I doing right? I tried to peer into the future but it was of course like trying to peer into a fog. Wryly, I said to myself that now I understood why some people turned to scrying.

Meanwhile, I just did what had to be done. I took the Brockleys to Sussex with me, along with Eddie, who drove Blaze between the shafts of our little carriage, to carry the baggage and give Dale a rest now and then.

I went to Withysham first, where I found all in good order though Robert Hanley was pleased to see me because he wanted to consult with me about what to do if the Spanish landed.

'They might not come here, madam, as we're not on the direct road to anywhere, but just in case . . .'

I gave the Withysham household, which was not large, the same orders that I had given everyone at Hawkswood. I spent a whole day checking the accounts and looking over the house and the home farm. The house was old, for it had once been a women's monastery, even before the Conquest. I had modernized it a good deal but it still had some rooms with narrow, Saxon-style windows and I had never been able to turn the hall, formerly a refectory, into anything really welcoming and friendly. Bright tapestries such as those that decorated the hall at Hawkswood, a blue and red Turkey carpet flung over the table, a plethora of candles, scented rushes underfoot made no difference. It was an austere place where prayer and silence and religious readings – Catholic prayers and Catholic readings – had sunk into the grey stone walls.

If the worst came to the worst, it would do very well as a setting for the prayers of a household under Spanish orders.

There were still things I needed to attend to, but I had made a start. The next day, accompanied by the Brockleys, I rode over to Faldene. Uncle Herbert and Aunt Tabitha were privately Catholic, though they made no show of it. They had formerly gone to the regular Anglican services in the nearby village but now, because Uncle Herbert had the joint evil in his knees and could neither ride nor walk, they had installed a chaplain. He was probably a secret Catholic but I preferred not to enquire. If he was, then if the Spaniards came, he would protect my uncle and aunt. I wondered what they would really feel about an influx of Spaniards.

Faldene House, three miles to the east of Withysham, stood on a site where there had been a house since before the Conquest. There had been replacements since then, however. This one had been built a couple of centuries ago. It had a thatched roof and it had the central hall common to all such houses, and the small windows of bygone times. In more recent years, a handsome gatehouse had been built, and there was a wing that had been new only just before I was born, with modern mullioned windows.

The house stood on the side of a hill, on the northern edge of the downs, with the village of Faldene and its church, which like our own church in Hawkswood village was dedicated to St Mary, down in the valley. Its fields, those of the home farm and those rented to the villagers, were spread over both sides of the valley, mingled with patches of woodland. As ever, I thought as we approached: *I could have had a happy girlhood here, except that . . .*

Except that my aunt and uncle, though they had housed, fed, clothed and even educated me, were never kind. They were angry with my mother for having got herself into trouble, as they called it, and they heartily disliked me. They were harsh to me in ways that they were never harsh to their own children. I sometimes wondered if my behaviour when I fell wildly in love with cousin Mary's betrothed, and eloped with him in the middle of a starry summer night, had a trace of revenge in it.

Not unnaturally, my relationship with my uncle and aunt had been fraught ever since. On one occasion I had even caused Uncle Herbert to be arrested, though at another time, when one of their sons was in danger, I had tried to help them. They no longer had any power over me, of course, and I didn't know what they thought of me now. For my part, I had learned to be thankful for the food, clothing, roof and education and I tried not to remember the disproportionate fury over little things, the birchings and hours spent locked in a cupboard, the frequent reminders that I was only in the house on sufferance.

I didn't always call on them when I was in Sussex and it was nearly three years since I had last seen them. Uncle Herbert was now seventy-five, and Aunt Tabitha perhaps two years younger. They had always insisted on efficiency in their household and on arrival, as usual, we were greeted deferentially by the gatehouse porter, who sent his boy to announce us; our horses were taken by grooms who appeared as if by magic, and the butler showed us inside in ceremonious fashion, leading the way to the hall, where my uncle and aunt were sitting.

I knew they would have changed since last I saw them, but I was shaken by how much. My uncle was now badly crippled. He had moved into a downstairs bedchamber and he had had wheels put on to his chair so that his valet could move him from there to the hall and back again. He had grown massive in body and his face had deep lines of resentment and age. My aunt, in contrast, had grown thin, almost stick-like. Her face was heavily wrinkled, and sour.

'So you're here,' said Uncle Herbert. 'We thought you might come, seeing the state the world's in. Come to see how we'll manage if we suddenly have Spanish soldiers at the door, hey?'

I rose from my polite curtsey and said: 'I have been worried.'

'We are all worried,' said Aunt Tabitha. The butler was hovering. She waved a claw-like hand at him. 'Wine and cakes, Bernard, and hurry.' He disappeared and she said: 'He comes of Catholic stock. If the Spaniards come, they'll find a good Catholic house here. But don't you go thinking we want it to happen. We don't want Spanish rule. Elizabeth's done well enough by her people and we're loyal English citizens. Well, get your cloaks off and sit down. You Brockleys as well. Ursula's always treated you as equals; can't see why but she was ever wayward. Don't suppose you'll want to stay the night, any of you.'

She was quite right. We didn't. However, I said: 'You didn't know we were coming so you won't have prepared anything, and I know it would put you out if we said we wished to stay.'

'That's right enough,' said Uncle Herbert and then moved uneasily, picked up a little brass bell from the table beside him and rang it loudly, causing his valet to appear at a run.

'Privy,' grunted my uncle, and added to me: 'Seems to be every five minutes, these days. Four times last night. Never get a night's sleep now.'

The valet wheeled him away. The butler returned with the refreshments. It came to me, as I sipped my wine, that if the Spaniards did invade, they might not find either my uncle or my aunt still here. This might prove to be a final parting, unspoken but probably felt by them as well as by me.

The Brockleys sensed my uneasiness and didn't venture to

speak, so to fill what had become an empty silence, I began to talk to my aunt, about Mildred, whom she had not met, but knew about, and Mildred's marriage and the loss of the child, and the sad events at West Leys. My uncle returned and I presented them with the gifts that I had brought: embroidered gloves for my aunt, an ivory chess set for my uncle. I was thanked with some graciousness, and we were urged at least to stay for dinner.

Dinner over, we made ready to leave. I knew by the way that my uncle stared into my face at the leave-taking, as though he were trying to memorize it. I saw that he too knew it was probably our last parting. They *had* housed, fed and educated me. There was no denying that. I kissed them both goodbye, before I left.

When we left, before taking the track to Withysham, we went down into the village of Faldene, where I visited my mother's grave in the churchyard of St Mary's. Brockley and Dale stood back while I went to stand beside the mound that covered her. I talked to her a little. I didn't leave flowers. Many people leave flowers for their dead, but the flowers only wither and die and it seems a pity. I just paid my respects, and then left her in peace.

Once back at Withysham, I still had much to do and plenty to think about, apart from the machinations of the Spanish king.

Over the years, I had made changes to the place. It had one small village and just one farm attached to it. This had originally had all its fields on the northern edge of the downs, sloping up the hillside and shadowed from the sun. They weren't especially productive for crops so I had let them go back to the wild, which meant that I and the villagers could use them for grazing. I had bought some better land, on the other side of the valley, facing the sun, and put that under cultivation instead.

Now I wanted to consult with the bailiff about changing the crops. Wheat did well in the new, south-facing fields; we should grow more of it and less barley, I said.

'Barley sells well,' said Master Barrow. He was about

forty, very fit and certainly skilled in all matters agricultural but fixed in his ideas. He looked at me pityingly and said that being a lady, I might well not understand some things, but . . .

I was obliged to put on a severe, *I-am-your-employer-and-you-will-do-as-I-say-whether-you-like-it-or-not* expression, state my wishes in a clear, firm voice and then walk away before he could do any more arguing. I had worried sometimes about the number of people at Hawkswood who were near retirement age; I now wished that Barrow was.

It all took time. Hanley had charge of the stables, and I instructed him to retire one of the heavy horses, because it too was getting old, and replace it with a young one. After that, I had another disagreement with Barrow, this time about bringing in a ram of a different breed, to improve my flock of sheep. He grumbled; I said firmly that I expected to find the new ram in residence before the end of the summer, ready to sire next year's lambs, and once more, I turned on my heel. It was like the steps of a dance.

While I was busy with all this, my groom Joseph rode in with letters, from Wilder and from Mildred. Wilder reported that all was well at Hawkswood, and that Mistress Atbrigge had twice visited West Leys to spend a few hours there and play with the children. She had always taken Hannah with her. He hoped that this was in order; in any case he had no authority to object.

Mildred's letter told me the same, saying that she had become very fond of the children during her visit at the time of Kate's death, and she hoped I would approve. On the whole, I did. Indeed, a faint idea which had begun to take shape in my mind since the day when we dined there now strengthened. It was too soon, of course. Christopher must have time to grieve. But he would need someone to mother his little daughters. Joan Janes couldn't do everything and though she was assuredly used to children, big, quick-tempered, loud-mouthed Joan, who would probably hand out cuffs as often as cuddles, wasn't an ideal choice as a nursemaid. In due time, Mildred might be. If she was now making friends with Christopher and his children, well and good.

Then, just as I was making plans to move us back to Hawkswood, a spell of bad weather set in. For three days, how it rained! A troupe of travelling players who had arrived the day the downpour began were virtually trapped in Withysham with us. However, they showed their worth by entertaining us. They kept us happy throughout one long wet evening by showing us card tricks and producing a length of pliable rope on which they demonstrated a variety of knots.

They wouldn't let us into the secret of their card tricks but were willing to instruct us in making the knots. Brockley turned out to be quite gifted and I wasn't bad myself, though Dale couldn't acquire the knack and Robert Hanley found it difficult as well. Anyway, we were grateful to our entertainers and I paid them off generously when at last the skies cleared and we could all be on our way. Between one thing and another, it was three weeks, not two as I had originally planned, before we could start for home.

Even then, the skies now and then clouded over and rained on us and the roads were deep in mud. Although we wanted to hurry, we took two long days over the journey. We eventually came trotting under the arched entrance to the courtyard in the late afternoon of the second day. By then, it was early in what was turning out to be a most capricious May. That day, we had travelled through intermittent sunlight that made us shed our cloaks, and sudden showers which had us scrambling out of our saddles to get them on again and drag the hoods over our heads. There had even been a hailstorm. But it was sunny when we rode in, and there were young leaves on the trees that crowded close to Hawkswood.

No one had apparently sighted us as we approached, because only Wilder and Harry were in the courtyard to welcome us and they had no smiles of greeting. Wilder, in fact, looked as wretched as though he were about to report that the Spaniards were in occupation already or plague had wiped out half the household. Harry was just tight-lipped and angry. My son was maturing rapidly, with every passing month bearing a stronger resemblance to the handsome, charismatic man his father had been, and growing more and more possessed of adult attitudes and emotions.

'What is it?' I demanded, slipping out of Jaunty's saddle before Brockley could dismount ahead of me and give me his customary aid. 'Wilder? Harry? What's wrong?'

'*Wrong!*' Harry burst out. 'Of all the ungrateful . . .! She's been acting silly for days; going about singing to herself and smiling in a secret sort of way but when Hannah came back and told us . . .!' His attractive, slightly asymmetrical features, so very much the features of Matthew de la Roche, with whom I had known physical joy and deep unhappiness, were suffused red with fury.

'You're not making sense, Harry,' I said. 'Wilder!'

'It's Mistress Atbrigge, madam. I am so sorry. I should have prevented it, whether I had the authority or no. But she's a widow, a woman in her own right and . . .'

'What has she done? Where is she?'

'Gone, madam . . . oh, madam!' He was nearly in tears.

'*Gone where? Wilder!*' I shouted.

'She left this letter.' He held it out. 'She's been going over to West Leys, to play with the children, so she said. I didn't know, no one knew, that Master Spelton had a guest there, someone I heard you mention after you went there, a Master Gomez . . .'

'*Gomez!*' My heart turned over.

'Yes, madam. He's been at West Leys and she's been meeting him and now she's run off with him. She's going to Brussels with him, and expects to be married before they get there.'

It seemed that I had only to turn my back for three short weeks and . . .

I took the letter from him and led the way indoors, signalling to Dale and Brockley to follow.

'The fool! The silly, romantic, gullible fool! Just what,' I said, turning to face them as we all went into the hall, 'am I going to do now!'

EIGHT
Pursuit

Inside the hall, various other members of the household had been waiting nervously for me. Among those present were Dickson, looking anxious; my senior maidservant Phoebe, looking stern; Bess, my youngest one, sixteen now, halfway between scared and excited; and for some reason Abel Parsons, one of my new grooms. Abel and his brother Jack were both sturdily built fellows, in their twenties, brown-haired and brown-bearded, with the quiet manners that give confidence to horses. Abel was the elder and was said to be courting a girl in Hawkswood village. I couldn't imagine what he could have to do with the disappearance of Mildred Atbrigge.

The hearth was lit. I stood with my back to it and Brockley, at my side, spoke for me. 'Will someone please explain to Mistress Stannard *exactly* what has happened!'

'Just yesterday,' said Wilder, 'Mistress Atbrigge went off in the afternoon saying she was going to West Leys and might stay the night. She took saddlebags with her. Hannah went too, on Mealy. They've been to-ing and fro-ing between here and West Leys . . .'

'And then,' Harry burst out, 'Hannah came back, leading Mistress Atbrigge's cob and bringing that letter that you're holding, Mother, and told us . . .'

I scanned their faces. 'Where is Hannah?' I enquired.

'Upstairs, I think,' said Peter Dickson quietly.

'She's frightened,' said Phoebe grimly, 'and with reason, I'd say.'

'So would I!' muttered Dale, who had come to stand near me along with Brockley.

'Fetch her!' I snapped.

'You go,' said Phoebe to Bess. 'You're quicker on the stairs.'

Bess departed and we heard her feet running up to the floor above. I looked at the letter in my hand but decided to hear what Hannah had to say for herself first. I heard her voice, speaking to Bess as they came down the stairs; she sounded tearful, as well she might. Then they came in together, Bess leading Hannah by the hand. Hannah was eighteen by now, a recent addition to my household. Hitherto she had seemed a sensible girl. She had become Mildred's maid, learning the work with surprising speed. She had become Mildred's confidante as well, apparently. Just now, there were tears of fright on her normally pretty face.

I was in no mood to be gentle. 'Hannah, come here! Tell me what has happened and why you allowed it to happen and never warned anyone!'

'Madam, I didn't know, not till it was too late. Please, madam, don't turn me off when I've nowhere to go. I didn't know! I had no idea . . .'

'All right. What *happened*?'

'After you went away, mistress, we went to West Leys twice in the first week. Mistress Atbrigge played with the children and so did I. And there was this Master Gomez there; he was ill, at first. He'd been on his way back to wherever it is he comes from, meant just to pass a night at the farm, only he fell sick with a rheum and a fever, and my mistress helped to look after him, taking him possets and changing his sheets . . .'

'I take it that he recovered?'

'Yes. He did. The second time we went there, he was up and about and it was sunny and he and my mistress walked in the field near the house, and talked and laughed. Then we came home and some days later we went there again – you had been away for nigh on two weeks then – and he was still there and he and my mistress they went walking together again, that time and the next as well. I stayed with the children; those little girls are so sweet and . . .'

'Never mind Christopher's daughters! Didn't *he* take an interest in all these talks and walks?'

'I don't know, madam. How would I know? Please, madam, it wasn't my fault, it wasn't . . .'

'She should have noticed! She should have known!' Dale was merciless.

'Very well, go on,' I said. 'You've only just begun the tale.'

'Yesterday, madam, my mistress said we would go there again and might stay the night. She brought her saddlebags upstairs and packed them, doing it herself, and I did wonder, after all, West Leys is just a farm, not a place for being fashionable but she packed a very smart gown and she took a farthingale with her, in its linen bag, and then she put that into one of your leather travelling bags and slung it on top of her saddlebags because it wouldn't fit into them and . . .'

'Then she's bound for somewhere that's no farm!' Dale said.

I knew what she meant. Farthingales are a nuisance when one is travelling. They are quite unsuitable wear for riding a horse, for one thing; they have to be packed and they won't fit into saddlebags. Mildred's and mine were whalebone wheels with an opening that let one get into it, and clasps to close it round one's hips. We carried them in linen bags, wide enough to accommodate the hoops in an upright position, and then put them into weatherproof leather bags that could be slung onto a horse like extra saddlebags. There would be no need of them at West Leys. One only needed them in places where formal dress would be worn.

'Didn't she explain why she was taking them?' I barked at poor Hannah. 'Didn't you *ask*?'

'It wasn't my place to ask.' Hannah was sobbing.

'Well, and then?'

'We set off, my mistress on her Grey Cob, me on Mealy, much like always. We went in the afternoon when it's mostly quiet and no one about much.' I nodded again. Afternoons, once dinner had been eaten, usually were quiet at Hawkswood.

'But before we were halfway,' said Hannah in anguish, 'we met this Master Gomez! He had a fine horse and another horse as well, saddled. Not a side-saddle. And the mistress greeted him, laughing, and she got off Grey Cob and put all her saddlebags on this other horse and then got on to it herself. She bundled up her skirts and I saw she had leggings on as well as her boots so that she could ride astride and the stirrup leathers wouldn't bite her knees. And she gave me that letter you've got there, madam, and told me to go home and take Grey Cob and not to worry, she was going to be so happy. I begged her not to go, I did, madam, but she laughed at me and wouldn't listen. What could I do? They rode off together and left me there.'

'I saw her collecting the saddlebags from where they hang in the harness room, madam,' said Abel Parsons, speaking up suddenly. 'I asked her if I could help her at all but she just smiled and said no, thank you. If I had guessed, I'd have tried to stop her but . . .'

'You should have stopped her! I'd have stopped her if I'd not been at my books so she was out of my sight!' said Harry, glaring at Dickson.

'I don't suppose anyone could have stopped her,' I said. 'She is my companion but I am no longer her guardian. She is a widow, a free woman, entitled to marry where she will. Very well, Hannah. I accept that you were taken by surprise.' I looked down at the letter I was still holding. It was rolled tightly and tied with cord. There was no seal. I pulled the cord loose, opened the scroll and read.

> My very dear Ursula, to whom I own I owe so much, I have at last found my future. I am going to be happy. Berend Gomez is to be my new husband. If you knew him as I have come to do, you would be glad for me and not anxious. We are going to Brussels. Berend has a letter to deliver there to the Duke of Parma, a letter from the queen herself. He would be there by now, had illness not delayed him, but if it had not, we would never have learned to know each other as we have, never come to love each other. We shall marry once we are across the Channel. Please be glad for me and don't pursue us. And please don't be angry with Hannah. She knew nothing about this until the moment when I told her to go home and take Grey Cob home as well.
>
> In haste, your loving Mildred.

'She is utterly out of her mind!' I shouted, crushing the missive in my hand. 'She says don't pursue her. Well, I must! Wilder . . .'

'Madam, as soon as Hannah came back with Grey Cob, I sent for Laurence Miller. I know what his position here truly is. I told him what had happened and we knew you'd very likely want to go after her, but that would mean going across to the Netherlands and you'd need consent, from Walsingham or Cecil. You'd be stopped at Dover if you went off without it, if you didn't have a passport from one of them. It's not like the old days when you had a passport all the time and could go anywhere. Things have changed, these last few years. Miller left at once. Driving that trotter Pharoah; he must have got there very quickly. I gave him a letter to deliver. Even if no one could see him at once, letters mostly get passed to whoever they're addressed to fast enough. And this morning I sent Jack Parsons off to West Leys to tell Master Spelton, being as it was under his roof that she . . .'

'You've done well, Wilder. What's that? I can hear hooves outside . . .'

There were voices as well; Jack Parsons and Arthur Watts talking rapidly, then a horse snorting and booted feet landing on the cobbles as someone threw himself out of his saddle. Wilder strode to the door and flung it open, and there was Christopher, distraught as I had never seen him.

'Ursula! Mistress Stannard! I have just heard! I never thought! I have been as innocent as my little Elizabeth! And much less sensible – the way they got on together – twice they took that walk up to the saddleback in the hill behind West Leys, the way I used to do with Kate, and she once did with Eric. It's a lovers' walk if ever there was one. I should have realized! He said he was testing his legs after being ill, because he must be on his way as soon as he could. He said it was pleasant to walk in company. I never, never dreamed . . .'

'No one did,' I said wearily. My own legs felt weak. I had been travelling most of the day and now this! I said: 'Brockley, bring the baggage in; Abel, help him and make sure that all our horses are being tended. Wilder, I want supper for us all, as quickly as possible. Dale, come upstairs with me. I want to get my boots off and change out of these mud-splashed things.'

'In your place, ma'am, I would give that silly lady's maid, as she calls herself, something to remember for the rest of her life.'

'I think Mildred deceived her until the last minute,' I said. 'She probably isn't to blame, though the fright she has had won't do her any harm. Anyway, she isn't the point. What is the point is catching up with them before they can marry. If I can get to Mildred I can at least argue with her!'

I put a hand to my head, realizing all too clearly that like Wilder and Phoebe, I was not as young as I had been. I not only didn't want all this; I hardly felt I had the strength to deal with it. But I would have to go, if I could get permission. I couldn't inflict such a task on Brockley. He wasn't that young now, either. The grooms hadn't the authority . . .

'Just a moment,' said Christopher. 'I think this task is mine.'

I turned to him with relief. I had been so distracted that for a foolish moment, I had forgotten that he was there. 'Gomez has done some deceiving,' he said, 'and in my house. I thought how pleasant it was for him to have someone to talk to as he took exercise and made his legs strong again. I never saw any harm in it. Mistress Atbrigge, a recent widow, and sorrowing for the loss of an expected child, would have no interest in another man, I thought. Not yet. And all the time, he was making love to her and she was responding! And now!'

'The horses,' I said. 'Where did he get the horses?'

'He'd have used a hiring stable in Guildford,' said Christopher. 'He always did if he passed this way. This morning he said he was fit enough to resume his journey. He rode off on a horse he'd got from the Guildford place; he said it was a wayward brute and he'd return it and hire a fresh one. He presumably hired two.'

'Where were they making for?' Brockley asked. 'Dover? Or wouldn't somewhere on the east coast be best for the Netherlands? Norwich . . . that's a river port, isn't it? Or London? Ships go down the Thames heading for everywhere.'

'Yes, and he does vary his routes; it's the sort of thing we all do. But this time he was making for Dover,' Christopher said. 'He told me as much. It's the nearest and I think he would have kept to that; I dare say he would want to get his stolen bride out of the country as quickly as possible, to make it harder to catch up with them. Although,' he looked at me gravely, 'does anyone have the right to haul her back if she doesn't want to come?'

'No,' I said frankly. 'But we can try. I tremble to think how I would explain this to her parents. I am sure that they at least still regard me as her guardian, even though I am not. Christopher, I fear for her! She will be a stranger in a foreign land, and one that may be at war with us before long. She may have plunged headlong into catastrophe! Anything could happen to her!'

'So someone must go after her. I anticipated that.' Christopher was decisive. 'And as I said, this is my task. If I can catch up with her in time, I can at least explain to her how perilous it is to go to Brussels now. I speak Dutch, I have that advantage. Mistress Stannard, I understand that you are just home from a long journey. There is no need for you to take the road in pursuit as well as me.'

I said wearily: 'I can't anyway. I have to wait for Laurence Miller to come back.'

And just then, from outside, there was a whinny, and the creak of wheels. 'I think he is back already,' Christopher said.

I wondered what I would do if Walsingham refused me leave to go. I half wished he would, and half wondered how, in that case, I could get to the Netherlands without leave. It was the last place, barring Spain itself, that I wanted to visit, but it looked as though Fate, mischievously, was bent on sending me there. Going after Mildred was my responsibility, even if Christopher was willing to go in my stead. My hands trembled as I undid the little scroll from Walsingham. But its few terse words granted me the right to travel out of the country. Stark, subtle Walsingham, relentless pursuer of Jesuits, ruthless interrogator who didn't mind going into the bowels of the Tower and listening to the sounds that his prisoners made on the rack, did have a human side. He knew how responsible I felt for Mildred.

He had also sent me a form of identification, to help me obtain an audience with the Duke of Parma if need be. It rolled out of the scroll and fell into my palm, a gold ring engraved with a lion and a dragon, the supporters of Elizabeth's coat of arms. Christopher, as a Queen's Messenger, had an identical one.

Walsingham had done his best for me. It was up to me now.

I hadn't the strength to shout for a horse to be saddled so that I could set out forthwith. 'We must leave at daybreak,' I said to Christopher. 'I can't go further tonight – I ought to but I can't.'

'Very well.' Again, Christopher was decisive. 'We may still catch them,' he said. 'They have a good hundred miles to go and I don't see Mistress Atbrigge staying in the saddle for all that way without stopping to eat or sleep; she is no royal messenger. They will have rested the night somewhere, and if they got to Dover today, they still have to find a ship. I suggest,' said Christopher, 'that we take a good supper, retire to sleep, and get into our saddles at dawn.'

'The supper will be on the table in half an hour,' said Wilder.

It was a cold daybreak. We had warm hooded cloaks but still the wind was chill as we set out, walking and cantering alternately, eastward, to join the main road to Dover.

For once, the Brockleys weren't with me. Dale could never have endured the long, hard ride that lay ahead and she had quailed visibly at the thought of going into possibly enemy territory. She never liked to see Brockley go off anywhere with me but not with her, but this time she said she understood the need. 'This is a terrible thing,' she told me and then bravely added: 'You will want Roger with you, ma'am, I know.'

I did want him but I knew quite well that he was even more tired than I was. Also, of late, his health had given cause for concern. He had recently suffered from a recurrent fever. It seemed to have passed now but I didn't think I should ask him to undertake foreign travel, and very fast travel at that. Brockley too must stay behind. I would just go with Christopher, I said. I took two well-filled saddlebags containing among other things one practical woollen gown and one more formal grosgrain gown. Both were open-fronted and worn above pretty kirtles. Inside the open skirts were secret, sewn-in pouches, in which I could carry such things as a small purse of money, a small sheathed dagger and a set of lockpicks. Unusual items for a lady's baggage, but the life I led was often unusual for a lady as well. To me, a dagger and picklocks were commonplace.

I also took my ruffs and a farthingale, in a separate bag. If we had to go as far as Brussels and confront Mildred inside the Duke of Parma's palace, I would need to dress correctly. For riding, I had an old black gown (with another hidden pouch), a grey kirtle that was loose enough to bunch up easily, and a pair of leggings borrowed from Dale. I too would ride astride. For fast travel, it was best.

Christopher, who had expected to undertake this journey, had come prepared. Like me, he had full saddlebags, augmented by a pack on his back. He said its contents included a smoothing iron. He too had considered the need to be presentable enough to appear at Parma's court. We hoped with all our hearts that we would catch up with Mildred before that. If we didn't, she might be married before we could reach her.

The first stage of our ride was exhilarating in its way. The horses were lively, snorting vapour into the chill air of daybreak, fretting at the bit, wanting to gallop. Christopher's big black horse Jet tried to buck him off, though without success. We were glad of their liveliness because it meant that we could make good time on the way to Reigate, over twenty miles away, where we would change to fresh horses. For the first stage, Abel Parsons rode with us, on Splash. It would be his task to lead Jet and Jaunty back to their homes once they had rested.

Dover was a hundred miles in a straight line but in order to get on to the Dover road we couldn't go in a straight line but must first go north-east and ride by way of Canterbury. It would add a good few miles to the journey. The only alternative was to go across country, which would mean muddy lanes, fields in crop, belts of pathless woodland, meadows with bulls in them, heathlands with bogs in them. If your horse went lame or cast a shoe where no farms were in sight, there was

no one to help you, and nowhere to change horses or get
something to eat, either. Well-used tracks were best and fastest
and any case, the road to Dover was familiar to us both.

We discovered quite soon that our quarry had chosen the
same route. The stableman at Guildford confirmed that Gomez
had hired two horses from him. We parted from Abel, set out
again at the best speed we could, and picked up their scent at
Maidstone, where we paused at an inn called the White Horse
to change horses again and snatch a quick meal.

I hadn't been that way for years and didn't know the current
landlord but he was clearly on familiar terms with Christopher.
He was a big, fleshy fellow, his shirt open beneath an old
doublet and a stained apron over his breeches. When Christopher
described the couple we were pursuing he recognized them at
once. Yes, they had spent the night before last there. He grinned
slyly and said: 'A pretty pair of doves they were, for all he
looked old enough to be her father.'

'He's thirty-three,' said Christopher coldly.

'Looked older,' said the landlord, undeterred. 'Not long
wed, I fancy. Or are they eloping? Is that why you're giving
chase? Fancy you might be too late; she had a wedding ring.'

I knew she had. Mildred had never taken Master Atbrigge's
ring off. She must be finding it useful now. The landlord was
suppressing chuckles at all this but Christopher looked at him
repressively and addressed him in a stern voice. 'They're not
long married, not that it's any business of yours, Jem Southey.
We've family news for them and it's an urgent matter. We
need fresh horses and we need good ones. Last time I hired
a horse from you, you palmed me off with a clumsy brute that
had a gift for putting its big stupid hooves into potholes. Twice
I nearly went over its head. It was a washy chestnut with white
socks on both front fetlocks, so I'll know it again.'

I strangled a desire to laugh. Master Southey looked hurt.
'I know the beast you mean. I've sold it to an elderly cleric
who wanted a quiet ride. Nice old fellow, rosy cheeks and
smiling eyes. He'll be all right with it; it wasn't clumsy at a
walk.'

'Food,' said Christopher brusquely. 'And small ale and our
fresh horses saddled and waiting. Cross saddles.'

'Sit you down and get those cloaks off. Table's over there. Ten minutes,' said Southey. In fairness to him, he produced hot meat pies and fried beans in not much more than the ten minutes, along with tankards of the small ale that refreshes one so well but doesn't go to one's head. Before long we were brushing crumbs off ourselves, swallowing the last drops of ale, picking up our cloaks and hastening out to the stable yard, where we found two sturdy animals waiting for us, ready saddled.

We continued to make good time. The weather was dry and so was the road, and there was warmth now in the May sunshine. Dusk was only just beginning when we finished the final stage and were coming into Dover.

'We'll go to an inn called the Safe Harbour,' Christopher said. 'Do you know it?'

'I haven't been there for a long time but yes, I know it. Bessie Ferguson is the landlord's daughter. If the landlord is still Ralph Harrison, that is. There was a to-do over Bessie marrying Duncan Ferguson. Old Hamish didn't think an innkeeper's daughter good enough for his son.'

'Bessie's a gift for any family. Full of good sense and good humour and her pastry's better than Southey's is. That meat pie lay a bit heavy on my stomach. Harrison always knows what ships are coming and going from Dover. Five more minutes and we'll be there,' said Christopher, shaking up his reins.

It was nearing nine of the clock and past sunset, but in the light of the flambeaux and lanterns that hung around its stable yard, the Safe Harbour looked just as I remembered it: built round two sides of the yard, thatched – the thatch was new, still golden – and with limewashed walls, crisscrossed by stout black timbers, and thick green-tinged glass in its windows, so that its rooms were shadowy but well protected from wind and rain. Candlelight glimmered within them.

The ostler was new to me but broad-shouldered, hearty Ralph Harrison looked exactly as he had the last time I had seen him, which was more than ten years ago. He welcomed us as old friends and he had information. Mildred and Gomez had passed that way. They had reached the Safe Harbour the previous day.

'But they were that wild to get away across the Channel,
bound for the Netherlands, where their home was, they said,'
Ralph told us. 'And there was a ship sailing today – this
evening, in fact – at eight of the clock, the *Arabella*, bound
for Oslo to pick up a load of pinewood but due to call at
Ostend on the way, had a cargo to unload there. God knows
what were in it,' said Ralph, grimly. 'It was supposed to be
ironware and tin ingots but the seaman who told me – he was
a crewman having a farewell drink with some shorebound
friends afore he left – said he'd helped to load it and one of
the box lids had broken open, and though everything inside
was packed in straw he could have sworn he'd seen gun barrels
poking through it.

'Some merchants,' said Ralph, 'will sell arms, even to folk
who might one day train them on us, just as long as they get
paid promptly. But anyhow, the *Arabella* was due to sail and
to the right place as long as Master and Mistress Gomez were
concerned. So off they've gone and you've missed them by
not much more than an hour. They went off hasty as you like,
hired a cart from me to carry their things and one of my lads
went with them to bring it back, and when he got back, he
said that yes, they'd got themselves passages and gone aboard.'

'Has the *Arabella* actually sailed yet?' I said urgently. 'It's
nearly nine, but . . .'

'Yes, she's sailed,' said Ralph, looking at our faces with
concern. 'I can see the shipping come and go, from my attic
window, and I often do go up to have a look at it. I saw her
moving out; a pretty sight, white sails turning pink in the
sunset, billowing out with a fair wind. Is it so very
important?'

'Yes. It is,' I told him. 'When is there another ship bound
for Ostend?'

'Not for three days, far as I know. The *Argenteus*, makes
regular journeys: carries tin and silver and woollen cloth and
there's tales about her too, about what's really in some of them
boxes supposed to be full of tin ingots, and what's wrapped
up nice and warm inside bales of pretty pale blue and peach-
pink and tawny and russet cloths to make winter gowns for
ladies.' Ralph was both wrathful and cynical.

'Would she take passengers?' Christopher asked.

'Captain Bridges, he'd take Old Nick himself, given the old devil paid up.'

But she wasn't sailing for three days. By then, Mildred and Gomez would probably be in Brussels.

We could do nothing but negotiate with this Captain Bridges, kick our heels for those three days, and like it.

NINE
Mildred Speaks

This part of the story is Mildred's. It isn't the incoherent tale that she told me when we finally met again; at that time I was too angry to listen to her properly. This is the account she gave me later when both of us had once more turned into reasonable people, and even then, she wrote it down rather than tell me aloud.

My dear Mistress Stannard, you have been endlessly kind to me, but I know that you have never understood how it was between me and Berend Gomez. I know you thought, *Oh dear, it's happening again. For the third time in a couple of years, that silly girl Mildred has fallen in love, and once again, as ever, with the wrong man.* Well, part of that was true. I had twice fallen in love with men who proved to be unsuitable. But I could remember well enough what that felt like and when I met Berend, it was quite different.

I want to say something about myself, for it has to do with what I know you will call my ill-judged romances. As you know, I was born to fairly well-off tradespeople in Devonshire. My parents were loving but they were Puritans and I grew up in a world where colourful clothes, attention to one's appearance, music, dancing and even interesting food were considered ungodly, wrong. As I grew from a child into a young woman I began to yearn for something else, something brighter, freer, merrier . . . I didn't quite know what. When I was nineteen, my parents found me someone to marry but I couldn't bear him. Well, you know all about that; you met him. He was twenty years or more older than I was, all bulging stomach and slobbery lips, and when I was shown his home and the things I would have to see to as his wife, I was terrified. I would have been expected to run a household ten times the size of the one I was used to, to understand recipes I had never heard of before, and to help on the farm as well, to help with lambing . . .

I refused to marry him. My parents were angry. Meanwhile, I had fallen in love on my own account. It came to nothing, in a very sad way, but I realized later that I had had a lucky escape. I also realized that when I fell in love like that, it was at least half because I also longed to escape from my narrow family, though I had no idea where or what I ought to escape to.

When you, Mistress Stannard, offered to take me into your household as your companion, I was glad to accept and I know very well that my parents were glad to be rid of me. And then I fell in love once more and that time it should have been all right. You approved! It was a respectable match. Daniel Atbrigge was no Puritan but he was a vicar, a man of God. He could offer me a comfortable home and a way of life which appealed to me, which I could understand. I married him and became Mistress Atbrigge and for a short while I was so very happy. Marriage suited me. It satisfied a need that I hadn't till then known that I had; the need for a man's company, for male caresses, for physical love.

His death, and again the circumstances were distressing, put an end to all that. I came back to Hawkswood to live, once more, with you. I miscarried the child I was expecting, and everyone around me took it for granted that I was racked with sorrow for my double bereavement, my husband and my child. For a little while, I was. And then it passed. It passed between one day and the next. I lay down one night and cried myself to sleep as I had done so often, and then awoke in the morning, free, recognizing that I was better off without Daniel Atbrigge and that I hadn't truly wanted to bear his child. Ursula, you promised that when I was ready, you would help me find a new husband. But I was ready much sooner than you knew and then . . .

How can I make you understand what I felt about Berend Gomez? It was quite different from the way I felt on those earlier occasions. I met him when he came to West Leys with Christopher Spelton and when we were introduced to each other it was like meeting an old friend. It wasn't exciting or breathtaking; no unseen angels played harps when he spoke. I didn't drown in his eyes or feel as if I had fallen down a well and emerged into the glorious light of Paradise. With Berend, I stayed safely in this world and talked of ordinary things. And wanted to go on like that for ever.

His looks appealed to me, certainly. He was handsome, his features clear cut, his skin smooth and tinged with brown, his hair as blue-black as any cock blackbird's plumage. He had dark eyes which always had a smile in them, a tidily clipped dark beard round chin and jaw, beautiful hands, strong and shapely, with a few dark hairs on their backs. But it wasn't just his looks that drew me. That was how it had been in the past, yes. On those previous occasions, the men concerned had looks that made my stomach turn somersaults. This was quite otherwise: quiet, sane, certain.

When you were away at Withysham I went several times to West Leys, and I found Berend there, recovering from an illness. When he was better, we walked and talked together. I told him about my first marriage and how it had ended; he in turn told me all about himself.

His father, Ricardo Gomez, was a Spanish merchant, bringing shiploads of oranges from Spain, and spices and silks from eastern countries, and taking metals back – tin, copper, iron, and tools and things made of bronze and iron. Oh, even in the days of the Protestant King Edward, there was trade with Spain. There is always trade, so Berend told me. Merchants look to their profits and leave others to argue about religion. Once, bringing goods to a market in Portsmouth, Ricardo met and fell in love with Jane Winter, daughter of Catholic parents, English merchants who lived in Portsmouth. Ricardo and Jane married in the May of 1551. Her parents had sought the match and were happy enough for Ricardo to take his wife back to Spain, to his home in Barcelona. Berend told me that he was born there in the January of 1555. He is much older than I am, I know. But just because of that, I felt safe with him. He knew the world. I wish now that I had known it better.

Ricardo Gomez died when Berend was just eight. His father

had been so often away on voyages, that Berend saw little of him and hardly missed him when he died. His mother Jane decided to return to her parents in England. She had some money; she was able to bring that with her and her parents were happy enough to have her company. Berend finished his growing up in Portsmouth and came to love England as his home. He married in England, when he was only eighteen. But his wife died after only three years of marriage and their one child, a daughter, died too.

Berend didn't wish to be a merchant. He took service with a gentleman who travelled at times to the court of the Duke of Parma. In fact, this man was one of Parma's agents. He was getting old and wanted, as it were, to train an apprentice. He chose Berend. Berend could speak Spanish, which would be a great advantage. His master retired; Berend stepped into his shoes. Yet his love for England dragged at his feet and when he was caught, he was actually relieved to become a double agent. Now he is paid both by Parma and by Elizabeth and has been able to rent a house in Brussels. He said he was beginning to put the past behind him, and to think of marrying again.

One early morning we walked up to the saddleback of that hill just behind West Leys towards the newly risen sun, and there, he asked me if I would be his wife. He was honest – at least I thought so. He admitted to me that of late, the duke had seemed suspicious of him, but he told me that he was now engaged on a confidential errand, which he was sure of carrying out, and if so – though he didn't think it was a case of *if* – the duke's trust in him would be restored. He asked me if I would mind the fact that he was an agent, that he would sometimes have to travel without me, and might now and then run into danger.

I said I didn't mind. You are an agent, Ursula. I thought of Berend as being just another such as you.

Then he said: 'The only thing is, that we need to do it at once for I must return to Brussels as soon as I am fit to ride, and that is now. I woke this morning knowing it. I must therefore leave without delay and I don't know when I shall be back in England. Will you trust me and come with me? I doubt if your duenna Mistress Stannard would give her consent so we must go without it. There is no time to linger and argue and arrange a wedding here. We can marry as soon as we set foot in Ostend. I know a priest there who will perform the ceremony. And, my darling, you will have to become a Catholic.'

I didn't object to that. I was the daughter of Puritans and throughout my girlhood, I had been starved of colour, of brightness, of beauty. I liked the idea of incense and lovely vestments and a world that exulted in stained glass instead of being slightly apologetic about it. There is stained glass in St Mary's at Hawkswood and the villagers love it and so does the vicar, Dr Joynings, but I knew from my parents that many people in England disapprove of such things; they are thought Popish. Berend was offering me something I greatly desired.

I don't mean that I suddenly wanted the king of Spain's Armada to invade and seize England; no, of course not. I didn't think so deeply. Well, I am but twenty. Though I have grown older inside myself. When I fell in love with Berend, there were many things that I didn't understand.

I knew, Ursula, that Berend was right when he said you would never agree to the match, at least not in such hasty fashion. Getting your agreement would take time that he couldn't afford. So I said: 'I trust you and I will come away with you. But if we don't marry in Ostend, I will go no further with you. I will bring funds enough with me to buy my passage home.'

'My love,' said Berend, and there in the sunshine on the hilltop, we kissed, and our marriage vows were in that kiss.

Then we became practical, settling details. 'After dinner, when the house is quiet,' I said. 'That would be best. Will it be today?' That did frighten me a little; I felt as though life were turning upside down all in five minutes. But Berend was holding me. I said: 'We must go soon anyway; Mistress Stannard has sent word that she is about to return.'

'We'll go tomorrow,' said Berend. 'I will leave in the morning and arrange about horses for us. We will need good ones; your grey cob won't be fast enough for the journey. We must ride fast, to keep ahead of any pursuit. Now, then. Halfway between Hawkswood and West Leys, there's a spinney. It stands alone in the midst of common land. You know it?'

'Yes. There's a stream nearby where we sometimes let the horses drink.'

'I will meet you in the spinney at three of the clock and I'll have a horse for you. Bring your maid with you, so that she can lead your cob back home. Pack what you need but remember, we will have only saddlebags or whatever can be slung on top of them. Bring a farthingale to wear at the ducal court.'

He grinned. 'It will be best if you ride astride; we're in haste, remember. Wear leggings as well as boots and loose skirts that you can kilt. Leave a letter, to say that we are going to marry, and are bound for the Duke of Parma's court in Brussels. Let us be as open as we can. Mistress Stannard will guess where we're going, anyway. There's no point in trying to hide that.'

I did as he asked. Yes, I did as he asked. It was that or lose him, see him go off to Brussels without me. If he did, I might never see him again.

Next day, at the last minute, I was seized with panic. I was going away with a man I was deeply in love with and yet scarcely knew, and we were going to a country that was under Spanish rule. I was by their standards a heretic. I was willing to become a Catholic but how would I manage to seem convincing? I considered changing my mind; failing to arrive at the trysting place. I was in a turmoil. In the end, when dinner was over and everything was quiet, I went to the still-room and stole one of Gladys' hemlock phials. It was marked with an H. It was stoutly stoppered but I wrapped it tightly in a piece of cloth for safety's sake before I put it in my belt pouch. If I were ever seized as a heretic and faced with a heretic's dreadful death, perhaps, if I were quick and determined enough, this would be my way out.

After that, I took a deep breath, and with it, my final decision. Just after three on the afternoon on that day, the fifth of May, I rode to the spinney, accompanied by an unsuspecting Hannah. I was suddenly afraid that he wouldn't be there, that he had only played a cruel trick on me, or that something had

happened, illness, a summons to undertake some sudden task
or other. He was an agent and sudden things can happen to
agents. I understood that because of you, Ursula.

But as we approached, he came out of the trees, seated on
one horse and leading another. I gasped with relief and we
both spoke at once.

'You're here! At the last moment, I was afraid . . .'

'So was I. Dear Mildred, I couldn't be sure . . .'

Then we were laughing. I slipped down from Grey Cob,
ran his stirrup up to the top of its leather, pulled his reins over
his head and handed them to Hannah. She started to say: 'But
what . . .?' but Berend interrupted her. 'Hannah, your mistress
is coming away with me, to be married. We are going to
Brussels. I mean well by her; have no fear.'

Poor Hannah just gaped at us. But I was already transferring
my saddlebags to the other horse and there wasn't any time
for long explanations. Then he said: 'Hannah, take the cob
home. Go now. Mildred, my love, can you mount without
help? Good, yes, I see you can.' I was already swinging myself
into the saddle, pulling my skirts out of the way, bundling
them round me and feeling with my right foot for the other
stirrup.

I said: 'Goodbye, Hannah. You knew nothing of our plans
until now so I hope no one will be too angry with you.' And
then we were cantering away. My horse was a lively chestnut,
tossing his mane and fretting to gallop. In moments, we had
left Hannah behind.

I was sorry for her; she would be fiercely questioned about
all this. But she really hadn't known what I meant to do. I hoped
that her innocence would protect her and in the letter I left on
my bed, I assured you of her innocence. As for me, I was
launched on my great adventure. I was so happy, Ursula!

TEN

Leaving the Past Behind

We were lucky with the weather, and as dusk was beginning, we came to the town of Maidstone, which Berend said was halfway to Dover. I wrinkled my nose at an unfamiliar smell and made him laugh. 'You don't know what that is?' he said to me.

'No, I don't.'

'It's the smell of a brewery. Or two or three. This is a great centre for brewing ale. Are you tired? We'll be inside a good inn before you know it. I know the route to Dover very well and I can recommend the White Horse.'

He was right about that. A groom was there the moment we rode into the yard and then a manservant came out of the inn to greet us and collect our saddlebags. The place was busy; this was evidently a popular inn. The stable yard was full of comings and goings and the grooms were having to move fast.

It was all interesting and exciting. A trio of gentlemen who had evidently been travelling together had waved the grooms aside and were unsaddling their own horses, while a short round gentleman with a bouncy walk and an impatient, slightly high-pitched voice was hiring a horse and refusing the one that had been offered to him; it was too tall for his convenience and he wanted something not over fifteen hands. The ostler he was talking to said something and gestured in a protesting way, and the short gentleman emitted a scornful laugh, like the bray of a donkey. I was amused by the little scene but I never learned the end of it because at that moment Berend pulled at my elbow and walked me indoors. Inside, we were welcomed by a broad-built landlord, wiping his hands on a well-used apron before offering handshakes to us. Berend presented me as his wife, and the landlord, who clearly knew him well, at once assumed that we were new-wedded and

congratulated us, beaming. I smiled and found to my delight
that I was now to be addressed as Mistress Gomez, 'or should
it be Señora?' our friendly host asked him.

'Señora would be best,' said Berend, and gave me a
reassuring smile as the man who was laden with our
baggage led us upstairs. He showed us into a bedchamber
suitable for two people, with a good wide bed, where he
deposited our bags. Berend slipped him a silver shilling.

When he had gone, Berend turned to me. 'I can sleep well
over to one side of the bed and put a rolled-up cloak between
us if you prefer. We aren't wed yet and that may matter to
you.'

'I don't think that would be fair to you,' I said. Oddly
enough, this aspect of our journey just hadn't occurred to me.
Perhaps because of the miscarriage that wasn't far behind
me, I had lost physical desire. It wasn't lust that had brought
me here with this man, just the need for love of the heart, and
a husband's company. I had experienced that once, and for a
time it had been good. I wanted it back.

'You are sure? I will not desert you. We *will* marry and if
we are lucky over finding a ship, it will be within days. And
I had the forethought to bring a small sponge with me, and
some vinegar.'

'I am sure,' I said, and once again, he laughed. Berend often
laughed. He had a joyous heart.

It felt strange at first. The man now sharing my bed was
still not that well known to me. For a moment I did want to
hesitate, wondering if I should be doing this, but the night
was chill and he was holding me, warming me, caressing me,
and feelings that I thought I had forgotten were returning.

'Don't worry about it,' he said. 'Be easy and I will do the
work.'

And after all, it was easy, and pleasant, although I didn't
reach a climax, as I had done in Daniel Atbrigge's arms. But
I thought it would come. I was out of practice. Berend was
happy, anyway. He sighed with pleasure, and held me close
until he began to fall asleep. I was as good as his wife, I
thought.

Next day we reached Dover, where we went to an inn called

the Safe Harbour and there we learned that a ship called the *Arabella* was due to sail for Ostend the next day and we might be able to get passages on her. Berend had a passport and a man has the right to take his wife with him when he travels. We went aboard late on the very next afternoon and we were on deck as the ship sailed out of the harbour. I saw her sails filling with a good south-west wind. I looked back, and saw the white cliffs which I had heard of but never before seen. I was on the other side of England from my parents' home in the shadow of Dartmoor.

We spent the night on board, in a cabin with four bunks and five fellow passengers, all of them men. We squeezed ourselves into one of the bunks but this time we had no inclination to make love. There were lanterns that gave the cabin an uncertain light, and perhaps I imagined the glances and winks but if our cabin mates were hoping for some erotic entertainment, we disappointed them. Anyway, as a simple precaution, we took our saddlebags to bed with us. The congestion in our bunk left no room for any kind of movement.

All this time, I had been buoyed up by excitement. Everything, the fast ride, the inns, the ship, was new and thrilling. At home in Devon, a wish for the stimulation of new things was frowned on. One accepted what God sent and to court eventfulness was another thing that was wrong.

I was so glad to escape, to come away with you, Ursula, and when I met Daniel, I found all the excitement I could want: life as a wife, life in an unfamiliar setting, physical love, a child. Only, those new things turned out to be the wrong ones. With Berend, I thought I had found the right ones. I was still in that wide-eyed mood when we landed at Ostend.

It was a clear, cool morning. I stood on the quayside, once more looking about me with great interest. The quay was crowded, with people, piles of luggage, crates of merchandise, porters staggering under boxes and hampers. At the far end, I saw a number of grooms holding horses and closer at hand a couple of carts were standing, one being unloaded, while sacks of something were being tossed aboard the other. Seabirds wheeled and cried. A family, father, mother and several children, who were apparently waiting to board a ship and had brought picnic food with them, were watching the birds and the children were throwing scraps to them.

All around me was a babble of unfamiliar languages, Dutch and Spanish, but others as well. Half a dozen fair-haired sailors unloading goods from another ship were calling to each other in what I thought must be Norwegian or Swedish and some swarthy sailors working on the deck of a very foreign-looking vessel were singing in a tongue with strange intonations, and to a tune like no other tune I had ever heard.

It was all marvellous. Not that I had lost my head entirely. I was ready, if I had to, to turn and seek a homebound ship. I wanted to be with Berend but I wasn't going to be fooled. I had at least learned enough about life and the world, not to let that happen.

It didn't. Briskly, as one who knew his way about, Berend led us to a kiosk where he spoke to an official who evidently knew him and simply nodded and said something I couldn't understand but it seemed to be permission to proceed. After that, Berend hired a porter with a handcart, who took charge of our baggage as we made our way off the quay and into the town. We went straight to the house of a priest who greeted Berend as an old friend.

He looked slightly shocked when he learned that we wanted a marriage without delay. But after a conference with Berend, in Dutch, which I couldn't follow, he complied. Berend paid the porter off, we left our baggage in the priest's parlour, and then he led us across the road to his church and the ceremony was performed, then and there. I gave Berend my first wedding ring and he gave it back to me, making it his. We were pronounced man and wife. We took the priest to dine with us in a hostelry.

After that, I waited in the priest's parlour along with the saddlebags, while Berend went out to get us horses from a hiring stable close to the quay. He had remarked on it while we were on our way to the priest's house. 'An ideal place for such a stable, where people are coming and going all the time. It's a big place, and does a healthy business.'

He brought the horses back within the hour, and to my relief I now had a side-saddle. I wasn't used to riding astride. We thanked – and paid – the priest, mounted, settled our saddle-bags and once more, were on our way.

'How far do we have to go?' I asked my new husband.

'To Brussels?' he said. 'About another hundred miles. I still think we'd better not waste time but at least we've put the North Sea between us and pursuit. We can spend a couple of nights on the road, if you're feeling tired.'

I said: 'I did a fair amount of travelling when I lived with Mistress Stannard.' Though you, Ursula, usually travel at a moderate pace. Now, we were in a continual hurry and I was wishing my horse, which in no way resembled the lively chestnut on whose back I had started the journey, would show a little interest in getting to wherever we were going. I kept having to encourage it with my heels.

'My poor Mildred! What have I done to you?' Berend had noticed the problem. 'I told the ostler that I wanted a lady's horse and I suppose he thought I meant a slug. Well, I'll make sure you do better next time.'

He sounded rather far away, as though something had distracted him and his mind was only partly on the business of our travel arrangements. 'Is everything all right, Berend?' I asked him. 'I thought you sounded worried.'

He turned to me with a quick smile. 'I am sorry. Do I seem distrait? It's only that when I was in the hiring stables, there was another fellow there, hiring a horse too. As I told you, it's a big place and he was quite a distance from me, just getting into his saddle. I could have sworn I recognized him. I thought he was a man called Nicolas Alvaro, someone I know at Parma's court. Odd, that. He's a recognizable sort – shorter than average, a trifle plump, with a high voice for a man, and a dreadful laugh, like a donkey. I heard this fellow say something to the ostler and I heard him laugh, too. That voice and that laugh both carry. He didn't see me. He was just leaving and he was away through the archway to the road a moment later.'

'Why did you think it was odd?' I asked. 'Perhaps he had business in Ostend. It seemed a busy place! I suppose members of the duke's court do travel about.'

'Yes, they do, but Alvaro acts as a courier between Brussels

and Spain just as I do between Brussels and England and he
does the journey on horseback. He never travels to Spain by
sea now – he was once on a ship that ran into a storm in the
Bay of Biscay and ever since then he's made the journey by
land. I can't think what can have brought him to Ostend.'

'Perhaps you were mistaken,' I said. 'Perhaps he was just
someone who was a little like . . . Señor Alvaro; have I got
the name right?'

'Yes. It was a very close resemblance, though, unless Alvaro
has brothers who look like him. And sound like him.' Berend
frowned. 'He is an unpleasant man and he has an old grudge
against me.' He didn't describe the grudge and I decided not
to ask. I was realizing that although Berend had told me much
about himself when we talked together back in West Leys,
there was still much I had to learn. He said: 'My good friend
Leonardo says that Alvaro doesn't wash often enough.'

I was remembering something. Then I said: 'I think this
man Alvaro may have travelled from England, like us.'

'Travelled from England. What makes you say that?'

'There was a man just like that, collecting a horse at the
inn at Maidstone. He was complaining that the horse was
too big and he wanted something smaller. I noticed the high
voice. And the laugh! It certainly did sound like a donkey
braying.'

'At Maidstone? Now, that really is strange. Well, perhaps
he has undertaken new tasks for the duke.' Berend shrugged
and then shook his reins to encourage his steed so that I had
to urge mine to keep up. He didn't seem to want to go on
talking about this Nicolas Alvaro, so I let the subject drop and
instead, I asked him what the duke's palace was like.

Berend seemed pleased with this new topic and enlarged
with enthusiasm. 'Ornate in parts and dismal in others. Big
reception rooms with rows of candle sconces and statues, some
life-size, of the Virgin and Child, and fauns and nymphs as
well, usually gilded, and there are marvellous tapestries on
the walls. The biggest reception chamber is the hugest room
I've ever seen; you could build a house inside it. And then
there are lots of narrow, twisting corridors with not enough
sconces and some with none at all, and they can put a shiver

in your spine if you have to find your way through them at night on your own.

'But don't worry yourself about that. You won't have to grope through any unlit passages. I have status enough to have a little set of rooms in the palace. The duke believes in keeping his agents sweet.'

Then I made a mistake and said something that I should not. I said: 'But Berend, you're not really one of his agents, are you? I mean, should you . . .?'

I stopped short because he had turned to look at me and for the first time I saw how his face changed when he was angry. He said: 'Don't be a fool, Mildred. If I suddenly refused to accept my pleasant suite, don't you think the duke might wonder why? Especially as – just as I have told you – the duke is already just a little unsure of me anyway. Agents do have to practise deception. You must get used to it.' He saw the alarm in my face and said, more gently: 'I suppose it's your Puritan upbringing. You will have to leave that behind now.'

'Yes, I see.' I made haste to repair my error. 'I'm sorry, Berend. Yes, I do understand what you mean.'

'I hope you do. You'll be sharing my suite at first, but when you're more settled and you've picked up enough of the language, you can live in my house in the town. I'll find servants for you – there's only a caretaker at the moment, a housekeeper called Klara, a kindly old biddy, she'll be a help to you.'

'I'll have to live there while you live at the court?'

'You'll see me often. It's the usual arrangement, for married courtiers and court servants. You're my wife now. You'll soon grow accustomed. Dear Mildred, don't look so nervous. Now let's see if we can shake some mileage out of these lazy animals. The inn I have in mind for tonight is still a long way off. We'll change horses before we get there, and a good thing too! On the way to Brussels, you'll see something of the Low Countries. They'll be strange to you but I like them very much and I hope you will too.'

The landscape was certainly strange to me. It was flat as far as the eye could see, threaded with waterways and with marshy patches. I saw farmhouses built of timber slats, and meadows with cattle grazing in them and there were windmills here and there, timber towers with huge spinning sails like inland ships.

We actually changed horses twice before we reached the little town of Neustad, where he told me we were to spend the night. By then I had grown very tired and I thought of you, Ursula, and I wondered what would happen if you caught us up before we got to Brussels. If we were there first, then we would be inside the ducal palace, and surely, there, you wouldn't be able to make too much of a to-do. I said as much to Berend.

'She won't be able to make any,' he told me. 'After all, we are now married, Señora Gomez.'

I said romantically: 'Oh, Berend. I love hearing you say that.'

Berend laughed.

ELEVEN
The Shadow in the Night

Captain Bridges was willing enough to take Christopher and me as passengers, but I spent the three days until the *Argenteus* sailed in a state of fuming impatience, unable to stay indoors, and walking restlessly around Dover, as though that would somehow make time go faster. I actually became angry with Christopher when he pointed out that even after three days, the *Argenteus* might not sail. 'If the wind is too contrary, or there's bad weather, she won't be able to leave port,' he said.

His eyes had a glint of mischief, which made me angrier than ever. But of course, he was right; we couldn't control the weather and nor could Captain Bridges, and I apologized.

I said: 'It's because I still feel responsible to her parents. They might blame me if harm comes to her.'

'I doubt if it will,' Christopher said. 'We have to make sure, to rescue her if she does fall into trouble. That's why I'm here. But Gomez is no adventurer. He has a home in Brussels where she can live and I don't think he's a philanderer. There's no reason why he shouldn't marry her.'

'Provided he does!' I said tartly. 'And even so, running off with her isn't the right way to go about it.'

However, the *Argenteus* sailed on time with a stiff following wind. I watched the white cliffs of England sink away astern and thought wryly that Gladys' scrying had told her true. She had seen me on a ship drawing away from white cliffs, and here I was. She had seen a wedding ring for Mildred, too, and might well be right about that. It was a pity that she hadn't seen any further into the future. I would have liked to know what was going to happen next.

The *Argenteus* sailed at dawn and we were in Ostend that night. We slept on board, went ashore at daybreak, dealt with the port officials and found somewhere for a breakfast of small ale, rolls and honey. At least, that was all I wanted, but Christopher had smoked fish as well. 'Kate always said I ate like a horse,' he told me. It was the first time I had heard him mention Kate as though it didn't hurt. Perhaps this new adventure was helping him to recover.

We hired horses, and set off again. I had been to the Low Countries before and I recognized a few things: a farmhouse here, a cattle pasture there, that windmill, that expanse of marsh. Not much had changed, and presently I thought I recognized the little township we could see ahead of us. 'We might get a change of horses there,' I said. But I had hardly spoken before I found myself drawing rein. 'Only . . . what's that? Christopher, look . . .!'

There was a column of smoke arising from somewhere within the town. The breeze blew it towards us and I coughed. 'Something's on fire.'

We had both halted and we both sniffed. Our horses were troubled, snorting, tossing their heads and moving uneasily, disturbed by senses that were keener than ours. Then I saw that the column of smoke was just that; it was a column, not a cloud, and it was limited to one place. It didn't look like an accident and yes, the breeze was carrying a smell. A stink. It was also carrying a sound. Somewhere within that town, someone was screaming, so desperately that the sound could carry all the way to us. And the smell was the stench of burning flesh.

'We're not going in there,' I said. 'We'll have to make for the next place where there's a stable. Let's get away quickly! Bloody Inquisition! I thought they didn't have it here. I thought Parma's policy was to make the Low Countries Catholic bit by bit, without coercion.'

'It is, but there are always people who won't keep their mouths shut,' said Christopher. 'There's always the fool who stands on a box and collects a crowd and harangues them about transubstantiation or the heliocentric theory or starts shouting about gluttonous cardinals getting fat at the expense of the poor. The Church doesn't need an Inquisition to clamp down on that kind of thing. We passed a fork about half a mile back. Let's try that.'

We retraced our steps and found that the left-hand fork seemed to lead past the town instead of into it. We set off along it at a fast canter, getting away as soon as we could from that horrible reminder that we were in Spanish-dominated territory.

That sense of fear and urgency was our undoing. Hard on our mounts and on ourselves, determined to spend only one night on the road, we pressed on too fast, not paying enough attention to the state of the track, which had become increasingly pockmarked. It looked as if heavy wagons had been along it ahead of us. When my horse stumbled in one of the ruts and lurched forward with its head down, I shot straight out of my saddle. As I went, I tried to clutch at the pommel but my own weight tore me away and I landed heavily on the uneven ground.

'I'm not hurt,' I said, scrambling to my feet and trying to pretend that it was true. I had relaxed all my muscles as I fell, just as I had been shown long ago when one of Uncle Herbert's grooms was teaching me to ride. I had bruised myself badly just the same. I had also failed to keep hold of the reins and the horse had set off on its own, probably to the next stop on the road, with which it was no doubt familiar.

Christopher, understandably, swore. 'Get up behind me!' he said but I found it impossible until he dismounted and I could use his left stirrup to help me and even then it was awkward because I needed to settle myself behind the saddle and not in it. After that, grimly and also rather slowly, for the sake of the burdened horse, we rode on until we reached another small town where we found an inn. We also found my errant horse and paid for it to be returned to its home stable. Christopher arranged for fresh horses in the morning and I ordered food and obtained an ointment for my bruises from the innkeeper's wife. By then, it was nearly sunset.

'We'll spend the night here,' Christopher said. 'We both need some sleep.'

'We're losing time!' I protested. 'They may be married by now!'

'They probably are.' Christopher was philosophical. 'But once we're with them, you can do some insisting about the way Mildred is to live, and demand an assurance that the ceremony was legal, and you can even offer a dowry if you want to – to be paid to her, not him, so that she will have protection if things go amiss.'

And now, once more, Mildred must take up the tale.

The inn at Neustad was built of dark timbers and festooned with ivy. Its upper chambers were reached by way of outside staircases and galleries. Inside, it was far from luxurious, and it was also very full. However, the landlord, a lanky fellow with an overworked air, said that we were lucky, there was a tiny bedchamber free, up in the attic. It was really meant for one but two could squeeze into it at need. Up there under the roof, the only other room was a long attic dormitory for men when the better accommodation on the floor below was full. I peeped into this and saw that it had a pile of blankets in the corner and some pallets on the floor, sufficient for a good number of guests.

Our room had little furniture but there was one clothes press, an upright chair, a small round table carrying a candle and tinderbox, and a bed with a straw mattress and no sheets. Still, it was fairly wide and had two thickly woven and gaily coloured blankets on it. There was a chamber pot beneath it. The walls and floor of the room were made of unvarnished wooden planks and there was a dormer window, glazed but without any shutters. Certainly not luxurious but good enough, all the same.

We sat downstairs with the other guests to eat a supper of broth and sausage and rye bread, and then Berend and I climbed the narrow and somewhat rickety outside stairs to our eyrie and our bed. Since this was an attic, the ceiling was simply thatch, and there were rustlings during the night. House martins were probably nesting in the eaves. But the long hours of riding had exhausted me. Martins might rustle and in the absence of sheets I lay with a rough blanket against me, but I fell asleep as though I had been stunned.

I woke in the depths of the night, suddenly and completely. The room was not quite dark for a half moon was shining in through the dormer window and casting a wedge of light across the bed and part of the floor. I wondered what had disturbed me and then realized that the small rustles I could hear had nothing to do with house martins. They sounded like paper. Across one of the moonlit wedges, a shadow moved. Someone or something was crouching on the floor. Berend, of course. He must have got up to use the chamber pot. But Berend was here beside me; I could feel his warmth, hear him breathing.

I shot up in the bed, exclaiming: 'Who's there? What is it?' and at the same moment, Berend woke and sat up beside me, and the shadow reared up and solidified into a human shape.

Berend was off the bed on the instant, grappling with someone. There were curses, shouting; I joined in by screaming for help. I scrambled out of the bed and groped for the candle and tinderbox. I found them but I was still struggling to use the tinderbox by feel when there were answering shouts from somewhere else in the inn and then the shadow broke away from Berend, hurling him to the floor, and fled through the door on to the gallery outside. It ran silently; where it went after that, I couldn't tell. Berend was scrambling to his feet. I went on struggling with the unco-operative tinderbox, spilling the tinder. Then I heard someone running up the staircase and the crash of the dormitory door being flung open. There was a flicker of light from a candle and the landlord's voice, shouting questions. Berend shouted something back, in Dutch. Suddenly the half moon cast a huge, gangling shadow across the floor and the landlord, a cloak flung over his night-shirt, appeared in the doorway. At the same time, running along the gallery, flinging cloaks and bedgowns hastily round them, came the men who had been in the dormitory room, several carrying candles.

On the instant, the room was full of alarmed but friendly people and also full of candlelight. It showed one of Berend's saddlebags, open, the contents strewn on the floor, and some papers half pulled out of a leather wallet. Berend promptly stooped, thrust his papers back into place and then pushed everything back into the saddlebag, while the landlord went back to the staircase and shouted down it to someone below to bring us all some wine. Berend and two of the other men went out to the gallery but came back shaking their heads. Whoever it was had escaped to the ground and fled before anyone else had arrived on the scene.

The landlord said there had been a late arrival at the inn, a fellow whose face he had hardly seen because the man's cloak had a hood that was pulled low over his brows. He'd just wanted a bed for the night and said he'd be happy with a pallet in the attic dormitory. He'd gone up with a candle and had evidently gone into the dormitory because two of its occupants said they had seen him come in, though they couldn't describe him. He had been just a vague shape with a candle. They had heard him spreading a blanket on a spare pallet near the door, and they thought he had lain down. They had fallen asleep, until the uproar broke out.

It was a fair guess that the assailant had visited the inn ahead of us, to reconnoitre, but there was no way to tell. He hadn't brought a horse into the stable but he could have left it somewhere outside. At any rate, he had got away.

'Only,' said the landlord grimly, and speaking English for my benefit, 'just what sort of a man are you, Berend Gomez, that someone wants to get into my inn at night to search your luggage?'

'He had a knife,' said Berend and pulled up his nightshirt. There was a thin red line of blood curving round his ribs and his left side. 'He tried to stab me when he realized I was awake.' He let his nightshirt fall again and I saw what in the vague light I hadn't seen before: a bloodstain that had soaked through the material.

'I see. So someone breaks in and not only tries to search your baggage, he tries to murder you as well!' The landlord wasn't inclined to be sympathetic. 'At this moment,' he thundered, 'I'd be mighty angry with you and suspicious of you except that you've stayed here a mort of times and been no trouble and I've been pleased to welcome you here again, you and your lady wife.' He was gracious enough to shoot me an apologetic look.

'I carry letters back and forth between my lord of Parma, and her majesty the Queen of England, as you no doubt know,' said Berend. 'Perhaps someone wishes to interrupt this service to the duke.'

There was nothing more to be done, except that the landlord did at this point call his wife, who brought warm water, a sponge and a salve, so that she and I together could clean Berend's cut. It had barely broken the skin; Berend had nearly evaded it altogether.

The matter would be reported to the proper authorities, but nothing was likely to come of it. The shadowy figure had vanished into the night, its mysterious errand having failed. Nothing had been stolen, said Berend, bland of face and voice and standing beside our saddlebags, which were both securely fastened. The wine the landlord had shouted for now arrived, brought by a young kitchen hand who was clearly sizzling with excitement. It was actually perry, but it was very good. We all drank some and then went back to bed. The landlord picked out the youth who had brought the perry, and one of the other servants, and told them to stay on the gallery and keep watch until the dawn. The rest of us, he said, could then sleep in peace.

Berend and I didn't feel much like sleeping. I wanted to know, even more than the landlord did, why anyone should want to investigate my husband's baggage, and was ready to kill if disturbed. I kept my voice down and tried to sound calm, but I know that I didn't quite succeed. 'What's behind all this, Berend? I want to know. And what about this man Nicolas Alvaro, that I saw in England and you saw at Ostend? Has he been following us? Could it have been him?'

Berend groaned. 'It might, I suppose. If the duke has been getting suspicious of me, he could have set someone on to follow me. A spy to watch a spy! But I can't see the Duke of Parma telling Alvaro or anyone else to creep into my room by stealth to rifle my baggage, let alone attack me with a knife. It's more likely that some miscreant recognized me as a man from the ducal court and thought I was carrying valuables . . . something like that. Courtiers often do carry valuables and have to look after them. There's a lot of unrest since the war. The countryside isn't as safe as it used to be.'

'But it could have been to do with your . . . your secret work. Couldn't it? Berend!'

'Perhaps. For the moment, it's a mystery. Oh, my darling, I should have given you more of a chance to withdraw, a chance not to marry me after all. Love is a dangerous thing, my sweet.'

'I wouldn't have wanted a chance to withdraw. I am happy to be married to you. But I want you to keep safe!' I hardly spoke above a whisper but heard the fierceness in my plea.

'The sooner we get to Brussels the better,' said Berend. 'We ought to be safe there. There is so much you still don't know about me, that I still have to tell you, should have told you. There's been so little time.'

'What sort of things? We talked for hours, back at West Leys. You told me you had been married before, when you were young, but that you were now a widower.' I sat up sharply. 'Don't say that you still have a wife somewhere and that . . .'

'No, no. Of course not!' Berend was indignant. 'I would never deceive you in such a way! One thing I didn't tell you, though, because it is a subject that will be raw for ever, was how our daughter died. We were both only eighteen when we married. We were very much in love. It was before I took the post with the gentleman who travelled to Brussels; to begin with, we lived with my mother. Eleanor came from a family much like hers; everyone approved of the marriage. We married in January and Alison was born just after Christmas in the same year. She died only last December, on her sixteenth birthday. She was so beautiful . . .'

'What happened to her?' I asked it very gently, for his voice had faded and I knew that there must have been a tragedy.

'Too beautiful, my lovely Alison. I named her for my mother. I brought her up as best I could, mostly alone, for Eleanor, my wife, died when Alison was very small. I was travelling to the Netherlands by then and I sometimes took my wife and daughter with me. Some of the low-lying marshy places in this country do breed fevers. I shall try to keep you away from them. Brussels is safe enough. Local people seem to have some immunity but my wife was English, like you. Eleanor had no resistance. I did my best for little Alison. I kept her away from marshy districts but as she grew up, I let her meet my friends, I wanted her to learn to be a hostess when I gave dinners. I hoped she might find a husband among my friends, here or in England. She was at home in both countries. But what she found was . . .'

'Berend?'

'I've never talked about this much before, but it seems natural to talk to you, love. One night – it was the August of last year – we were in England, staying at an inn where I had met a friend – I thought he was a friend – among my fellow guests. I was already one of Elizabeth's agents and he was one of her agents, too. I knew him quite well. He had twice dined at my home in Brussels. Last August, he had been on an assignment in England and was on his way back to Brussels. We met at the inn in Maidstone, where you and I spent our first night. I was going the opposite way, bound for the English court. We dined together, this other man, Alison, and me. It was summer, a warm August night with a crescent moon in the west and a sky full of stars. There's a garden behind the inn and Alison went out after dark to walk there, to enjoy the starlight and the night-scented flowers. She came back distraught, her clothes torn, blood running down her legs . . . she had been attacked and violated, out there in the dark. There was a patch of lawn, newly scythed. She had been thrown down on a heap of the cut grass. She said he had been hooded, the hood pulled down, but the moonlight had caught his features just for one second, and she knew him. He was my friend, who had visited my home, who had eaten with us in the inn.'

'What was his name?'

'Better that you don't know, that you know nothing of this, better that you can if need be deny that I ever told you.'

'But, Berend . . .!'

'Listen. Back in Brussels he had pestered Alison, apparently, but she hadn't told me. She was ashamed, thought it was somehow her fault. Just because she was beautiful, she attracted men. That fellow Nicolas Alvaro actually asked me for her hand when she turned fifteen, but I refused; she was too young to marry and I didn't like him anyway. That I said no and never gave him a chance to speak to Alison himself is the grudge that he has against me. Believe me, with him, grudges last. This other man, though, didn't even have the manners to ask me for her hand!'

'It definitely wasn't this man Alvaro who . . .?'

'No. He was innocent of that. He was in Brussels at that time, and this happened in Kent. The fellow who did it had pursued Alison behind my back and while she was struggling with him, he'd accused her of tempting him. Weeping, shocked and in pain, she cried to me that she had not and she kept repeating it, begging me to believe her, obviously afraid that I would not. Perhaps I had been too strict. I had tried to bring her up to be honest, chaste, as I thought Eleanor would have done but perhaps I went too far. It was only for her protection! I had told her that to have a love affair before marriage would be a dreadful thing, against the laws of God and man and not forgivable; a girl who did such a thing had better go into a nunnery. There are nunneries enough in France and Spain. She was afraid to tell me that he was annoying her, poor, poor Alison. I could have protected her, but she feared me too much to give me the chance.

'Afterwards, when it was too late, I did all I could to help and reassure her. The fellow fled from the inn that same night . . . I don't know where he is now. But he got my poor Alison with child and she miscarried at just over four months. It killed her. As I said, she died on her sixteenth birthday.'

'Oh, Berend!'

'I've never known what I felt about that,' Berend said. 'He was the child of rape . . . and yet he was my grandson. He was my daughter's child. It was a boy – I had called a midwife and she told me that. I never saw . . . it . . . him. I couldn't have borne to. Alison's child and yet also the child of that damnable man. What should I feel about him?'

He was almost crying. Feebly, I said: 'Oh, Berend. Please don't.'

'What is one *supposed* to feel? Should I have been relieved, or grieved? I've never known. Mildred, in you, I have found a hope for the future, a way of making a new beginning after so many years in a kind of wilderness. But I have business that I must still finish. I have not been able to find the man who raped my daughter. I have had duties to do; I couldn't abandon them to go after him. But if I ever do catch up with him, I shall kill him. If that happens, you must appear to know only that I had a daughter who died. That is the tale I have told to others. Only a few know what really happened to her. Alvaro does! He would. How he manages to hear things not meant for him is a wonder. I marvel that I have told you as much as I have, except – yes, it's because I want my wife to know me completely. I must not have secrets from you. Which means,' said Berend, 'that there is something else that I must tell you . . .'

TWELVE
No Turning Back

'We shall be in Brussels today,' Berend said as we mounted our horses the next morning. He gave me his beautiful smile. 'You're a wonderful girl,' he said. 'Last night must have been a bad shock to you. It's the sort of thing that can happen to men in my line of work but it's hardly what you were reared to expect.'

'You warned me,' I said. 'At West Leys, that early morning, up on the saddleback of that hill behind the farm, when you asked me to marry you. I told you then that I wouldn't mind.'

'Easy enough to say but last night you were faced with the real thing.'

'I don't suppose you were expecting it either,' I said, trying to sound cheerful. I didn't want to talk. I was still trembling inside because of the attack in the night, and I was still trying to absorb the last conversation we had had before trying – and failing – to go back to sleep. Now, I felt dreadful, from fright and sheer sleeplessness, but I didn't want Berend to know it. First thing in the morning, he had made the most tender and affectionate love to me. I thought he was trying to reassure me of his feelings for me, and I was willing to be reassured but now I wished with all my heart that he would stop talking and let me concentrate on staying awake in my saddle.

But he was answering my last remark. 'No, I wasn't expecting anything like that to happen, but it's true that I have been uneasy. I told you, did I not, that I thought the duke has been growing suspicious of me? My friend Leonardo Moreno warned me before I left the court last time. He had heard something, or overheard it; I'm not sure which. The duke has apparently noticed that some of my reports to him weren't accurate. A few months ago, I gave him a misleading account of the number of warships being built in English shipyards. The bad joke is that what I told him has turned into the truth since then. Elizabeth's navy is now even bigger than I led him to believe it would be. What I reported about Catholic support in the north of England – or rather, the lack of it – certainly *was* the truth. I just hope he believed *that*! I am half afraid that he'll think the confidential letter I am carrying to him from Elizabeth is a forgery! If any of Philip's agents has suspicions about the correspondence between the duke and the queen, it could account for last night though I most sincerely hope that it was just an attempt at an ordinary robbery. But, Mildred, you will not forget what I told you last night? It's better that you know.'

'I understand,' I said, and inside my head I heard again the things he had told me in the chill darkness before the break of day.

'Don't go to sleep yet, sweetheart. And don't be afraid; we're safe enough now. Someone is on watch. Just listen. I have told you that I am on a confidential errand. It consists of carrying a very secret message to the Duke of Parma from Queen Elizabeth. And not only that. She has also charged me with finding out some information for her. Her agent Standish, in Spain, has reported that if Philip succeeds in raising an Armada, he is anxious to avoid a battle with our navy. He wants to fight for England on land rather than on the sea. He wants to land his forces quickly, and deal with the opposition by horse and foot. Elizabeth wants to hold him off before one single Spanish soldier sets foot on an English beach and she wants to know how he intends to confront seaborne resistance. She wants to know his battle plan; how he will position his ships. Standish apparently hasn't managed to discover that. She thinks that Parma may know it and she has asked me to try to find it. I agreed to try.'

I asked if it would be written down. 'It's surely very secret,' I said.

'On the contrary, I think it would have to be written down; it's not the kind of thing easily carried in a man's head. And it can't be all that secret; many people will need to know it. I have some knowledge about the workings of the court and I know where copies of such documents may be kept.

*Though I must be careful. The duke may be in confidential correspondence with Queen Elizabeth but that isn't the same as actually handing King Philip's plans – about his vessels or anything else – over to her. I fancy that if he helps her, it will be more by **not** doing things rather than the contrary. If anything does go wrong, when we are back in Brussels, if you can get away, you may have to take that plan back to England.'*

'*But . . .!*' He had told me that he had a confidential errand, but not that I might be involved! I was angry and frightened and I started to protest. But he placed his fingers on my lips, closing them. '*Yes, my love. I know. I must apologize. But no one knows of my commission to copy the battle plan. In all probability, nothing will go wrong. You agreed, back at West Leys, that you were willing to share the life of an agent. Such things are part of it.*'

I had thought of it in terms of you, Ursula. You are an agent but you have never endangered me. But I had made my choice. I couldn't go back on it now. I had married him.

But no wonder I lay awake all the rest of the night, utterly appalled by the world of dangerous intrigue into which my husband appeared to be leading me.

He did stop talking in the end, and we rode on quietly. I was determined not to show my fear, not to show that I felt ready to fall out of the saddle because of tiredness. My mind and body didn't want to go on with this adventure and were capable of trying to call a halt on their own, if I were weak enough to let them. I must not.

After a while, I forced myself into making a few harmless remarks. I asked if the dresses I had brought would be really suitable for the ducal court and if not, what fashions I should choose for new ones. I commented on the scenery we were riding through, which was now becoming less flat and marshy, more like an English landscape. I also asked Berend to describe in more detail the house he had in Brussels. I now understood that I might be alone in it for quite a lot of the time, except for servants. Berend would visit me rather than share it with me. I found this a depressing prospect.

By then I was finding a good many things depressing. I

loved him. Yes, I loved him. His touch made me tremble and yearn. But things were emerging that I hadn't known, despite all those hours of talk we had had in England. Then, he had talked of the Dutch countryside, the dinners we would attend at court and what we would eat, the kind of shops I would find in the town of Brussels. He had told me of his childhood, in Spain at first until his father's death, and then the journey to England when he was eight and how strange England had seemed at first, and later, how much he had come to love it. I had told him of my home and my upbringing and my first marriage. It now seemed that for all our endless conversation, Berend had left a great deal out.

At length, Berend said: 'Look ahead. Straight ahead, between your horse's ears. That's Brussels. And there's the palace.'

I looked. The city was still a long way off and there was a haze of chimney smoke over it, but nevertheless, in the far distance, beyond the nearer roofs of the town, I could see the pinnacles and spires of a palace. They glinted in the sunshine. Berend had talked about the Duke of Parma's home but my first glimpse of it, even so distantly, was nearly as frightening as the midnight intruder had been. I suddenly realized that when Berend talked of the ducal palace, he really did mean a palace and I recoiled from the prospect. A palace! Me! I wouldn't know how to conduct myself in such a place. It wasn't for me, Mildred Atbrigge, widow of an English country vicar, daughter of a Puritan dye-master and his wife, and brought up in a little Devonshire village.

Ursula, I had been impressed by your home of Hawkswood and even more impressed the time when we went to stay with Sir Henry Compton and I saw his manor house. But judging by what I could now see of the Parma's residence, both Hawkswood and the manor house at Minstead could have been dropped inside it and lost. The spires and pinnacles of Parma's palace seemed to stretch half the width of the horizon.

I would have to go through with this. There was no turning back, not now.

When we were actually face to face with the palace, it was worse. First there was a gatehouse, where Berend presented a small metal disc in some dull bronze metal. I had seen it before, because he wore it on a chain round his neck, but I had never asked what it was. I had had too much else to think about on our journey. It was apparently a pass and anyway, the gatekeeper seemed to recognize Berend. We were nodded through.

Next, came a lengthy, tree-bordered track, and then we were right in front of the palace itself. It made me gasp. It seemed to stretch for ever, left and right, with rows and rows of tall, elegant windows, three floors of them at least, and an over-powering principal entrance. This was topped by a graceful soaring arch that culminated in a pinnacle, and had immense doors inlaid with a pattern in gold and approached by a flight of stone steps, long enough to count as a staircase. In the porch at the top were two well-armed guards. Berend seemed to sense my feelings.

'People leaning on walking sticks have to use a side entrance,' he said. 'Even if they're emissaries from King Philip or the Pope. Even if they *are* King Philip or the Pope. We have to use a side entrance as well, not because we're decrepit but because our social standing isn't high enough for the front door. This way.'

He turned us to the right. After a little way, I saw the roofs of some kind of building also to our right, facing the palace, and as we drew near, I realized they were the roofs of a stable yard. We turned in through an archway and the next moment, there were grooms coming to take our horses and promising that our saddlebags would be taken to Berend's room, and greeting Berend as someone they knew. They looked at me curiously and Berend introduced me as his wife. One of them said something that I thought was probably Dutch for *congratulations* and there were smiles.

Then Berend was leading me out of the yard, and after a short distance, we came to another palace entrance, without steps this time but again with a massive and ornamental door and a pair of guards. But Berend said cheerfully: 'Here's our side door,' and stepped up to the nearest guard, holding out his pass. Again, we were nodded through. We went inside, into a vestibule with passages leading off to either side and a staircase ahead. We started up the stairs and Berend said: 'It's a bit of a climb. We're on the second floor.'

The stairs were steep. Once we had reached the right floor, Berend turned us to the left and after that I became hopelessly lost. We went along a passage which seemed to lead round a central courtyard, and then took another turn and after that another . . . most of the way was well lit because there were windows nearly everywhere, but there were one or two sections without windows, where the way was lit by oil lamps.

From time to time we passed other people; hurrying servants, ladies in immense and elaborate dresses, gentlemen in quilted doublets with huge puffed sleeves slashed with gold and silver satin, and colossal ruffs, not so much wide, I noticed, as tall, stretching the wearer's neck upwards. It wasn't a fashion I had seen before and it looked most uncomfortable. There were doorways here and there, mostly inset into small alcoves. At last, Berend stopped in front of one of them. 'Here we are,' he said.

He took me into a suite of rooms. The main chamber was in two parts; one furnished as a parlour, with settles and stools, small tables, a sideboard and a hearth, and then, beyond a wide arch, the place became a bedchamber. This held a tester bed, halfway between single and double, a couple of clothes presses and a washstand. On the left there were three doors, standing open, two from the parlour, one from the bedchamber. I peered through them. The one off the bedchamber revealed a study, with bookshelves, and a desk with a writing set on it; the two that opened off the parlour respectively showed what looked like a servant's small bedchamber, and a privy. This also contained a water storage tub and a brazier full of charcoal. Then I realized that we were not alone; a black-clad manservant – presumably the occupant of the little bedchamber – had come in behind us and was saying Berend's name.

Berend turned. 'Ah. Hans. Someone ran ahead to warn you, I imagine.' I had thought the gatekeepers were somewhat casual but I had been wrong. My husband drew me forward. 'Hans, this is Señora Mildred Gomez, my wife. She is English.' He spoke English as he said it and Hans evidently understood. He inclined a polite head and said: 'Welcome, Señora.' He was a small man with dark eyes, though his bare head was sandy. He had the air of being active and alert and the dark eyes were bright with intelligence.

Berend said: 'Please serve my wife as willingly and deftly as you have always served me. You can begin by finding a maidservant to assist her, until I can arrange a regular maid. Mildred, this is Hans Hendriks, my manservant here. Our bags will be delivered soon, I hope; Hans, if they're not here within the hour, go to the stables and find out why. Seb was the groom who took charge of them. Meanwhile, we would like some wine and will you also get the water tub filled. I must try to see the duke if he is available; I have something to deliver.'

If I had been Hans, my head would have been spinning with all these orders, which sounded as if they were to be carried out simultaneously, but he seemed to regard everything as normal. He smiled at me, turned to a sideboard, took out two blue and white earthenware goblets, filled them from a keg of wine standing on the floor beside the sideboard and set them on a table. Berend handed one to me.

We sat down to drink. Meanwhile, Hans hurried out of the room and presently came back shepherding a pair of scullions carrying buckets of water, which they emptied into the tub in the privy. They went off again and shortly returned with another two buckets. They worked skilfully and there was no slopping. Berend nodded his approval and dismissed them. Then he drained his goblet and said: 'Hans, is the duke in residence at the moment?'

'Yes, sir. Listening to music in his private apartments, I believe.'

'Thank you. Mildred, my love, the message I have to deliver, from Queen Elizabeth, must be handed to the duke as soon as possible, so for a while, I must leave you. I must try to see him at once. I can't take you. You'll be formally presented to him in the morning, when he gives audiences. As one of his confidential messengers – that is my official title – I have a certain status, and would be expected to present my wife in formal fashion. I won't be long, my dear.'

'Will you not first change your riding garments, sir?' Hans

asked, looking shocked. His English was fluent. 'You will surely not present yourself before my lord with the dust of the road still upon you?'

To my amusement, I saw that the manservant sometimes gave orders to the man. Hans fetched water from the tub in the privy and poured it into the basin on the washstand and I withdrew tactfully from the bedroom to let them get on with it. Presently, from the sound of it, Berend was having his hands and face washed as though he were a small boy. When they emerged, Berend was clad in doublet and hose, quilted, puffed and slashed like the garments of the gentlemen we had passed on the way here, a mighty ruff which Berend was grumbling about and a green velvet cap with a jewelled brooch in it. He gave me a kiss and then he was gone, and I was alone with Hans. I felt a little shy.

Hans wasn't at a loss, though. 'Do please take some more wine, Señora. I will find you a maidservant. This house is well served. There is always someone available for extra duties. Please make yourself at home until I come back.'

'Thank you, Hans.' I was glad to be alone for a while. I could feel the size and weight of the palace all around me and I wanted time to get used to it. I was afraid of it.

Hans wasn't gone long, however. He came back with a young maidservant, an amiable girl with a round pink face whom he introduced as Greta and at the same moment a groom appeared, hung about with saddlebags, and delivered our belongings to us. Hans and the groom then withdrew and Greta, compensating efficiently for her lack of English, indicated that she wished to help me wash and change. She led me to the washstand in the bedchamber and then poured imaginary water into the basin and wiped her palm over her face.

Then she lit the charcoal brazier, set a pan of water on it to heat and started to unpack my bags. Soon, I had a wash in hot water, which was more than poor Berend had had, and was freshly dressed in the one respectable gown I had brought, light blue, and made of a fine wool that didn't crease much. I had a modest but well starched ruff to go with it, and the small farthingale that had travelled with me in its linen bag, slung across my saddle.

Greta had just finished with my hair when Berend came back. He dismissed her with a glance. I looked at him anxiously. He was not happy.

Timidly, I said: 'What is it, Berend? Did you find the duke?'

'Yes. He left his music to attend to me. I had an audience five minutes long, standing up, on a landing. He took the queen's letter over to a window and read it, and nodded. Then he said: "So you are in good standing at the English court, Berend. I wonder just how good. I hope this message is genuine. Some of the information you have brought me in the past was not. That may not have been your fault, of course. You may yourself have been deceived. I must think it over. Return to your rooms. I will see you in audience tomorrow." He still isn't pleased with me, Mildred. I don't know quite what that could mean. I don't know what he knows or what he just guesses; who has said things to him as Leonardo warned me before I left for England. I truly believed that by conscientiously delivering that letter from the queen would set me right with him. Now, it looks as though I was wrong.'

'But we – you – have to find that battle plan . . .?'

'Yes. The duke is right to distrust me.'

'It's horrible!' I expostulated. 'Everyone spying on everyone else, all in secret, all underhand, people creeping into a bedchamber at an inn and going through saddlebags and attacking you with a knife . . .!'

'Yes, my love. That is the world of the secret agent. It's a more dangerous and a more complicated web than you realize. Truth to tell, the moment I saw that man Alvaro at Ostend, I started to wonder. And when you said you had seen him at Maidstone, I was nearly sure. If the duke has had serious suspicions about me, he may indeed have sent Alvaro to follow me, to find out if they're justified. It's the sort of thing Alvaro would be good at. I didn't want to say too much to you. I didn't want to frighten you. I wanted you to grow accustomed to my world, gently, gradually. But today, the duke's manner towards me, well, I think I will have to be plain with you. Alvaro is a spy for the duke and not only for the duke. He has two masters. He is King Philip's man as well. He is Philip's eyes and ears in Parma's court. Philip doesn't trust Parma.

Oh, the duke knows that well enough. He prefers to know who Philip's chief spy is, and to keep him in view; that's why Alvaro has never been dismissed. But if Nicolas Alvaro has got wind of the letters I have carried between the duke and the queen, well . . .'

'So it *could* have been him who attacked us in the inn.'

'Yes, it could. I didn't want you to be afraid so I made light of it, talked to you of commonplace robbers . . .'

'You didn't convince me,' I told him. 'Nicolas Alvaro, the man you obviously didn't like, the man I saw at Maidstone and you saw at Ostend, he was obviously a possibility as our intruder that night. And he *was* trying to search your baggage. But how could he have known about the letter? Surely it was given to you in private?'

'I've believed hitherto that Alvaro did his travelling between here and Spain, but it looks as though he has been travelling to England too. The duke could have arranged for him to have the entrée at Queen Elizabeth's court. I have never seen him there but I am rarely there myself and never for long and he is as cunning as a snake. As for how he might know of any secret letters – Elizabeth's court isn't as wary as she thinks it is or as it ought to be. The servants of the council members, the maids of honour with nothing in their heads but pretty gowns and what jewels to wear to the next masque, and *Ooh, my dear, have you heard* this *bit of gossip?* and the careless young courtiers who don't have much in their heads either, except the fumes of wine, any of them may sometimes hear council members talking together – in passages, anterooms, stable yards, at tennis matches – and they pick up scraps of this and that, and make guesses and whisper about them. Alvaro could well have learned that the queen and the duke are exchanging secret letters. I think he was searching my baggage for evidence to send to King Philip, to warn him that Parma can't be relied on if Spain makes war on England. Mildred, I must remind you that here, for your own safety, you are a Catholic. I'll give you a rosary and teach you how to use it. Do you understand?'

'Yes, Berend.' I shivered. And then realized that I was hungry. Mundane nature was announcing her needs. I said so.

'We take supper in one of the general dining rooms,' Berend said. 'It's suppertime now so we can go along at once. You must try to remember how to get there, and back. You need to learn your way about.'

THIRTEEN
A Stranger in a Strange Palace

I tried to memorize the route but it was difficult. The place was such a warren. However, I did note that we went down to the floor below and I also realized that the room we finally entered didn't overlook the same courtyard that Berend's quarters did. I never did work out how many courtyards this amazing labyrinth contained. The room to which he brought me was a big dining chamber, with trestle tables and long benches and sawdust strewn on a wooden floor, the sort of place you might find in a large inn. Servants in a blue and white livery were collecting dishes from a serving hatch at the far end, and serving people at the tables.

'Sit down,' said Berend, nudging me towards a bench. 'This is the dining chamber for all the common herd of people who don't have cooks and kitchens of their own.' He looked round. 'There's my friend Leonardo over there; I'll just have a word with him. If you're asked to order, just shake your head. The servants don't speak English. I'll be back in a moment.'

'Very well,' I said. I was a little muzzy from the wine I had drunk with Berend. The room was filling up. Nearly everyone, even if they were, as Berend said, part of the common herd, was well dressed in velvets and silks and brocades, and the high-piled ruffs that I had noticed before.

There was a good smell of food but I could also smell human sweat and a mixture of perfumes. A man in a huge doublet that made his shoulders look as though he were wearing a barn door tried to take a seat on the end of the bench to my right and I tried to dissuade him.

'Forgive me,' I said, trying to sound both polite and firm. 'That is my husband's seat. He will be here in a moment; he is over there, talking to someone.' But I said it in English as I had no other language and he clearly didn't understand me.

I pointed to my wedding ring and then to the disputed seat and then to my husband, some yards away. The barn door individual remained obtuse, but across the table from me a man who had just taken a seat there suddenly leant across the table and said something in Dutch whereupon Master Barn Door withdrew.

I recollected things that Berend had said to servants in the inns where we had stayed, and said: 'Danke,' to my champion, who replied, 'You have to be very firm,' in perfect English.

I looked at him in surprise, not just because he spoke English but also because I had recognized that slightly high-pitched voice. He had his back to the light and it took a few moments for me to realize that he was short and chunkily built. Then I put it all together. He was the man I had seen in the stable yard of the Maidstone inn, wanting to hire a fifteen-hand horse.

It was Nicolas Alvaro and his grey eyes were hard, and seemed to be absorbing me.

He could evidently speak English, though. I said: 'I am new here and I haven't yet learned much of the language. I shall have to set about learning it in earnest.'

'You'd do better,' he said, 'to worry less about fitting in, and make for home as quickly as you can.'

'What?' I wasn't sure I had heard him properly. There was a good deal of noise; talking and munching, the clattering of feet in smart shoes.

'You may need help before long.' He smiled, displaying uneven teeth. 'I shall be willing to give it. I have glimpsed you before, my dear, and who wouldn't want to help such a beautiful young lady? If you need assistance, turn to me. For the time being, until my duties send me away, I shall be easy to find; I take supper here every evening.'

He smiled again and then added: 'I would charge for my services, of course, but my price won't be beyond your purse.'

I stared at him, too startled to attempt any reply. Speechless, in fact. The hard grey eyes were appraising me and in them, I read, quite clearly, the form that his charges would take. This was outrageous! I had barely arrived and already the sticky threads of the spies' web were being spun round me. I wanted to spring up, get away from the table, away from this champion turned enemy as quickly as possible. I knew quite well who he was but I chose to be a lady offended by a stranger and said: 'Who are you? What is your name, sir?' He merely displayed his teeth again, stood up, stepped over the bench behind him, and went away. I saw him making for the door and then he was gone, and Berend was back.

'I've ordered for us. Smoked mackerel, ham, bread, honey, and a little cheesecake each. And some wine. I've paid for everything. What's the matter, Mildred? You look so white. Are you well?'

He sat down beside me, looking anxious, and I told him about Master Barn Door and then, haltingly, told him that Alvaro had sat down opposite to me and spoken to me. I was about to enlarge, but he stiffened, and then, in a near whisper, he said: 'We can't discuss this here. Eat your supper. Then we'll go back to my rooms.'

We ate. Berend talked of our journey, said that in the morning, after he had presented me to the duke, he would take me to his house and introduce me to his housekeeper. 'Klara speaks some English, and you can discuss with her what other servants you need to employ. I'll arrange for them once you have decided. Klara will cook and see to the linen but you will probably need a maid to clean and to help with the cooking, and a manservant to do any heavy jobs. The rate of pay . . .'

I listened and made suitable answers. The seat opposite to us remained empty for a while and then a pleasant-looking young man came to claim it and Berend hailed him by name. 'This is Leonardo Moreno. Leo, this is Señora Mildred, my English wife. I spoke to him just now, as you saw, Mildred, and asked him to come to our table.'

'There were people I had to detach myself from first,' said Moreno. Smiling, he leant across the table to say words of welcome to me and shake my hand. He was brown-haired and broad of shoulder and he had a calm, deep voice that reminded me of Roger Brockley's voice. I thought: *If I needed help at any point, this man is the sort I would ask.* His eyes were hazel, very much like your own, Ursula, and they were kind.

He and Berend then had a short conversation in Dutch, which I couldn't follow, though I looked at their faces and noticed their tones, and realized that whatever Señor Moreno had to say to Berend, it wasn't anything cheerful. Then supper ended, and we were all saying good night and Berend was leading me away. We went back to his rooms.

The moment we were inside, he shut and locked the door after us, turned to me and seized my shoulders. 'Now, tell me everything! You're sure it was Alvaro? And he started talking to you! Just what did he say?'

'He told me not to worry about fitting in, but to go home as soon as possible. Then he offered to help me, but there would be a price and I could tell, from the way he looked at me . . .'

'You need not say any more. Oh, how he would love to seduce my wife. I shudder when I think that he tried to marry my Alison. It was Alvaro last night, for sure. My God! Well, he had little chance of finding anything. The commission about the battle plan was given to me by Walsingham himself and by word of mouth only and the queen's letter was in the hollow heel of my left riding boot and *that* was tied to the leg of the bed on my side. No one could fiddle with it without waking me. I always do that when I have something in one of my heels. I made sure that even you didn't see me do it. Hans knows nothing of my hollow heels, either. He complains because I never let him pull my boots off, but I take no notice.'

'I had no idea,' I said, astonished.

Thoughtfully, Berend said: 'I don't think Alvaro can know of the battle plan commission. Yes, Elizabeth's court is a mass of gossip and Alvaro has a real gift for hearing things he shouldn't. But the idea of the battle plan arose very suddenly and nothing is on paper. The confidential letter is another matter. The secret correspondence between the duke and Elizabeth has been going on for months though this is the first time I have been the courier.' Berend let go of me and started to pace the room, muttering. Then he swung round to face me.

'If Alvaro has been making journeys to England, spying into what ships are being built, and what supplies England has of her own and what vital armaments, foodstuffs and so forth have to be imported, then his reports probably would differ from my own! No wonder the duke has been noticing the flaws in mine. Alvaro has been helpfully pointing them out. I suspect that he has been dropping poison into the ducal ears. I just hope that while I was still in England he didn't catch sight of Christopher Spelton, or at least didn't recognize him. Spelton is dubious company for a respectable ducal spy! It was unwise to fraternize with him. Though heaven knows we only met by chance in the first place.'

'Isn't it true that an agent was murdered in England recently? Mistress Stannard told me. Someone called Juan Smith?'

'You know about that? It's true, yes.'

Again, I determined not to show my fear, to keep my words light, witty. 'I think you might have warned me that I should be prepared to wake up one morning and find you stabbed to death at my side!'

'I didn't think it would encourage you to marry me! Though,' he added thoughtfully, 'I may have underestimated the danger. Alvaro resented it so very much when I refused to let him marry Alison. He told me to my face that one day he would get even with me. He *loves* to bear grudges. He cuddles them to him like a happy mother with her first baby. I've no doubt that he would like to frighten my bride into fleeing for home, and how he would enjoy taking my place in her bed!'

I was very frightened indeed by now. I had married expecting to be a straightforward wife, respecting my husband's work without being part of it. Instead, here I was in a vast, strange palace where I could not only get lost, but might meet an enemy round any corner. I was like a tree entangled in ivy, choking in it and without means to defend myself.

Berend said: 'You will see the duke tomorrow. Try to make a good impression. I must consider the best way to get hold of that battle plan. I must talk to Leonardo, in case we have to make a hasty flight.'

'Who is Leonardo? I mean, what does he do?'

'He is one of the Masters of Horse. The duke has three or four of them – for his own horses and the ceremonial ones, and for the light harness horses, and for farm horses and in Leonardo's case for the animals that are kept for guests. Everyone doesn't arrive on their own horse, any more than we did. Leonardo buys and sells, keeps an eye on the grooms, doctors the horses himself if necessary, recommends suitable animals for various guests. Things like that.'

'What did he say to you at supper tonight, in your own tongue?'

'Oh, he was only warning me that I am under suspicion! As if I didn't know! Apparently, gossip about me is winging round the palace. *Ooh, the duke's messenger boy has been up to things he shouldn't! He's going to be in trouble!* But I was grateful, he meant it kindly. Damn Alvaro to the hottest part of hell. But I must still get on with the task appointed to me.'

He stopped pacing and sat down on the settle. 'About that battle plan. A great many men will have to know about them, or they can't be put into effect. Captains and crews have to know what they're doing. Parma wouldn't be part of the Armada, he's supposed to meet it, which isn't the same thing. But Philip might reasonably want Parma to know what his plan is, to have a picture of it in his mind, to understand what kind of array he is supposed to reinforce. The queen obviously assumes that Parma will know about it and if so, he will have informed his chief officers and ships' captains. One thing I have found out, is that so far, Parma hasn't had any warships built. Just a number of vessels suitable for use in a river, or maybe for a short sea crossing. Parma may be arriving at his own decisions. All the better. I don't want to see England under Philip's heel, believe me.' He seemed to lapse against the back of the settle. 'Dear God, I think I am growing weary of this way of life and it's hardly fair to you. If I can just get back to England with the plan . . . I wonder if I should simply stay there. We could live there very happily, as Spelton does. Would you like that?'

'Yes,' I said fervently. 'I would.'

'Maybe we should consider it. I must appear to settle you in my Brussels house, though. It will look innocent. But when I go back to England, *if* I go back to England, you will come with me, and perhaps we won't return to Brussels. I must think it over. My darling, it is time for bed, our first night in Brussels.'

*   *   *

He made it a night to remember, a night of love, of need.
Entwined and joined, we were one flesh, as the priest who
married us had said. We didn't use the vinegar-soaked sponge
this time and I wondered if we might engender a child, and
then shrank inwardly, thinking that if Berend did not after all
choose to give up his secret work and stay in England, I would
have to bear our child in this terrible world of his, peopled by
strangers who whispered secrets and crept into other people's
bedchambers at night. Carrying knives.

But then Berend's warm body and his caresses overwhelmed me again, enfolding and claiming me, lifting me
to astonishing heights and keeping me there until I cried out
because I had reached the pitch where pleasure and pain
were one, and then releasing me so that something gave way,
burst out, like a great flower of joy, while a mighty pulse
throbbed within me and I felt a warm wetness, his seed and
my welcome combined.

After that, he slept. But for a long time, I could not.
Lovemaking, no matter how splendid, could not quiet my sense
of dread. Once Berend was asleep, I felt as though I were
alone, on guard, with one ear open for a murderous intruder.
I felt so very far from home. I yearned for you, Ursula, and
for Hawkswood. When I did finally sleep, I dreamed of it.

I woke at dawn and turned over, reaching for Berend. He
wasn't there. I sat up. We hadn't closed the shutters and a
faint grey daybreak was creeping in. I looked at the empty
place beside me and felt the sheets. They were cold. He had
left me again, gone away about some secret business. How
long had he been gone? I looked about me and saw his night-
shirt lying across the foot of the bed. He must have dressed
and gone out. Where was he and when would he come
back and what was I to do if he didn't?

I wasn't even sure that I could find my way to the dining
chamber for breakfast without Berend there to show the way.
Berend, where are you?

Beyond the wide arch that divided the bedchamber from
the parlour, I heard a faint click. A shadow moved. I caught
my breath and then Berend was there. He was wearing the

breeches and loose-fitting doublet he used for riding but his
feet were slippered. He sat down on the side of the bed. 'You're
awake?' he said.

'Yes. Where did you go? I woke up and you weren't here.'

'I hoped you wouldn't wake before I got back.'

'But where *were* you?'

'In the Secretaries' Room,' said Berend.

'In the . . .?'

'The duke has two private secretaries,' said Berend. 'They
work with him in his study. That's not actually within the
duke's suite. It's just outside. Next to it is a room for the clerks
who do the dull work, making copies of things that have to
go to several people, making file copies, all that. Some of
them act as secretaries for men about the court who don't have
their own, though most of them do. That's the Secretaries'
Room, anyway. I thought it might be a likely place to look
for that plan. It's locked at night, of course, but I have picklocks. And I found what I wanted! I found the plan! Lying on
a desk, where a clerk had been making copies of it. There was
a parchment original and two copies on paper and one half
finished. The work was horridly fiddly – here.'

His riding doublet had an inner pocket. He pulled out a
piece of paper and gave it to me. He opened the shutters to
give me some light, and I stared at the plan in complete bewil-
derment. There were blocks of letters, arranged in a kind of
crescent. Then I saw that at one side there was a key, explaining
which letters stood for which kind of vessel. I could now
understand it. I also saw how very fiddly it must be to copy.
Nervously, I handed it back.

'There were some spoilt copies in the waste bin,' Berend
said. 'It's such a tricky business, even for the clerks. I couldn't
risk stealing one of the finished ones; there were only two and
the clerk would have noticed. I think he'd paused in his work
when the light faded. Candlelight wouldn't be good enough.
Only, I had to make do with it and it wasn't easy. I started by
using the quill the clerk had left and the damn thing had
already been worked hard. It started to spatter and spoilt my
first attempt. I had to prepare another quill. That and all the
trickiness are why I took so long. It was just beginning to get

light as I came out of the room, and I'd only got a few yards
before I nearly walked straight into a sentry!'

'Berend!'

'I said nearly. There are guards at night in the passages
close to the duke's private apartments. They prowl those
passages all night long. A few steps from the door to the
Secretaries' Room, the passage goes round a sharp corner and
opens out into a long salon. I heard the guard's footsteps before
he came in sight.'

'But, Berend . . .'

'Just before the corner, there's a deep alcove, furnished like
a little room – table, chairs, a settle with its back to the wall.
Gatherings are sometimes held in the salon and there are
always a few folk wanting to slip out and talk in private; men
with business in mind, amorous couples – well, you can
imagine. I dodged in there and went down flat behind the
settle. The sentry went past and then, I got up and darted round
into the salon. He must have heard something then because
his footsteps halted and turned – sentries don't have slippers
on; they have boots. There are more settles in the salon so I
repeated my trick and dropped down behind the nearest. Whew!
It was a bad moment. He came back round the corner and
stood there, looking along the salon but after a little while, he
turned away, and that time I didn't stir until I was sure he was
really gone.'

I let out my breath in a sigh, and realized that I had been
holding it for some while. 'What time is it?' I asked.

'Six of the clock, or round about. Hans won't be on duty
yet. But he should have left us some ale and laid a fresh fire
in the hearth. If you can light it, you could mull some ale for
us. I must dress properly.'

'I'll heat some washing water for you.' I looked at him.
'You have ink on your fingers. You must get rid of that. You
need shaving water, too. How is the cut round your ribs?'

'Closed and dry. Hans made a point of cleaning and salving
it yesterday. Even my exertions last night haven't opened it.'
He grinned at me.

I shook my head at him, pulled my bedgown on and went
to set the water to heat. By the time Hans arrived, Berend was

washed and shaved with neatly brushed hair, and I had him dressed for the day in doublet, hose and ruff, with a velvet cloak and matching cap to hand. We were sitting side by side on the bed, sipping the warm ale. Beyond straightening our (decidedly rumpled) bed, there wasn't much for Hans to do. With amusement, he said: 'Sir, now that you have a wife, I am nearly out of a job.'

FOURTEEN
No Time to Breathe

I used some of the water I had heated to wash my face and hands, but made no haste to dress. I thought we would have time to sit and talk before I need prepare myself for the day. But to my surprise and regret, Berend said: 'I have a further appointment with the duke, first thing this morning. I am sorry to leave you but I shan't be long, and I will be back to accompany you to breakfast. Yes, breakfast is provided. Hans, call Greta. My wife must be ready for her presentation; she will need the help of a maid.'

Then he was out of the door and gone, and within five minutes, Hans had fetched Greta, and I was in her charge.

Despite her lack of English, she found no difficulty in getting me out of my nightgown, after which I was washed again, this time from head to foot, except for my hair, because there was no time to get it dry. She explained this by showing me a wet sponge, pointing to my hair and then shaking her head at the sponge. I grasped the point. She indicated approval of my light blue gown, which was just as well, since I had no other that could be called formal. Then we had to select the jewellery to go with it.

I had thrown my jewel box into a saddlebag at the last moment. I held up the fresh-water pearl necklace and discreet matching earrings that I had worn at supper the previous evening, whereupon Greta shook a determined head and out of the box, plucked a much more dramatic set of lapis lazuli and pearls, with drop earrings that were not at all discreet.

You gave them to me last Christmas, Ursula, and you also gave me a hood lined with silk and covered in chestnut-coloured velvet and adorned with a bright row of blue agates and fresh-water pearls. I had worn it at supper the previous evening, as well, but when it was enhanced by lapis lazuli and a few deep-sea pearls, it seemed quite different. I looked at myself in Greta's mirror and was astonished. I looked so elegant.

What I had not thought to bring with me was perfume. Greta, after dabbing imaginary scent on her own wrist, raising her eyebrows and then looking dashed when I shook my head, had an inspiration, ran from the room, and came back with a phial of rosewater, her own, I presumed. With this on my wrists and behind my ears, I was ready, I hoped, to impress any number of dukes.

After that, I sat waiting and wondering what breakfast would consist of. I was relieved when at last Berend reappeared. He was beaming. He closed the door after him, came to me and swung me off my feet.

'As I told you, I gave the queen's letter to the duke yesterday, and lo! He is going to entrust me with the reply. He has not yet written it but he will give it to me later today and I shall have to leave without delay after that but as I have the battle plan, that's nothing to worry about. For the moment, we are to take breakfast and then I am to present you, and after that settle you in my house before I collect the letter and a horse and set off. Come along.'

For a moment, I hung back. 'You said . . . you would have to leave at once and you're going to settle me in your house? You're going to leave me here alone?'

'This time I must. It would be hard on you to have to ride as fast as I shall ride, going back to England with correspondence for Elizabeth. But I shall come back for you and perhaps then we'll plan our escape to England. God, I am so thankful. I am back in favour.'

He picked up one of the goblets from which we had sipped wine the previous evening. 'Did Mistress Stannard ever tell you about this blue and white ware? I don't believe that I did for all our hours of chit-chat at West Leys. I used to carry samples of this to England and collect orders for the man who makes it. It was my way of accounting for my presence in England, and useful to him. I'm quite a good salesman. I would come back with orders and he would see to getting them delivered – by somebody else. Even carrying samples meant taking a pack pony with me; transporting orders for ten serving dishes, two bowls and twelve goblets six times over, and maybe little orders for three bowls here, six goblets there, a pair of serving platters somewhere else, would need a cart. Earthenware is heavy. But before my latest trip to England, I gave it up. I was very doubtful of my standing with the duke. My position with him might be coming to an end. Though I did think that if I were dismissed from his service, my useful acquaintance with the kiln might employ me to travel about and sell his wares. I would have a living. However, after all, I don't think it will be necessary. Now, don't worry about being left in my house. You'll settle easily. Klara will help you and Leonardo's wife will call on you. I know you'll like her. I'll be back before you miss me. Meanwhile, aren't you hungry?'

I was, but I felt breathless. Things were happening too fast. I had been looking forward to seeing Berend's house and taking charge of it but it would be some time before it ceased to be strange to me. I wasn't ready to be installed in a strange house in a strange land and then left there. He had told me that when he left for England again, he would take me with him, and perhaps we'd stay there. First he said one thing, then another. I didn't know what to believe.

Breakfast was an informal affair and sparsely attended. A long table was set out with breads, slices of cold meat, cheeses, little bowls of spiced dips, butter and honey, and some jugs of milk and small ale. There were some wooden platters and drinking cups. Most people seemed to eat standing up, though there were tables where one could sit. We collected our food and took a table and then, to our annoyance, Señor Alvaro came into the room and strolled over to us. He wished us good day. Then he said: 'I congratulate you, Señor Gomez, on your marriage to such a beautiful wife. I hope you will take better care of her than you did of your daughter. Had you let Alison marry me, she would be alive to this day.'

Berend started furiously to his feet but Alvaro was already sauntering away. 'May he die of the pox,' Berend muttered.

He looked at me. 'The horrible thing is, it could be true. But Alison would not have been happy.'

And then it was time to meet the duke.

'He holds an audience of some sort on most mornings,' Berend told me. 'There are always people wanting to speak to him. He speaks English. You address him as Your Grace. This way.'

He led me through a succession of passages and then down a long and ornate staircase to a lower floor. Here, I caught a glimpse through an open door of one of the enormous reception rooms he had mentioned to me. It took my breath away because it didn't look like a room at all; it was far too huge and it glittered so with mirrors and gold ornaments that where the sunlight through the tall windows glanced off them, the reflection dazzled. But I had no time to stand staring at it for Berend was hurrying me on. There were other people in the passageway, too, nearly all going the same way, and all splendidly dressed.

Eventually, we came to a large anteroom where, in company with many others, we had to wait. It was a long wait and there was nowhere to sit down. Every now and then an usher, dressed in black velvet hose and doublet, instead of the dark blue and white that I had by now realized was the livery worn by most of the servants, would come in through the huge double doors at the far end and call a name. Then he would escort someone into the duke's presence. I thought, as the morning dragged on, that it would be time for dinner before we had our turn.

But at last the usher called: 'Señor and Señora Berend Gomez!' and we were led through the double doors into a spacious audience chamber. Many of those who had preceded us were still there, standing about in small groups. They glanced at us with casual interest. There were two doors, I noticed; the one by which we had entered and another at the far end of the room. Both had guards standing on either side.

The usher conducted us to where the duke was seated in a throne-like chair on a dais. Berend bowed. I curtsied. I hoped that my finery was fine enough. However, the duke smiled and beckoned and we went up the two shallow steps on to the dais, where the Duke of Parma reached out to take my hand and kissed it.

In clear if accented English, he said: 'Welcome to our court, Señora Gomez. You have had a long journey from England, have you not? How brave of you to commit yourself not only to a husband but to a new country. We all hope that you will soon be at home here, and feel yourself to be one of us. Señor Gomez, you did not tell me that your wife was so beautiful. She will be an ornament to our court, I feel sure.'

'I think I wanted her to be a surprise to you, sir,' said Berend, and nudged me.

I said: 'Thank you, your grace. I am happy to be here.'

I rather liked the look of the duke. He was dressed in a massive doublet in greeny-gold velvet, thickly quilted and with huge puffed sleeves, slashed with gold satin. His ruff was colossal, tall enough to push his chin up, and nearly as wide as a cartwheel. Yet, the face that smiled at me from the midst of all this bulky clothing had small features and a delicacy that was almost feminine though the thickly bearded chin was masculine enough. He had dark, wiry hair and dark eyes that smiled. I could not help smiling back.

'When you return from your next journey to England,' he said to Berend, 'we will hold a masque, as a way of saying a proper welcome to your lady. Meanwhile, I will see you, Señor Gomez, in private in my study at three of the clock this afternoon. My letter to Queen Elizabeth will be ready for you then.'

He gave a nod, and Berend bowed again. I took the hint and made another curtsey, and then we retreated backwards down the steps, which I found unnerving because I was afraid of losing my footing. Berend drew me off to one side. The duke leant sideways to speak to the waiting usher, who at once set off to summon the next appellant. We moved over to the wall. 'What now?' I whispered.

'We wait until it's all over and then the duke will leave through the anteroom and the crowd will drift after him. He'll go wherever he's going and people will gradually fade away to go about their own affairs as well.'

I thought it was an exhausting way just to be introduced to someone but decided that it would be tactless to say so. We stood where we were for some time. One or two people recognized Berend and nodded to him. One of them was Leonardo Moreno, who was in a group on the opposite side of the room. The sudden arrival, through the further door, of a tall, black-gowned individual, accompanied by Nicolas Alvaro, caused a stir, because it clearly wasn't expected. The usher hurried over and spoke to the two of them in low tones. The guards who were on duty by the door joined in. Then the usher and Alvaro went towards the duke, leaving the black-gowned man with the guards.

Parma had noticed what was happening. He dismissed the gentleman to whom he had been talking and beckoned the usher and Alvaro forward. They spoke together and I saw the duke's brows draw together in a frown. Then he nodded and the usher went to fetch the black-gowned man and also one of the guards. He led them on to the dais and I saw the duke begin to question them.

And under his breath, Berend swore. 'What is it?' I whispered.

'That guard. Difficult to tell; in their helmets and uniform jackets they all look alike, but last night when I was hiding from that sentry, I caught a glimpse of him. I could only make out his shape but that one there could easily be the same man; he's the same build, anyway. He's had time to eat and sleep and come back on duty. That other fellow, all in black, is a clerk. From the Secretaries' Room. All the clerks dress like that.'

Again, I felt afraid and beside me, I sensed the tension in Berend. Presently, the usher escorted the black-clad clerk away and the guard also went away, but instead of resuming his post, he left the audience chamber as if upon some errand. Then everything went on as before. No one looked our way. 'It's probably nothing to do with us,' I whispered. Berend said: 'I hope not.'

We had to stay where we were for another half-hour until the duke rose and went out by way of the anteroom and everyone followed. There were some disappointed hopefuls still in the anteroom, who now gave up hope and blended with the crowd as we all followed him out. Berend seized my elbow, turned us into a side passage and then hurried us up some stairs and into another passage. I once more lost my bearings.

Then we were back in his rooms, where he slammed the door behind us, went to the cupboard where we had put our small store of clothing, pulled out one of his riding boots and twisted its heel. I watched with concern. This was where he had hidden the queen's letter. Had he concealed the plan there as well? He unscrewed the heel and I saw that it was hollow. There was nothing inside, however. My heart turned over and I looked at Berend in alarm.

He understood my expression. 'I didn't hide the plan here. The heel was meant to be empty. I use it sometimes when I'm travelling but not as a hiding place here. It's a trick that too many people know about, including most of the duke's agents. I have a trick of my own, though, as a way of checking whether anyone has been through my belongings. I leave my heels not quite screwed home. Not *quite*. I doubt if any searcher would notice. But most of them would be working in haste, and they'd most likely screw the heel back fast and properly. This heel has been screwed back properly and that's not the way I left it. And, Mildred, my love, on the shelf at the top of the cupboard, you had put your hat at one end. It is now in the middle. I saw it just now when I opened the cupboard. While the duke finished his leisurely audience, this room was searched. That guard was probably sent out with orders to do just that.'

'Oh, dear God! Where did you hide the plan, then?'

'You're wearing it, sweetheart. While you were washing your face this morning, I hid it under the lining of that pretty hood you have on your head. I am handy with a needle. Where the lining and the stiff outer covering meet, I made a slit, pushed the folded plan inside and then stitched the slit up. Tiny stitches, also right under the edge of the stiff outer covering. Invisible, I think, even if anyone examines the hood which they can't have done, as it's on your pretty head. And now . . .'

He held a hand out to me and drew me over to sit beside him on the bed. His face had changed, not as it changed the time I made him angry, but in a pinched, taut kind of way. Where was my Berend, so ready to laugh, so splendid a lover? This Berend was afraid, bracing himself for something. But before he could speak, there was a knock on the outer door. It made us both jump.

Berend began to say something to me, but Hans emerged suddenly from his bedchamber and was opening the door. Leonardo Moreno came hastily in. 'Berend!'

'What is it?' Berend came to his feet.

'I came to warn you.' Moreno sounded breathless, as though he had been running. 'My friend, you are under suspicion again. What have you done?'

'Nothing that I know of.' Berend sounded convincingly bewildered. He said: 'My things have been searched, though I don't know what for.'

'Don't you? In God's name, Berend, what are you about? You are suspected of having stolen – well, copied – King Philip's plan of battle. The clerk who was making copies of it yesterday found this morning that his desk had been disturbed. Things had been moved and there was a nearly new quill on his desk. The clerk is saying that the one he'd been using was almost worn out. Oh, he reported everything to the proper quarters but of course there were other clerks by when he first looked at his desk, and Nicolas Alvaro was in the same room, collecting some message or other that the duke wants to send to Spain. He heard all the exclamations and came over to look at the desk for himself. He would! The clerks begin work early and all this happened before any of us went to have breakfast. And it seems that during breakfast he stopped to speak to you and noticed that you have ink beneath your fingernails.'

'Ink beneath . . .!' Berend held his hands up to the light. He had washed himself well when he got back to our room in the early morning, but it was true. Some of his nails still had dark ink under them.

'Anyone could have inky fingernails!' I said indignantly. 'My husband writes letters sometimes. That means nothing.'

'As you well know,' said Leo, addressing Berend, 'the duke, of late, has had doubts about you. He thought they had been dispelled but now he is once more wondering. Alvaro is talking about you to various cronies of his and that's what he's saying. And his friends, of course, are spreading it all round the court. Alvaro seems pleased with himself. Anyone would think he was an excited child.'

'Alvaro has reasons for hating me,' Berend said. 'And he is spiteful. What else is he saying?'

'It seems that he has now informed the duke that in England recently you were seen in questionable company.'

'I see. Yes, I do see,' said Berend. He sounded convincingly bitter, like an innocent man who had been slandered. 'I have been restored to favour with the duke and Alvaro didn't like it. He's probably been waiting his chance to smear my name and sheer chance has presented it to him. He was in England lately. While he was there, he probably saw me with a man called Christopher Spelton, who is an agent for Queen Elizabeth. We chanced to fall in together on the way to Queen Elizabeth's court, and later, I took shelter in his house when I was ill. Oh, this is maddening. It is worth my while to cultivate Elizabeth's agents; Alvaro knows that perfectly well. But it so happens that the moment I get back here, there's a rumpus over this battle plan, or whatever it is, and then, oh, what a pretty weapon my meeting with Spelton has placed in his hand! I've no doubt that he's spun a fine tale out of that.'

Moreno said: 'I am not asking you whether you did or did not interfere with the clerk's desk. I don't want to know. Nor do I know whether or not you are in danger of arrest. I am just concerned for you. Is there any proof that you touched that desk?'

'Of course not,' Berend said. 'There couldn't be. I've never even heard of this battle plan, let alone stolen it!'

'For your own sake, I hope not. But I don't think you will be allowed to go to England again. That's being bruited round the court, as well. As your friend, I wanted to forewarn you. No one has told me not to.'

'I see,' said Berend. His face now was that of a stern stranger. I stood rigid. Things were certainly happening too fast. He said: 'Leo, my friend, I thank you for your warning. Please leave us now.'

'God be with you,' said Leo, and went. The stern stranger with whom I had spent such a night of passion, turned to me. 'Once more, Mildred, I have things to tell you,' he said.

FIFTEEN
The Nightmare Truth

I am not likely ever to forget what he said to me then. He said: 'The duke won't entrust me with his reply to Elizabeth now. I can forget my nice little private meeting with him in his study at three of the clock this afternoon! If I am really accused of trying to copy or steal that plan, then I will certainly not be allowed to leave the palace. It's too serious. The plan is in your hood, Mildred. You will have to take it to England for me.'

I had half foreseen it, but when he said it aloud, I was terrified and began to protest. 'How will I manage, travelling to Ostend without you? I don't know the language! And when will I see you again? I shall have to come back after I've delivered the plan . . .'

'Hans will see you to Ostend and see you onto the boat and as for coming back . . . Mildred, my dear, I don't know what will happen to me now but it may well be worse than mere dismissal. It was a wonderful relief when I thought for a short time that the danger was past, but Alvaro has made it return in even greater force. If you once get back to England, stay there. Forget me. Marry someone else. Since the day I said I wouldn't let him get his hands on my Alison, Alvaro has longed to find a way of doing me harm. I've evaded his efforts so far but I think that this time, he has triumphed. He's a bad enemy. My poor daughter. She was such a picture, so lovely. Any man might want her. I rue the day that ever Alvaro set eyes on her. From the moment I undertook to find the battle plan, I realized that it could be dangerous. But I meant to be cautious, and I hoped – I was sure – that because Queen Elizabeth had entrusted that letter to me, that simple fact would overcome the duke's doubts, would count as evidence of my good faith. And for a while, it did! But now, alas, the fears I

had back in England were justified and I was right to act on
them if I could. You see, my dear, when I fell ill at West Leys
on my journey back to Dover, and you were there . . . I saw
a way, through your delightful self, I saw a way to ensure that
I could fulfil my duty to the queen, even if I couldn't do it in
person.'

'You . . . what?' My mind went numb. I couldn't believe
what I was hearing. Was he saying that he married me so
as to have a substitute courier if the need arose? Was he
saying *that*? No, I couldn't believe it. Then a new and appalling
thought came into my mind.

'If I leave you to go to England, what if someone guesses
that perhaps I am carrying the stolen plan! I shall be pursued,
brought back!' Visions of armed men seizing me, of being
shut in a dungeon, even . . . I wanted to throw myself onto
the floor and howl because what was happening to me was
unbearable and I wanted it to go away.

'I made two copies of that plan,' said Berend calmly. 'One
is in your hood but the other's inside the buckram lining of
my thickest doublet. If you are in danger, I'll let them find it.
That may well distract their minds from you. Darling, do this
one thing for me. Take the plan to England. And then, dear
Mildred, find another husband and be happy with him. I truly
wish you well.'

My mind was reeling. What was he saying? Find another
husband? Had he gone mad, or had I? 'But we're married!
Even if I wanted to, I couldn't just marry someone else, unless,
unless . . .'

'Unless I were dead? And once in England, you might
not know if I were dead or alive. It's all right, Mildred, my
love . . .'

'Stop calling me your love! You obviously don't care a
straw for me or you wouldn't have dreamt of . . . using me
as you have and . . .'

'The world of the secret agent is hard beyond your under-
standing, though I think your good friend Mistress Stannard
understands it. To do our duty, we sometimes have to be ruthless, have to ignore our tenderest feelings. It doesn't mean
that we don't have tender feelings; it's just that sometimes

they don't and can't come first. But I did take thought for this. Darling . . .'

'*Will* you stop calling me things like that!'

'. . . we are not lawfully married,' said Berend, quite placidly, as though it were the most reasonable thing in the world.

'Not . . . What in God's name do you mean?' I shouted. 'There was a priest, a church, we took our vows . . .'

'There were no witnesses. Under Spanish law, a marriage without witnesses is void. The Netherlands are under Spanish law.'

I gasped. Tears sprang to my eyes and began to run down my face. And then I screamed some wild insult or other – I can't now recall just what I said – and lashed out, trying to strike him, but he caught my wrist and stopped me. Afterwards, there were blue fingermarks there, bruises as his farewell gift to me.

'You can do that later,' he said. 'Down in the stable yard. I expected some outrage and some floods of tears on your side . . .'

'Expected outrage? Expected . . .?'

'Yes, of course,' said the unemotional monster who had once been my husband and my lover. 'I expected you to be furious – it's only natural and it will be a great help in getting you safely away if I am prevented from returning to England, as I fear I will be. We can use this to get you out of here in a fashion that won't at all suggest that you're taking – er – contraband with you. Lose your temper with me by all means but don't hit me here, not until we have witnesses . . .'

'*What?*'

'Just pack, fling your cloak and your saddlebags around you, rush to the stables, *now*, and demand a horse. I will follow you, shouting, pleading, you will bawl that I have deceived you, that I care nothing for you; you won't stay with me a moment longer. No need for details about the nature of my offence! In public, you can hit me and welcome. I, a perfect gentleman, being reasonable though you are not, will exclaim that you can't go alone, at least let me see you to the boat. You can scream that you would rather be escorted by Satan himself. Hans will come after me; I shall see to that, and I shall insist that he goes with you – you will have just enough sense to agree and to wait, fuming, for him to fetch his things. He'll have them ready.' He went to the door and bellowed: '*Hans!*'

Hans was always at hand, sometimes in his tiny bedchamber, and sometimes, as I now knew, in a room close by where he and some other menservants congregated when off duty, to play board games and talk though not, Hans had quietly told me, to gossip. He appeared at once and glanced at me in a startled fashion, understandably, for my tears were still pouring and I dare say I was scarlet with rage and hurt.

'Pack your saddlebags,' Berend said to him. 'You are to help us to enact a little drama down in the stable yard. Then you are to take my distraught wife to Ostend.'

I was distraught, that was true enough. But in that terrible situation, Ursula, I thought of you and wondered what you would do, and I knew that you would want to get that beastly battle plan to England at all costs, that with you, that would come first. So it would have to come first with me, even if it felt like tearing my heart out of my body and stamping on it.

Oh yes, to begin with I cursed and protested and swore that I wouldn't be a party to all this deception, but in my heart, I knew from the first that I would have to agree and so I did. With a mad feeling that I was acting when I was only showing my real feelings and showing them to the world in a way that I would never have done if it hadn't been forced on me, I performed Berend's drama. I stuffed my saddlebags and the farthingale bags to go with them. I slung it all around me and rushed out of Berend's rooms, sobbing, which was easy for I was already doing so, and I ran down the stairs, somehow, miraculously, finding my way to the side door through which we had first come, all quite openly, ignoring the people I brushed past and sometimes bumped into, ignoring their astounded faces and indignant exclamations as well and rushed out of the palace, on to the surrounding track and then head-long into the stable yard.

Berend pursued me, shouting my name, but carefully didn't catch up until I was there. He came running in behind me, exclaiming things like: *I'm sorry! You're being unreasonable! Mildred, I can explain, let me explain! Please, Mildred, don't be silly* . . .

I screamed: 'Don't call me silly!' and slapped his face, hard. That wasn't acting; I meant it and I put my strength behind it. Berend, standing like a rock, said: 'Very well, but you must let me escort you to Ostend, you can't go alone. Not after the war, not after the rebellion there has been here.'

'The rebellion is over!' I shouted. 'Will someone saddle me a horse! I *am* going to England but not with you beside me; I would rather ride beside the devil himself!'

Berend went on with his argument, at the top of his voice. 'War is a living monster, it swallows lives, homes, and like other living things it passes ugliness from its entrails. The dead, the wounded, the bereaved and the furious, all those are left behind from the rebellion and I tell you that you can't and mustn't . . . Hans! There you are! Madam, will you let Hans ride with you?'

'Yes, yes, anyone, anyone but you! *Where is my horse?* Hans, you can come but get ready as fast as you can. I won't linger here a moment more!'

'Do as she says, Hans!' shouted Berend. 'I say it too – put your things together and escort her to Ostend and on to a boat for England! If she changes her mind on the way, bring her back by all means! But keep her safe!'

'I shan't change my mind! May I never set eyes on you again, you . . .!'

I will not repeat the epithet I used. I was myself surprised that I had ever heard it before, let alone understood it. I had learned a lot from my husband Daniel's villagers. There were some foul mouths among them. It had a remarkable effect on the grooms. They looked at me in horror and two of them even backed away from me. I glared at them and once more demanded a horse. They hurried off to fetch one, no doubt relieved to think that such a termagant as I had proved to be would soon be off the premises.

'Fifteen minutes, Señora, no more,' said Hans. He had timed his arrival skilfully. He ran out of the stable yard and while he was gone, a horse was at last produced for me, complete with a side-saddle. When Hans returned, in considerably less than fifteen minutes, I was mounted, with my saddlebags all slung in place, and a second horse had been saddled for him. Berend was hovering, alternately trying to plead with me and condemning me for an unreasonable, unjust, unforgiving disaster as a wife. I ostentatiously ignored him. Hans arrived with his bags, got onto his horse, and with that, we were on our way. I didn't say farewell to Berend, although he said it to me. I didn't know then and I still don't know, just how much real feeling he had for me. Nor do I understand what kind of feeling I had – and still have – for him.

I did take with me the memory of that glorious and passionate night, his caresses, my surging, exultant climaxes, the huge pulses within me, the relief and the joy of them. I have never forgotten any of that. But how much they meant to him remains forever a mystery.

When Hans and I were on the road, I said to him: 'This must all seem very strange to you, Hans. Please don't ask too many questions. I am thankful for your protection, that's all.'

'I understand more than you know, Señora,' said Hans. 'I also understand that we must lose no time. Just in case.'

I didn't ask him just in case of what. I knew the answer to that and so, no doubt, did he.

SIXTEEN
Mounting Impatience

During that last day of our journey to Brussels, I asked Christopher if he had ever visited the Duke of Parma before. As a Queen's Messenger, I knew he had sometimes gone abroad. 'How did you become a Messenger?' I added. 'I've never asked.'

'My father was a Messenger,' said Christopher. 'And when I was a boy, he encouraged me to study languages and as it happened, I had a talent for them. I know French and Dutch quite well, and can manage with Spanish and Italian. I was never too good at Latin and I never attempted Greek. But knowing the languages of today made me very suitable as a Messenger and I followed my father into his calling. Knowing languages raised my pay, as well. And yes, I have been to the Netherlands before, but I've never been sent to the duke. It was always to people with whom the queen or her council had dealings. Merchants sometimes, bankers and so on – carrying letters to do with money or trade. In late years, most of my work has been inside England though lately I made one journey with a letter for the delegates who are in Ostend just now, dragging out interminable peace talks that aren't meant to come to anything. And I once went to Portugal, before Philip annexed it.'

'Oh, yes, I've been to Portugal once,' I said reminiscently. 'Also before Philip got at it. Pray God he doesn't annex England.'

That was what everyone dreaded, though few people said it aloud. It was hard to keep one's spirits up. The day was grey and chilly and my bruises were troubling me. In the fashion of bruises, they were more painful now than when I first incurred them and they had delayed us. Because I was in such obvious pain, we had had to spend an extra night on the road and in a town called Neustad. I wanted to press on hard, but Christopher was insisting that we should not.

'We can canter in patches and walk in between,' he had said, as we started out on what we hoped would be our final day of travelling. 'No trotting; it will hurt you, rising up and down. And best not gallop, even if these nags *can* gallop, which I doubt. We can't reach Brussels before this evening, but what of it? Even if they aren't married yet, we can't stop them. We have no right. She's a widow and a free woman. She can please herself.'

'She has no sense!' I snapped at him. 'She falls in love at five minutes' notice – she keeps on doing it – and she just flings herself into the man's arms without any thought for the kind of life she's going to lead, and I am still in a way responsible to her parents for her safety. They consigned her to me and she is still very young. She's only twenty. And a secret agent like Berend isn't right for her, you know he isn't!'

'I'm a secret agent and you never said I wasn't right for Kate and Kate was your ward once.'

'You're English and at that time we weren't on the brink of war!'

'Calm yourself,' said philosophical Christopher. 'You're exciting your horse.'

'This horse wouldn't be excited if someone let off a cannon behind it,' I said glumly. 'It's another damn slug.'

'At the moment, all the better for you,' said Christopher, irritatingly. 'Mine's as bad as that mare you're on. He's so broad in the back that he makes my thighs ache.'

We therefore rode on at the steady pace that Christopher recommended. The sky cleared and Christopher did his best to make pleasant conversation, mostly about West Leys, where he hoped there had been no heavy downpours of late.

'I've been concerned about the drainage in the six-acre field,' he told me, and I did my best to look interested. 'That's the one that's on the flat ground at the foot of the hill. My bailiff is new – the one I had before died suddenly just after Christmas. John Brinkman is a stranger from Hampton way. The Brentvale vicar also comes from Hampton and knew him from childhood. He recommended him – Brinkman was looking for a better post than the one he had. He seems like a good man, but he doesn't yet know West Leys intimately.'

'I'm sure he'll manage very well,' I said, attempting comfort. 'Brinkman's an unusual name. Did his ancestors live on the edge of a cliff, I wonder.'

'Why should they?' said Christopher, obviously not seeing the joke, if it was a joke. For all I knew, it could have truth in it. I didn't try to explain but secretly I sighed a little for Brockley. Master Spelton was as solid and reliable as an escort well could be but he didn't have Brockley's sharp-edged sense of humour. Brockley would have picked up that play on words at once. I changed the subject and said: 'There in the distance – are those pinnacles? Would that be Parma's palace?'

It was, though it was still far away, and long before we even drew near to it we came across another interesting sight. We were drawn to it by the sound of a trumpet in the distance, and a man's voice shouting what sounded like orders.

The track had been running along the crest of a long, low hill and the sound seemed to come from below us, on our left. We rode a little off the path to find out what it was and found ourselves overlooking a stretch of flat land which was being used, apparently, as an arena. There were squads of men, grouped into a number of squares, wheeling and turning, dissolving into columns and then back into squares, in response to the shouts and trumpet calls of the officer in charge. We could see him, a tiny figure on a horse, standing still.

'That's astonishing,' Christopher said. 'He's moving those men about as though they were pawns on a chessboard! He's *wielding* them.'

We went on watching. There came a change. The men had been released from their formations and arranged in simple lines, and some of them had been detailed to fetch what looked like images of human beings, which they set up in a row opposite to the waiting ranks. Then we saw the first row of soldiers charge the images, swords out, amid battle cries and the trumpet ringing out orders again.

'If that's a sample of the army that Parma possesses, we don't want him on Philip's side,' said Christopher. 'No matter

how expensive the bribe has to be.' We rode on in sober
fashion.

By the time we had ridden through the town of Brussels
and drawn close to the palace, the shadows were lengthening.
I was used to Elizabeth's palaces, and shouldn't have been
intimidated by this one, but I was tired, the spectacle of the
soldiers in training had been alarming and the astounding
height and length of Parma's residence was alarming too. It
loomed up before us in a most unwelcoming fashion. I had
been impatient to get the journey over, and now I found myself
baulking at the very moment of arrival. I admitted it.

'I don't feel like storming those battlements – I mean
pinnacles – this evening?' I said candidly. 'Can't we find a
hostelry in the town and come back in the morning?'

'You would rather do that?' Christopher asked.

'Yes, I would! What a place! Did you ever see anything
like it? Getting ourselves inside that palace at all would probably take until midnight, anyway! It's too much for me just
now. Don't laugh at me, Christopher. Let's come back
tomorrow,' I said.

'I'm not laughing. I feel just the same,' he said.

We found a hostelry and by the morning, having slept well
in between a good dinner before and a good breakfast after,
both served in our rooms, we dressed for visiting a palace.
One of my saddlebags had been entirely filled by my formal
grosgrain gown of mixed silk and wool, in pale grey and deep
rose, to be worn over a rose-coloured kirtle embroidered
with little silver flowers. The separate sleeves, also of rose
embroidered with silver, had travelled folded inside.

I had hung gown, kirtle and sleeves up overnight in the
hope that the creases of travel would drop out, but they hadn't.
Christopher came to my rescue with his smoothing iron. He
habitually carried it when travelling. There was a small table
in my room. I padded it with a blanket and a sheet from my
bed while Christopher went to find a charcoal brazier. When
he brought it, we lit the brazier and I put the iron to heat,
while I spread some of my gown skirts over the padding and
put another sheet over it. I splashed everything with some of
the water that the inn had supplied so that I could wash, and

set to work. It took a long time, because my skirts were so big.

However, it was done at last, and one of the inn's maidservants kindly helped me into it, fastened the sleeves, adjusted the farthingale, and even tried to spruce my one ruff a little. I had a hood to go with the gown and kirtle, rose-coloured velvet studded with moonstones and pearls.

My outer skirt, like most of my skirts, was open and had a hidden pouch, but I left my picklocks and my dagger in my riding skirt – surely I wouldn't need such things inside the palace! – and carried only a handkerchief and a small purse with a few Dutch coins in it, acquired during our journey from Ostend.

Christopher had a quilted doublet in a dark green silk with white silk slashings and hose to match, puffed and striped with green and white. Such garments didn't need an iron; the quilting and the stripes more or less buried any creases. We donned our cloaks and mounted our unimpressive nags. In order to look respectable, I had arranged a side-saddle for this last stage of my journey. I managed to accommodate my farthingale, somehow, though with difficulty. Since we weren't sure what kind of reception we would get at the palace, we retained our rooms and left our baggage there. Then we set forth.

Obtaining entrance to the palace really was rather like storming the battlements. We were glad we hadn't attempted it the night before.

First of all, the lodge keeper wasn't at all impressed by our gold identification rings, and when he finally consented to let us present ourselves at the palace proper, he was grudging about it and insisted that we were escorted by a guard who had to be fetched from the palace by the keeper's errand boy. We had to wait until the guard arrived.

The guard bristled with weapons as a hedgehog bristles with spines. Sword, dagger and knife were all in evidence and he had a helmet and breastplate as well. Apparently, a middle-aged couple, respectively on a ewe-necked mare and a cob with the wide back and hairy fetlocks of carthorse ancestry, were regarded as potential assassins who might at any moment run amok with swords or handguns. However, the hedgehog guard did lead us to the main entrance where we were confronted by a flight of stone steps and more guards. We showed our rings – we both wore them on the long fingers of our right hands – but the guards just glanced at them, made nothing of them, and brusquely ordered us round to the stable yard and thereafter, we gathered, to another entrance.

'We're like barbarians at the gates of Rome,' I said to Christopher. However, when we finally arrived at the stables, things improved. At least there were grooms to take the horses and they directed us to a secondary entrance where we once more presented ourselves. That was where the improvement came to a halt and so did we.

There were servants about, mostly dressed in dark blue with white ruffs and some of them with white sleeve slashings. It seemed to be a livery. We were allowed to enter and one of the servants took us across a vestibule and out through a further door into a cold passageway. Here, there were some benches. We were invited to sit down. Then we appeared to be forgotten.

Time went on. I was unpleasantly aware that every time one of the servants came through the vestibule door a cold draught blew in. There was a fair amount of traffic through the door in both directions but we were treated as though we were invisible. Then Christopher lost his temper.

Suddenly he rose to his feet, seized the arm of a passing manservant, jerked him round to face us, shook him hard and thundered a stream of Dutch at him. I made out the name of Elizabeth, heard my own name, saw Christopher thrust his ring into the man's face and point emphatically to mine. Then he shook his captive again, swung him round and released him with a shove between the shoulder blades. The fellow went off at a near-run.

'That may get results,' said Christopher.

'What in the world did you say to him?'

'I shouted at him that it was an utter disgrace that a kinswoman of Her Majesty the Queen of England, and an accredited Messenger of that same queen, should be left sitting in a draughty passageway for over half an hour because the duke's flunkeys are all so ignorant that they can't recognize an official identification when they see one, and would he kindly fetch someone in authority to attend to us. *Now!*'

'Whew!' I said. 'I hope it works.'

It did. After quite a short time, a tall individual with a gold chain of office came to us, spoke to Christopher in Dutch and then, in English, said: 'Welcome, Señora Stannard; you are a sister to Queen Elizabeth, I believe. Please come this way.'

We were only too happy to comply and we certainly needed his guidance. The palace was enormous and we were taken through so many passages and galleries, round so many corners and up so many stairs that I became completely bewildered. But finally we found ourselves in a small reception chamber where we were confronted by a man with haughty eyebrows and an even more resplendent chain of office. He was apparently the butler for the duke's private quarters and he spoke English. On the duke's behalf, he made us a speech of welcome and told us that as the duke was holding an audience in an hour's time, we could present ourselves to him then. Meanwhile, perhaps we would care to go to the guest quarters where we would be offered some refreshment.

He glanced behind him and snapped his fingers and from behind an ornamental screen, a fair-haired page boy emerged. 'Johannes will take you,' he said.

The guest chambers turned out to include a parlour where we could once more be seated but this time on a settle with cushions. Maids took our cloaks, and the page fetched us a tray of wine and little cakes. Some time later, he reappeared to show us the way to the anteroom where we waited to be called into the audience chamber.

It was crowded with other people also seeking an audience but Christopher's outburst had apparently sent our status up. We were called within a few minutes, to the visible annoyance of some elegant gentlemen in enormous ruffs, who had been there before us. There were many people too in the audience chamber, standing about here and there and they stared at us when we were announced as Señora Ursula Stannard, kinswoman to Her Majesty Queen Elizabeth of England, and Señor Christofero Spelton, Accredited Messenger of the English Queen.

I suspected that they also stared because although we had done our best to dress suitably, my farthingale was only half the width of those worn by the few ladies who were present, and neither of us had what seemed to be the obligatory huge ruffs. Everyone probably thought we were an odd pair to be representatives of a queen.

'We must hold up our heads and look as though we are the well-dressed ones, and they have all overdone it,' I whispered to Christopher, as we were led forward.

Our names had aroused fresh interest, which I sensed as we crossed the black and white flagstoned floor towards the dais. I glanced about me. Two ladies were whispering together and looking sideways at us and a short, rotund little man was staring particularly hard, to the point of rudeness and I saw him turn to speak to someone beside him and then emit an unpleasant braying laugh, almost certainly at our expense.

Christopher noticed too. 'That chubby little soul is sneering at us. I'd like to call him out for that piece of insolence,' he muttered to me.

'I dare say you would, but you can't, not here,' I muttered back as a liveried usher beckoned us to mount the dais.

We did so, making polite obeisances. Parma greeted us affably, in accented but otherwise fluent English, and apologized for the bad reception we had had earlier. He recognized our rings but admitted that some of his staff did not; such rings had rarely been seen at his court. My impression of him was very much the same as Mildred's when later on she told me of it. I too saw small, almost delicate features above a neck-stretching ruff, and dark eyes with a friendly expression. I kept it in mind, however, that this man was a nephew to King Philip of Spain. I would be wise to be careful.

'And now,' said the Duke of Parma, 'I take it that you have business with me?'

'Mistress Stannard is the one with the business,' said Christopher. 'I have given her my escort and we had royal permission to make this journey. May the Señora speak?'

'Certainly.'

I told him of my concern for Mildred, describing her as my ward. Explaining the complications of my relationship with her would have been too difficult. 'I don't know if she has reached this court; I can't be quite sure even that she and Berend Gomez were coming here but we have traced them most of the way and as he is one of your messengers . . .'

'Was,' the duke interrupted me. 'I am sorry, Señora. The man Gomez was arrested yesterday on a charge of treason. Treason to me is also treason to King Philip of Spain. He will be tried here, however. I regret to say that it is also very likely that he will in due course be executed here. His wife, the Señora Mildred Gomez, left him, very abruptly, yesterday morning, shortly before his arrest. I understand' – there was a flicker of laughter in the duke's voice – 'that she created a disturbance in the stable yard, though from what I have heard, it wasn't clear what had made her so angry. Not his treason, I think. She apparently shouted that Señor Gomez had in some way deceived her. She was leaving him and going home; she was demanding that a horse be saddled for her. It must have been quite a spectacle and I rather wish I'd been there.'

'What . . . what finally happened?' I asked, suddenly afraid that Mildred too was under arrest and also vaguely irritated by the rotund man who seemed to be edging round as if to get a better view of us, though he was far out of earshot and couldn't overhear anything that was said on the dais. I watched him out of the corner of my eye. He was either blatantly inquisitive or had some special interest in us. The first possibility was impertinent and the second was alarming. Meanwhile the duke was answering me.

'Oh, a horse was made ready and the lady started for Ostend. She did finally allow her husband's manservant, Hans Hendriks, to go with her; it would not be wise for a lady to travel alone. You must have passed her on the road. I dare say you will wish to dash after her, but . . . it's fortunate that you are here, a kinswoman of Queen Elizabeth and one of her Queen's Messengers, and ready to start for home at once! I want to take advantage of such good fortune.'

He leant back in his chair. 'This is the position. Señor Gomez, the man your ward has married and a man that I trusted, has now been caught committing treason. It is just as well that your ward has abandoned him. But there was an errand I had planned for him. You, if you will, could act in his stead. He brought me a confidential letter from Queen Elizabeth. I wish to send her a reply, also in a completely confidential manner. Would you be agreeable?'

With one voice, we said we were. We could do no other, though we were already chafing to be away, and hot on the heels of Mildred.

'I will speak with you both in my study after this audience is finished,' he said. 'In the meantime, you can wait in my Green Parlour. It is in my apartments and no one will disturb you – or attempt to speak to you – there.'

He signalled to an usher, murmured some instructions, and with that, our audience was over. We followed the usher out through a further door, through a further tangle of passages and galleries, up some more stairs and finally through a guarded door where the guards, seeing the usher's livery, grounded their halberds and saluted. We found ourselves being shown into a parlour where lavender was strewn among the rushes, imparting a sweet scent to the room, and there were stools and a couple of walnut settles, softened by green velvet cushions that echoed the principal colour of a big tapestry. This, which had the popular design of a hunting party riding through a leafy wood, covered most of one panelled wall. There were a couple of small tables where a backgammon set, a chess set and some packs of cards had been placed. There was a shelf of books too, though when I examined them, they seemed to be all in Dutch or Spanish.

It was a room where one was clearly expected to while away time, until summoned to duty of some kind. We sat down and Christopher reached out for one of the card packs. 'Shall we play something?'

'Do you know any card tricks?' I asked him. 'Some strolling players who sheltered with us in Withysham recently, during a patch of bad weather, showed us card tricks. But they wouldn't explain how the tricks were done.'

'I know one or two. And I don't mind showing you how I do them,' said Christopher and we were still engrossed with card tricks when the page Johannes came to take us to the duke's private study. Here, we were handed over to a tall, thin gentleman in a smart version of the blue and white livery, with quilting and silk slashings and a ruff quite as immense as any we had seen in the audience chamber.

He introduced himself in English as Señor Diego Sanchez, one of the Duke of Parma's secretaries, and then, stalking ahead of us on his long legs, led us through a further door into the presence of the duke. He had to duck his head to get through the door. The duke was seated at a desk. In front of him, on the desk top, was a sealed scroll. He greeted us courteously, and then picked the scroll up. He hesitated between Christopher and me and then handed it to me.

'It is utterly private. No eyes may see it until you place it in the hand of Queen Elizabeth or at least in the hand of one of her foremost and most trustworthy ministers. You understand? No one but yourselves may touch it or even know of its existence until then.'

He seemed to sense my impatience for he smiled at me and said: 'Ah, yes. You are anxious to catch up with your errant ward. You can leave this afternoon, though I hope you will take some food before you go. That will hearten you for a hard ride. And I will call upon Almighty God to protect you on your way.'

He nodded to Sanchez, who stalked out of the room and returned a few minutes later with a chaplain, who pronounced a blessing on our journey, invoking the protection not only of God but also of various saints. I wondered what Walsingham would have thought of it.

After that, Johannes, who had been waiting outside the door, was summoned to take us back to the Green Parlour. In halting English, he explained that food was about to be served. It arrived promptly and consisted of a bowl each of a thick, steaming vegetable soup along with little fresh-baked, crusty rolls of bread, a dish of veal slices fried in breadcrumbs and accompanied by salad, a cheeseboard and jugs of wine and water.

When we had finished, Johannes reappeared and offered to show us the way to a privy, an offer which we gratefully accepted.

But all the time, I kept on thinking of Mildred, going further and further away from us, though presumably bound for England. I would catch up with her there, of course, but if only, if only, I hadn't had that fall, I might have caught up with her here. I might have been in time to take her home myself. With her husband a prisoner and perhaps about to lose his life, she would surely welcome the presence of somebody she knew. Even somebody who was angry with her and liable to berate her as a wantwit.

The duke came to us just as the maids were handing us our cloaks. 'So now you are on your way.'

'We are indeed,' Christopher said. 'Especially as the two horses we arrived on, and will have to use on the first stage of our ride to Ostend, aren't the fastest in the world.'

'Are you returning them to Janssen's Hiring Stables? That's where people mostly change horses for the first time on their way to the coast.'

'Yes, your grace,' Christopher said.

'Shame on Janssen. He buys cheap horses and expects his clients to put up with them. I have heard complaints before. I will give orders that you are to have two of my horses – I have many guests, who don't all arrive on their own steeds. I keep horses for their use and they're all good ones. I would prefer you to get to England and deliver my letter as soon as possible. One of my grooms will go with you on the first stage and bring my horses back. Where are the Janssen horses now?'

'Here, your grace. In your stables,' said Christopher.

'I shall give orders that they are to be returned to Janssen's at once. I don't want them in my stables. By the sound of them, they're lowering the tone,' said the Duke of Parma with amusement.

SEVENTEEN
Five's a Crowd

By mid-afternoon, we were on our way. Parma had kept his word, and our mounts were excellent. The groom who came with us said he would have a lively time leading them home again, but he was grinning when he said it. He was proud of his mettlesome charges.

We had to make one short diversion, back to the Brussels inn where we had spent the night, to collect our saddlebags and change into suitable clothes for riding. I hoped we would meet no danger on our journey, but was glad to feel the reassuring weight of the picklocks and the little dagger in the pouch of my riding skirt.

Setting off in earnest, we made the best speed that we could. 'If we press on hard, we may still reach Neustad by nightfall,' said Christopher after we had parted from the groom and started off on the second stage. Janssen, a thickset, pink-complexioned Dutchman whose grooms addressed him as Mynheer, was impressed by the sight of a groom in Parma's livery, and gave us much better horses this time.

Reaching Neustad was too optimistic, but we found a small inn where we could spend the night, and where the horses we were using could rest. The inn couldn't offer us a change of mounts but the night's recuperation meant that we could take them on for the first stage in the morning. It was a Sunday and the innkeeper clearly disapproved of Sunday travel but we had no time to waste. We ignored his long face, set off early in the morning and were in Neustad in time for dinner. We went to the same inn as before, as we could change horses there. The landlord spoke English too. Christopher asked if a gentleman called Hans Hendriks, escorting a lady, had passed that way.

'Oh, surely,' said the landlord. 'They're still here. They

arrived on Friday, at noon. The lady wasn't well and they couldn't ride on that day, so . . .'

'Wasn't well?' I snapped.

The innkeeper looked surprised. 'She is better now but the manservant who is escorting her insists that she should rest until tomorrow. You're friends of theirs?'

'Very much so!' I said. 'The Señora is my ward. You say she has been ill?' I avoided mentioning her surname. If she had parted from Berend in a rage, she might not be calling herself Gomez.

'I fancy it was exhaustion, Señora. I understand that she and her escort had been riding hard. My wife has tended her. On Friday she and her servant – yes, his name is Hans Hendriks – were here in time to dine but the Señora could not eat and said she was too tired. She said that Hendriks must eat and she would just have some milk and would rest for two hours or so. They must travel on quickly, she said, because she was in great haste. My wife finally persuaded her to take a slice of cheese-cake with her milk, but when she rose to put on her cloak and start out again, she fainted. Then she brought everything up. Since then, she has rested in bed. But this morning she took breakfast – light ale and bread and honey, nothing more, but no harm came of it. She is now partaking of a light dinner.'

'Will you ask if we may see her? I am Mistress Stannard and my companion is Master Christopher Spelton. She knows us both very well. It is imperative that we *do* see her, in fact.'

Ten minutes later, I was at last face to face with Mildred.

She was not in the attic room where Berend had been attacked. She described it to me later but I never saw it myself. This time the inn was evidently not so crowded and she had been given a pleasant bedchamber on the first floor. We were shown up the outside staircase to the gallery on the first level, and there, I knocked on the door and called my name. After a moment, we heard a bolt being withdrawn, and then she let us in. Behind us, we heard the landlord retreating down the staircase.

'Well,' I said, as Christopher and I stepped into the room. 'So we've caught you up. We hear you've been unwell.'

She was dressed, but she certainly looked wan. The moleskin cover on the bed was slightly rumpled as though she had been lying on top of it, and I was probably right for now she turned to the bed and sat down on it.

'Are you now recovered?' I enquired.

'I think so. But Hans says I mustn't press on until tomorrow. He is a good man and is taking the greatest care of me. I wanted to ride on today but he wouldn't have it and it's true, I don't feel really capable of it. It would be so awful if I fainted when I was riding and fell off the horse. Oh, Ursula, I am so glad to see you!' said Mildred, and then she got off the bed and threw herself into my arms.

I didn't hug her back. I wasn't in an affectionate mood. I set her back onto the bed and said grimly: 'You may well be. We've chased you across the Channel to Brussels and back again, hoping to find you in time. I don't know whether I am in time or not. What name are you calling yourself? Are you Mistress Atbrigge or Señora Gomez?'

'I thought I was Señora Gomez but Berend has told me I was wrong.' Mildred had sensed my anger and her eyes were brimming. 'I went through a marriage ceremony with him but the day I left, he told me it wasn't legal! He told me I was still Mistress Atbrigge! I don't know what to believe.'

There was a tap on the door. Christopher opened it and found a small man, sandy haired and dark eyed and dressed in black, on the threshold. 'Excuse me,' the man said, 'but I am Hans Hendriks, escort to Señora Gomez. I heard voices and the sound of people entering her room. It is my duty to protect her, especially as she has been unwell. May I know who you are?'

'It's all right, Hans, they're friends. Oh, come in, do, please!' Mildred acknowledged him at once. 'This is Mistress Stannard, with whom I lived in England, and her friend Master Christopher Spelton, who is a Queen's Messenger. I am in no danger from them.'

'You addressed her as Señora Gomez,' I said. 'Is she or is she not married to Berend Gomez?'

'As far as I know, Señora, yes.'

Whereupon, Mildred emitted a sob and said: 'Berend told

me I wasn't! He said our marriage wasn't lawful. How would I know? I don't know what the laws are in the Netherlands. He said that because there were no witnesses, just us and a priest, the marriage was invalid! He said he did it on purpose . . . because he thought he was in danger, because I might have to finish an errand for him on my own . . . that was why he married me at all, only it *wasn't* a marriage. Oh, I wanted to scream! I wanted to kill him! I ran away from him! Didn't he tell you?'

'Not everything, Señora, and I haven't felt it my place to ask you questions. Señor Gomez said to me that you were carrying something to England for him, because he probably wouldn't be able to take it himself, and that you were going to pretend to be leaving him in a temper because that would discourage any suspicions that you might be acting as his substitute.'

'It was no pretence!' Mildred snapped at him. 'It was because of what I said just now! He told me that because we had no witnesses at our marriage, it wasn't legal. What's the truth, Hans? Tell me the truth!' The last few words were a pitiful wail.

Hans, standing stolidly, foursquare like a small bull, said: 'If only you and Señor Gomez and the priest were present at the ceremony, then it wasn't lawful. A marriage without witnesses is against Spanish law, and Spanish law is upheld in this country.'

'That's what he said to me. And so, when I screamed and cursed him in the palace stable yard, I wasn't acting!' Mildred reiterated.

'You are safely out of a bad business,' I told her. 'And I do mean safely.' I steered her back to the bed and sat her down on it. I hesitated a moment and then decided that here was another situation when telling the truth might be best. 'Mildred, I have some news that may distress you but I think I should tell you that Berend Gomez has been arrested on a charge of treason. It sounds as though he expected it, which is why you are here and not still in Brussels. And the sooner you are back in England, the better.'

'There I most heartily agree,' said Christopher and Hans nodded emphatically.

'I am Señor Gomez' personal man,' he said. 'I know nothing of treason. Señor Gomez never spoke of such things to me. He travelled to England sometimes, usually with earthenware goods to sell, though sometimes he said he was acting as a messenger for the duke. I obeyed his orders and didn't wonder about them. He has charged me to see this lady, whether or not she is his wife, safely to Ostend and on to a ship bound for England. You will not object, I trust, if I travel on with you all the way to Ostend.'

'No, of course not,' I said and Mildred, hiccupping, but brushing away her tears, said: 'Hans has been most kind, and most competent, dealing with the landlord and making his wife bring me things to drink and the like.'

I studied Mildred, who certainly looked unwell, and said: 'What was the cause of your illness?' I lowered my voice and both Hendriks and Christopher moved tactfully away. 'You were not with Berend all that long, but is it possible that . . .?'

'No,' said Mildred. 'It's the opposite. It doesn't usually make me ill, but I have been so angry and so exhausted . . . I have definite proof that I am not with child.'

'I'm glad to hear it.' My hard tone seemed to brace her up, which was a good thing. 'That would have been a complication! However, from the look of you, I would advise you to wait until tomorrow before riding on.'

'It might be best,' Mildred agreed, 'though just to see you, Ursula, has made me stronger. Everything has been so strange for so long . . .'

She was about to dissolve into tears again, and I found that I had to put a reassuring arm round her. I was still angry with her – I stayed angry for a long time – but I realized that it would be cruel to show it too much. She was bitterly regretting her rash behaviour, that was obvious. I wouldn't rub salt into her wound. At least one disaster had been spared us.

Christopher was saying something about ordering some food for us, and Hans, agreeing, was turning to the door to go in search of the landlord. But before he reached it, it was flung open and a complete stranger strode in. Or . . . no, he wasn't a complete stranger because I remembered seeing him in the audience chamber though I had no idea who he was. He hadn't come near me in any way.

He was the short, bouncy individual with the high voice and the braying laugh.

I saw at once that Mildred knew him. So did Hans. They both exclaimed his name at once. 'Señor Alvaro!' That was Hans, using a polite enough greeting, but with an angry scowl on his face. 'Nicolas Alvaro!' That was Mildred, using a more familiar term, with a gasp of sheer fright.

'How did you get in here?' demanded Christopher, who had no idea what was going on but had instantly sensed that Alvaro was an enemy.

Alvaro slammed the door behind him, using his heel, and then swung round to push the bolt home. He pulled off his cloak, tossing it onto the floor. 'I wear the Duke of Parma's livery, Hans Hendriks. I told the landlord I had a message of the greatest urgency for you and Señora Gomez, and let him glimpse the edge of my dagger, and he stepped out of my way. Now, there is no need for noise or disturbance, or for anyone to be injured. I am aware, Señora Stannard, that you and your companion Señor Spelton are carrying a letter from the duke to Queen Elizabeth of England. It is a treasonous letter which King Philip would very much like to see. The duke saw you in private after you were presented to him in audience, and I know for what purpose. If you will hand that letter to me quietly, now, I will go away and there will be no trouble; you may continue your journey to England in peace. I have nothing against you, Hendriks. You may continue to escort the Señora, or return to Brussels as you will. Now, the letter.'

'Of all the insolence!' Christopher was furious. 'How dare you walk in here and make such a demand! If anyone is carrying any of the duke's correspondence then we would certainly not hand it over to anyone but the person to whom it is addressed. And before you brandish that dagger at us, I would point out to you, Señor whoever you are, that you are alone. It's four to one. Two are men, who are very ready to give a good account of ourselves, and I wouldn't underestimate the two ladies, who I am sure are thoroughly offended.'

Yes, we are! I thought, and pressed my left hand to my side, feeling the outside of my dagger in its secret pouch.

'Four is company,' Christopher said. 'But five is a crowd. Why not withdraw with dignity?'

'Oh, really!' said Alvaro, sounding like a slightly scandalized hostess who has heard someone express a foolish opinion or utter a coarse phrase across her dinner table. He stepped smartly across the room, seized Mildred, wrested her off the bed and sat down in the one chair that the room contained, with her on his lap, whisking his dagger out of its sheath in the process. His left arm gripped her round the body and his right held the blade to her throat. Above the dagger, Mildred's mouth was open and her eyes bulged. She was whimpering faintly.

'Now,' said Alvaro, 'the letter, if you please.'

My hand dropped away from my side. My hidden dagger wouldn't help anyone now. In what I knew to be a doomed attempt to establish our innocence, I demanded: 'What letter?' in a loud, indignant voice.

No one heeded me. 'If you cut the Señora's throat,' said Christopher, while Mildred's eyes widened still more, 'then you won't have a hostage, will you? You will be open to attack.'

'But the Señora will be dead,' said Alvaro, and emitted his ghastly laugh. He seemed to find the situation amusing.

I repeated: *'What letter?'* in a still louder voice and Christopher said: 'As it happens, none of us are carrying a letter of any kind. Why do you imagine that we are?'

'I know you are. Ah well, if you are going to be difficult . . .' He seemed to consider. Then he said: 'I can make Señora Gomez very uncomfortable without actually killing her.' He moved the dagger from Mildred's throat but applied the point to her right thigh. 'I made some preparations in case you tried to be foolish,' he remarked. 'Señora Stannard, please go to my cloak, which is there on the floor. It has a pocket inside and in that, you will find some pieces of cord. Fetch them out.'

I hesitated and Mildred cried out. I saw a little blood seep through her skirt, around the dagger. I went to the cloak and found the cords.

'Splendid,' said Alvaro. 'Now, I hope you are a capable woman who can do, efficiently, what I require you to do next. Señor Spelton, go and sit on the bed, close to the bedpost at the head of it. Do it!'

Christopher had noticed the blood as well. He obeyed. 'Good,' said the unspeakable Alvaro. 'Señora Stannard, go to Señor Spelton and tie his hands behind his back and also tie them to the bedpost. Tie proper knots. Keep your hands where I can see them. Then do the same with Señor Hendriks, who must now sit at the other end of the bed, also next to a post.'

Mildred's distended eyes were begging me not to argue. I did as I was told. My hands shook and I muttered curses about my own clumsiness while Alvaro cursed me for being slow. Christopher's wrists were thick and I found it hard to tie the knots properly. When I had finished and turned to Hans, things were no better because his bony wrists were simply awkward.

'If you have a letter, give it to him, for the love of God, or he will hurt the Señora to make you,' Hans whispered to me as I fumbled, and Alvaro snapped: 'Delaying won't help, my lady. Hendriks is right. I do mean to force your hand by means of Señora Gomez. There's nothing you can do about it.'

Mildred let out a gasp and her eyes met mine as though she were trying to pass a message to me although I had no idea what it was. As I finally moved away from Hans I glanced towards Christopher and his left eyelid drooped in the ghost of a wink. Then his attempt to follow the instruction I had muttered to him between my curses, as I tied his hands, worked. A finger and thumb got a grip on the loose end I had left, pulled at it and freed the knot. Silently I called down blessings on the strolling players who had amused the household, one wet afternoon at Withysham, by showing us how to tie knots. Including trick ones.

At this point, matters took a startling turn. I had of course hoped that Christopher, once freed, would be quick enough to take Alvaro by surprise and overpower him before he could do any more harm to Mildred. Hans would be releasing himself in the same way, ready to help. I could only hope they would be quick enough. But before I had had time to think further, Christopher looked towards the door, his eyes widened as if in horror and he let out such a shout that we all, even Alvaro, turned our heads to look at whatever he had seen. In that moment, Christopher freed his hands, and then his sword was out and it was all, shockingly, over.

I had never thought of Christopher as a swordsman, but now he proved his skill. He drew his sword at an astounding speed, the blade swept, flashing, and Alvaro's head was on the floor. It was done so quickly that the gap between life and death was less than a split second. One moment Alvaro was sitting in the chair, grinning, his dagger against Mildred's thigh and the next, he was headless, sagging sideways amid a torrent of blood, and Mildred was falling off his lap. She toppled to the floor, and for a few heartbeats there was utter silence, and then Mildred screamed, because hot blood was splashing down on her. She rolled away, retching and sobbing. The air was suddenly full of the stench of blood, sweet, metallic and revolting. Hans was now free and was on his feet, staring. 'You've killed him!' he said to Christopher, gazing at Alvaro's body almost as though he were not sure if the man was dead.

'I had to,' said Christopher, wiping his sword on the moleskin coverlet of the bed. 'He could have hurt the Señora badly if I hadn't attacked so fast.'

'But what are we to do with him?' I asked, my voice muffled, for my hands were at my mouth, to prevent me from retching like Mildred. I sat down on the bed, well away from the place where Christopher had cleaned his blade. 'We can't . . . leave a body just lying there . . .'

'No, we can't,' Christopher was calmly in control. 'Now, up you come, Mildred . . .' He put a hand under her arm and lifted her to her feet. 'You're safe now, though you will have to change your clothing.'

'I'm all over blood,' Mildred sobbed. 'It stinks and ugh . . .!' She looked back at what a moment ago had been Alvaro, and then stumbled to the window, pulled it open and was sick into the bushes below.

'Is there water in that jug over there in the jug and basin?' Christopher asked, and walked over to the washstand to find out. 'Yes, good.' He drew the shuddering Mildred back inside.

'Here, my lass, drink some water and wash your face and hands. Ursula, get up for a moment.'

I stood up and he pulled the moleskin coverlet off the bed and threw it over Alvaro's body. It was big enough to hang down and conceal the fallen head. Once they were out of sight, the sense of horror in the room grew less, and so did the smell.

Christopher said: 'Mildred, I take it you have fresh clothes in your saddlebags. Get out a gown – even if the only spare one is your best – then close those bedcurtains and retire within them to change. Ursula, help her. I will roll up the bloodstained things, inside out so that not much blood will get onto other things, and stuff them into your saddlebags. Señor Hendriks, if you can manage to appear normal, go downstairs and bespeak food and drink – say for five, as though we are entertaining Señor Alvaro as a friend who has just delivered an important message. But try to be very helpful and carry the trays up yourself. Make haste, ladies!'

Mildred, though shaking hopelessly, mopped her face and hands with a towel that the inn had provided, and emptied the stained water out of the window into the bushes. She found a clean gown and cap and we both withdrew behind the bedcurtains. It was tricky, changing a gown while standing on the uncertain surface of the bed but nevertheless, we did it quite quickly. We emerged to find that the lingering smell of blood was being challenged by the smell of hot sausages and fresh, warm bread. Hans was coming in at the door with a tray in his hands. There was an inn servant behind him with another but Christopher, smooth and smiling, stepped past Hans, relieved the serving man of his burden, thanked him and then, still smiling, closed the door on him. I doubt if anyone was hungry except Christopher who, as usual, ate with apparent enthusiasm. He caught my eye and said apologetically that he liked this good plain food. The rest of us just made ourselves swallow a little, though we all drank the perry which seemed to be what the inn served as wine, and we probably all felt better for it.

'Now, Hendriks,' said Christopher, 'the Señora is dressed and I suggest that we get that sorry object out from under the coverlet and put it into the bed. We can then restore its head to its proper place on top of his neck. We'll put the coverlet back – blood won't show up too much on that dark brown fur. Then we leave, and we ride fast to get well on our way before Alvaro's body is found. We tell the landlord that Alvaro rode all through last night, is very tired and is asleep in this bed, and has asked not be disturbed until supper time. We also tell the landlord that Señora Gomez – for his benefit we'd better call her that – is much better and also, the message that Alvaro brought contained an urgent reason why she should make all haste to get to England. Then, off we go and hope that Alvaro's body won't be found for a long time.'

'It sounds chancy,' I said. 'We could be pursued by a hue and cry, just as we would be in England.'

'Can you think of anything better?' Christopher asked, reasonably.

Mildred had been cocking her head. 'What's that noise?' she said.

EIGHTEEN
Dangerous Secrets

For one awful, muddled moment, I thought that Alvaro's severed head had come to life and said something. Then I realized that it was a trick of sound, and that the voice I had heard was somewhere down below. Besides, Mildred had recognized it and her expression was joyful. The sound increased, to a babble; there must surely be half a dozen men down there. Hans, who also seemed to have recognized the principal voice, opened the door. I came behind him and there were indeed four or five men in Parma's livery clustered at the foot of the staircase and one man halfway up. When he saw us, he called out: 'Is Señora Gomez there?' and from behind me, Mildred's voice cried: 'Is that you, Señor Moreno?'

'Yes!'

'Oh, come up, do, we are in such trouble!'

'I imagined that you might be,' said the stranger, arriving at the door. Christopher was exclaiming: 'Señora Atbrigge, what are you about? Who is this man?' and Mildred was saying: 'It's all right, I know him, *let him in!*'

Then he was in, brushing Hans and me aside as though we didn't exist and Mildred, greeting him with a joyful embrace, announced to us all that this was Leonardo Moreno, Berend's good friend and he would surely help us.

Since Señor Moreno hadn't yet said why he had come, but had certainly brought with him enough men to arrest us all, if he was so minded, I think we all considered this a simple-minded statement and Christopher pulled Mildred away and began to reprimand her for it. But Moreno laughed and shook his head and declared in English that he was indeed Berend's friend and meant no harm to any of us, at which point, he suddenly noticed the strange heap in the corner of the room, where what was left of Alvaro was hidden under the moleskins.

His nostrils twitched, sensing the metallic tang of blood beneath the more wholesome smells of broth and bread. He walked straight to the place and lifted up the coverlet. Then he stopped, drawing in a sharp breath.

In English, he said: 'So that bastard did catch up with you. I feared he meant harm to you. When I realized he had saddled up and gone off at a gallop, not long after you, Señora Stannard, I feared the worst.'

He turned from the horrid heap in the corner and looked at me directly. 'I don't know what your business is and I don't want to know. But it's known to the whole court that you and Señor Spelton there, strangers from England, were with the duke in his private study for a long time yesterday. And that you, Señora Stannard, are in some way linked to Señora Gomez.

'You left yesterday afternoon, on two of the best horses in his grace's stables. I am one of his Masters of Horse; I had instructions to have two such horses saddled, one for a lady. Alvaro has his own horse but nothing happens in the stables that I don't know about and when I heard he had gone off at speed that same evening just after your departure, Señor Spelton, Señora Stannard . . . well, he is a ruthless man. I didn't like it. There has been bad blood between Berend Gomez and Alvaro for God alone knows how long. If you, Señora Stannard, have a link to Señora Gomez, then you are also linked to her husband. There was a pattern that I didn't like. Well, I not only buy and sell horses and arrange their training, I train men as well. I announced an unexpected exercise – I do that sometimes – and came after you. If you didn't need help, well and good. We'd all go home again. If you did – then I would do my best. You seem, however, to have dealt with Alvaro yourselves. Just what happened?'

It took a long time to explain. I was careful in what I said and so was Christopher, but we couldn't explain Alvaro's pursuit without admitting that we were carrying something he wished to intercept. Moreno, however, only shrugged and said that he never poked his nose into the duke's affairs. If what we were carrying had been confided to us by Parma, it wasn't his place to interfere. He had no wish to be entangled with dangerous secrets.

Moreno said that his men would be providing the landlord with good custom downstairs, though their ears would be open in case he called.

'If I'd walked in here and seen that . . . *thing* . . . holding his blade across the Señora's throat as you tell me he did, one shout would have had enough armed men in here to deal with ten of him.'

'He might have cut my throat before they got up the stairs,' protested Mildred.

'I trust not. What would be the point? Alvaro wasn't a fool,' Moreno said blithely. I wasn't so sure and never have been and from Mildred's expression I don't think she was sure either. However, the danger was past and gone, lying in two pieces in a corner of the room, shrouded in dark brown fur.

Moreno turned to Mildred. 'Señora, I understand that you parted from your husband in anger, but please, whatever he did, forgive him now. He is under arrest.'

'Mistress Stannard has told me,' said Mildred. 'And I am very sorry.' Her lips trembled. 'I wouldn't have wished that to happen to him or to anyone. I'm afraid for him. Exactly what is the charge? Mistress Stannard said treason.'

'Yes. He has confessed to making a copy of King Philip's battle plan for his fleet, and intending to take it to England. He shouted it out as he was being taken away. But there is also talk of heresy – because he married a heretic – you, Señora. I think the idea is that you suborned him. *That*' – he pointed to Alvaro's body – 'was talking privately to the duke before he set out after Mistress Stannard. I saw him at it. The duke had summoned me, to instruct me about providing the horses for Señora Stannard and Señor Spelton but I had to wait while Alvaro finished talking to him. I wonder what he was saying. Maybe the accusation of heresy was planted in the duke's mind by him. It's possible. He still harboured resentment about an old quarrel with Gomez.'

'Yes, he did,' Mildred said fervently. But she said no more and none of us asked.

I had been puzzling over something. I said: 'How is it that Señor Alvaro knew that the duke meant to see us in private after our formal audience with him, let alone why? He told us when we were on the dais in the audience chamber, talking to him at close quarters. No one else was near enough to hear. I can't understand it.'

'I can,' said Mildred.

We all looked at her.

'When we were all in here with him and he was making you tie Hans up, Hans whispered to you that he knew Alvaro meant to use me to force you into giving him your letter. Just after that, Alvaro said to you that Hans was right and repeated what Hans had said . . . isn't that right, Hans?'

'Yes, it is, Señora, and it struck me as strange. I had whispered it so softly.'

'Are you sure he was nowhere near when the duke was talking to you in audience, Ursula?' Mildred asked.

'He was in the room, like a lot of other people,' said Christopher. 'But not close by. He couldn't have heard anything at all of what passed between us and the Duke of Parma.'

Moreno said: 'He's a man who often seems to know things that he shouldn't have known; it's one of the reasons why people are afraid of him. He's said to have the hearing of an owl and owls can hear the tiniest rustle of a field mouse in the grass.'

'When the duke saw us in audience today,' said Christopher insistently, 'he couldn't possibly have overheard anything. Nobody could. No one was near enough. Not this man Alvaro or anyone else.'

'That's true,' I said.

'I think he could read people's lips,' said Mildred. 'Just like an old deaf man I used to take provisions to, when I was a vicar's wife. His family wouldn't be bothered with him because he couldn't talk to them, and they just wouldn't or couldn't understand that he could read their lips, the movements of their mouths, as long as they shaped their words plainly. I soon realized that if I did that and always faced him directly so that he could see my mouth, we could talk quite well. He was so thankful to be able to talk to somebody, poor old fellow. I keep wondering who is looking after him now and if anyone else has learned how to make themselves understood.'

'Good God!' said Christopher. He and Moreno were looking at each other.

I said: 'He could have seen Hans' face while I was trying to tie his hands. And in the audience chamber he was certainly staring at us. Thank God that when I muttered to you, Christopher, about how to free your hands, I was so positioned that Alvaro couldn't see my face. If he had, he'd have known what I was saying! If Mildred is right, we've had a narrow escape! And you could well be right, Mildred. Wouldn't that explain the other times when he's known things that he shouldn't have known? It makes sense!'

Moreno pushed the bedcurtains back and sat down, uninvited, on the edge of the bed. He was frowning in thought. Then he said: 'Yes. If he has taught himself to read lip movements, then it explains many things. People fear him because they can never be sure that their secrets are secret from him. He has pointed the finger at more than one English spy and more than one dishonest courtier. The duke himself fears him. So that was his dangerous little secret! A useful skill for a spy.'

'He's still dangerous,' said Christopher. 'To us, I mean,' and explained his plan for disposing of Alvaro's remains.

'Oh, we can deal with that,' said Moreno easily, and I saw that he had probably dealt with similar situations before. The ducal court was harsh, and a law unto itself in ways that Elizabeth's was not. Moreno said: 'I will order my men go out and buy a big, stout sack and some rope. Alvaro's horse must be in the stable here. I know it by sight; it's barely an inch over fifteen hands, dark bay with a white sock on the off fore. We'll saddle it, make a bundle of Alvaro's remains and throw him over the saddle. We'll make sure that the landlord doesn't actually see the bundle. If he doesn't see it, he won't ask questions about it. Then we'll all set off together, towards Ostend. Before long, we'll pass close to a useful marsh. We'll dump the sack there and Alvaro's saddlery as well. We always carry a halter or two so we'll lead his horse a few miles further on and turn it loose. Somewhere near farmland. If a farmer sees a strange horse loose on his land, he'll take it in. He might try to find out who owns it, or perhaps someone will recognize it and claim it on Alvaro's behalf but even if it is identified as Alvaro's horse, it will look as though whatever happened to Alvaro, happened a long way from Neustad. Most likely it will never be recognized and the farmer will either sell it or use it. It'll find a home all right and Alvaro's fate will be a mystery for ever, either way.'

'But the mess . . . the . . .' Mildred pointed to where a stream of blood had oozed from under the moleskin shroud.

'It will appear that we all rode off together. Alvaro's horse will be gone. The innkeeper can make what he likes of the blood,' said Moreno. 'And get it cleaned up.'

'There'll be questions asked,' I said. 'If Alvaro just vanishes, his superiors at the palace will want to find out why.'

'They may ask,' said Moreno calmly, 'but there need not be any answers. The innkeeper won't like the look of the blood and he won't have an explanation for it. He won't want suspicion pointing his way, either! If men from the palace come asking questions, there won't be any sign of the blood and they'll probably be told that Alvaro rode off in perfect health. I'll give the landlord a good-sized gratuity, anyway. I expect he'll take the hint. Alvaro will ride off into oblivion. And good riddance.'

'It's rather shocking, though,' Mildred ventured. 'Even such a man – ought he not to have a Christian burial?'

We all looked at her. Christopher smiled. 'You're a good woman,' he said. 'But not used to the underside of the world. We can say a prayer for him before we immerse his body, if you like. Marsh or earth; is there much difference?'

'Had he a wife?' Mildred persisted, but Moreno shook his head. 'He had no family. He won't be mourned.'

'That's sad,' Mildred said. Her face stiffened. She said: 'What of Berend, what will happen to him? I was so angry with him but I wouldn't want . . . Oh, tell me that the way I ran away from him didn't have anything to do with his arrest?'

'No, it didn't,' Moreno assured her. 'It's as well that you did leave Brussels; you might have been taken in for questioning too. As it is, well, it's best you forget him. I know you were married to him but . . .'

'In our last quarrel, he said we weren't married. That there were no witnesses and so the marriage was invalid.'

Moreno looked at her sharply. 'You mean the ceremony was conducted by a priest but no one else was present besides you and Berend?'

'Yes.'

'Then it's true. You aren't legally his wife. You are still – whatever you were before. Señorita . . .'

'Señora Atbrigge,' I said. 'Mildred was a widow.'

'I still felt as though I was his wife,' Mildred said. 'Señor, you didn't answer my question. *What will happen to him?*'

'I don't know. There will be a trial, but I think he will be found guilty – of whatever the final charge is, treason or heresy or both. Alvaro is dead but I don't know what he was saying to the duke just before I went to attend to your horses.'

'Heresy!' Mildred whispered and I trembled too, remembering the smoke and the smell on the wind when we turned back from that little town at the start of our journey from Ostend to Brussels, and the distant screams.

Mildred seemed to collect herself. 'Señor Moreno,' she said, 'can you get in to see Berend? Will you be allowed? You are his friend, after all.'

'Probably. Yes, I might. I can bribe his turnkey, anyway, or I think I can. They're nearly all bribeable. They're badly paid and it's more or less taken for granted that they'll take bribes as perks.'

'Then . . .' Mildred was feeling in her belt pouch, though with distaste. 'It's in here – ugh! There's blood on my pouch as well. I must get a new one – here it is.' She had taken out an object wrapped in a piece of cloth. She undid it and revealed a phial. She glanced at me. 'I took it from Gladys' shelf before I left Hawkswood. It's hemlock. I was timid about coming to a country that is supposed to be Catholic. I brought this as a kind of safeguard.'

She wrapped it again and held it out to Moreno. 'If you can get in to see him, give him this. Tell him what it is. A sip or two will ease pain. Swallow all of it and it will kill you.'

Moreno's eyes widened but he made no protest. He took

the phial and put it in his own pouch. 'I will see he has it. Thank you.'

'And would you tell him . . . tell him . . .?'

'That you love him, and forgive him, and will not forget him. I will say all that, Señora, whether or not it's true.'

'It is true,' said Mildred.

NINETEEN
Against Time

It wasn't the first time I had returned from a journey and been thankful to see the white cliffs of Dover rise out of the sea. Those cliffs meant home. They meant safety. They meant familiar things, like Hawkswood and the English tongue. They meant hills that sloped at a certain angle, with patches of woodland on them; they meant fields all kinds of shapes, spread over the land like a patchwork coverlet, patterned with green and brown, and, in harvest time, the gold of English corn, all subtly different from the crops and hills of other lands.

My bruises were fading and no longer hurt, and there, ahead of me, was home. Except that it was a home under threat. If Philip of Spain had his way . . . and once again, I could feel the Spanish Armada like a rising darkness in the mind.

I longed to forget the stains of blood we had left for the landlord of the Neustad inn to find and the greedy gurgle of the marsh as Alvaro's remains sank into it. And then the white cliffs took on a new significance. That whiteness was cleansing; a counter to the sickness in my memory.

To me it was a wonder that we had got away. We were kept in Ostend for days before we could get a ship for England. I kept expecting that we would be pursued and seized and dragged back to face accusation, trial, retribution. But nothing of the sort had happened. When I expressed my fears to Moreno, he smiled and shook his head.

'My livery and that of my men would be some protection for you and we won't leave until after you have sailed. Besides, what did the landlord find? Bloodstains, but no corpse. He never saw the sack being carried out and piled onto Alvaro's horse. I made sure he didn't. I was indoors with him at the time, paying our bill along with a gratuity that he would have known very well was some kind of bribe. Anyway, as I told you before, what kind of innkeeper wants his inn to get a reputation as a place where guests disappear, leaving blood-stains behind them?'

Not the man in Neustad, it seemed. No one came hunting us. Leonardo Moreno and his men were on their way home by now while Mildred, Christopher and I were safely aboard a ship called the *Dainty Jane* – an English vessel with an English captain – and before nightfall we would once more be on English soil.

'It may be quite late in the day when we land,' Christopher said, crossing the deck to stand beside me. 'We'd better spend the night at the Safe Harbour. But after that, we ought to make what speed we can. We have a letter to deliver for the queen. We shall have to go through Walsingham, of course, and I only hope that he'll be easy to find.'

Quietly, so that we didn't hear her approach, Mildred had joined us. 'I too have a message for the queen,' she said. 'I hope you'll let me go with you, Master Spelton, because I don't know how to present myself at the English court. Will it be like Parma's?'

Christopher and I both turned to stare at her. '*You* have a message for the queen?' I said.

'There was no point in mentioning it before,' said Mildred. 'And wiser not to speak of it until we were all well on our way home. But you heard Señor Moreno say that Berend . . . poor Berend . . . had confessed to making a copy of the battle plan for the Spanish fleet. It's true. But he made two copies. I have the other. He said that he was sure he wouldn't be allowed to travel to England again, so I must carry it in his stead. But he had a copy of his own and kept it so that if the duke found out what he had done, he could admit to it and then perhaps no one would suspect that there was another copy, on its way to England with me. And he said we must put on that great show of me leaving him, with all that shouting and to-do.

'Not that it was difficult.' I could see that Mildred was trembling. 'When he told me that before he even left England, he had foreseen that he might not be able to come back and that was why he married me, I thought I would lose my mind. He did it so as to have a replacement courier if necessary – and so he made sure there were no witnesses at our marriage. So that I could go free of him. He admitted it. He *used* me. I was so angry . . . I didn't know I *could* be so angry. I wanted – when we acted our scene in the stable yard, I hit him and I enjoyed it . . . only, he just let me, he didn't care that I was leaving him, didn't care that I hated him. I really, truly, *wanted* to kill him!'

Christopher and I were silent for a moment, taking this in. Finally, I said: 'My poor Mildred. He betrayed you in the most unkind fashion. You are well out of that marriage, and well rid of him!'

'I still love him,' said Mildred pitifully. 'Can you believe it? I really do.'

Christopher, more practical, said: 'Where is the battle plan you carry? What made Berend make a copy of it at all?'

'The queen commissioned him to do it,' said Mildred, sounding surprised, as though she had expected us to take that for granted. 'He went to court – he went with you, Christopher – and while he was there, he was asked to find the plan and get it to the queen if he could. I think there was to be a good reward.'

'There might well be!' said Christopher. 'You have it with you, then. Well hidden, I assume.'

'Sewn into my best hood.'

The sea wind lifted Christopher's hair. 'When we're in the inn at Dover and there's no danger of bits of paper getting blown away,' he said, 'we'd better get it out and look at it. I'll escort you to the court and bring you to Walsingham and the reward will rightly be yours.'

At the Safe Harbour we were received as old customers ought to be, with smiles, welcoming glasses of strong, warming sack, a groom for the pack mule we had hired to carry our baggage from the ship, servants to carry our bags upstairs, and comfortable rooms, one big one for me and Mildred, another for Christopher. 'A bit of a cubby-hole,' Ralph Harrison said apologetically, 'but I've a crowd here waiting to take a ship to Norway tomorrow morning. There wouldn't be room for you two ladies except that I always keep a bit of accommodation spare in case there are ladies to provide for. You'll want supper in your room, I fancy.'

'We'll all take supper there,' I said, 'Master Spelton as well. We have things to talk over.'

Our last meal had been taken early in the morning in Ostend. We were tired and we were hungry. Hot mutton pie, beans fried in onions, a dish of salad followed by a bread-and-butter pudding flavoured with ginger and cinnamon, all washed down with the aid of a good-sized jug of wine, put strength into us. But when we had finished, and a maidservant had taken the empty dishes away, Christopher said: 'Well, Mildred, let's see this battle plan. Did you stitch it into your hood yourself?'

'No, Berend did it. He told me about it afterwards.'

'Best make sure it's really there, then. Where is your hood?'

Mildred got it out of her saddlebag and put it upside down on her bed, revealing the lining. 'The stitches are right at the edge. But they're there all right.' She pointed.

Christopher pulled out his belt knife but Mildred was before him, with a small pair of shears from a little workbox in her luggage. Her fingers were slim. She found the stitches and cut them, carefully. Then she slipped two fingers into the slit. She withdrew them with a paper between her fingers. 'Here it is.'

The paper was not rolled but folded flat. She opened it carefully and smoothed it out. Christopher and I peered at it with interest. There were very few words on it. Instead, there were groups of small symbols, tiny circles, squares, triangles, oblongs. They were arranged in a broad semi-circle with one or two outlying groups. There were just a few words written in a column at one side. The lettering was very small but after staring at it for a moment, I realized that it was a key to the symbols. The little circles represented one kind of ship, the squares another and the same with the other symbols.

'Interesting,' Christopher said. 'It's a defensive arrangement. It's designed so that any attacking fleet will have to come within the half circle if it's to do any real attacking at all, and it can then be bombarded from the sides as well as from in front. All right. Put it back in your hood, Mildred, and stitch it up again. It will be safe there until we can get it to the queen – well, Walsingham.'

Mildred was examining the sheet of paper closely. 'There's a second sheet under this one,' she said. 'Look.' Gently, she lifted a corner of the plan and revealed another paper below. The two sheets were very thin. She parted them with care. 'It's a letter! Or something. It isn't addressed to anyone . . .'

Christopher picked it up. 'It's a confession!' he said. He read it aloud.

> I doubt if I will ever be able to return to England and I am concerned in case some innocent person has been accused of something that I did on my last visit there.
>
> In a Lincolnshire lane on the 16th of March in this year of Our Lord 1588, with a crossbow, I, Berend Gomez, shot dead a man called Juan Smith. He was a spy codenamed Magpie. But that has nothing to do with the reason why I killed him. It was Juan Smith who last August raped my fifteen-year-old daughter Alison, getting her with child, and thereby killing her, for neither she nor the child survived its birth. To my mind he murdered her. An opportunity to deal with him was long in coming but it came at last. I know how to use a crossbow and I know where to buy such things. I bought one. I stopped him in a lonely place, told him why I intended to kill him, for I wished him to understand his own perfidy, and to be afraid and beg for his life, and then I loosed the bolt. I threw the bow away afterwards.
>
> I repeat, I write this confession in case any innocent person should be accused of what I did. I will not say accused of my crime, for to me, the slaying of Juan Smith was justice, and no crime. I seek no forgiveness.
>
> Berend Gomez.

I said: 'That too must be delivered to Walsingham. Juan Smith was known to him; his death had importance in high places. We will all three go to Walsingham. He will question you as to what happened to us in the Netherlands and to complete the story, I had better be there.'

*   *   *

To begin with, we had to go to Hawkswood because we didn't
know where the court was to be found. Laurence Miller, the
watchdog that Cecil and Walsingham had inflicted on
me, could be trusted to know and he could tell us. We made
the utmost haste but it still took two days to get there. We
needed to call at West Leys on the way, even before we went
to Hawkswood, so that Christopher could assure himself that
all was well with his children, and collect his own horse. After
that we made good speed to Hawkswood, where Miller told
us that we would find the court at Richmond. It was too late
that day to travel on at once and it was a Sunday evening
anyway. We slept at home that night but made an early start
on Monday morning. By now we were all reunited with our
own horses, for which we were thankful.

We reached Richmond in the afternoon, where we learned
that the court had just moved to Whitehall. For once, Laurence
was behindhand with the news.

I had a curious sense of urgency for which I couldn't account
but it was strong enough to make me say that we must continue
to Whitehall at once, which we did. It took up the rest of the
afternoon. We left our horses at a nearby inn and presented
ourselves at the main gate. We all had identification and we
were quickly brought to an office where we could state our
business and ask to be shown to Walsingham's quarters.

Walsingham was not there. He had fallen ill and was at his
home in Seething Lane, some distance away. We couldn't
inflict ourselves on a sick man. He was probably suffering
from an attack of his bowel trouble. I asked instead if we
might be brought to Sir William Cecil. 'Is the queen in
residence here?' I added.

I had been recognized by this time and the White Staff
official we were speaking to was helpful. The queen was at
St James' Palace and Cecil was living at his house in the
Strand, attending at Whitehall or St James' as required. He
had been at Whitehall that day but had now gone home.

We said thank you, withdrew, and went on foot to the Strand.
I was known at Cecil House but we were told to wait because
Sir William was in his study, still working. However, at this
point we had some good fortune, for while we were talking

to his butler, Sir William left his study and passed within
earshot of the entrance lobby. He recognized my voice and
suddenly appeared on the top of the nearby staircase.

'If that is Mistress Stannard, send her up. And whoever is
with her.'

'I thought, my lord, that as you were working . . .'

'Mistress Stannard wouldn't be here at this hour without a
reason. She represents work herself! Come up, Ursula, and
bring your companions with you. Come to my study. We can
be private there.'

The study was a secluded place, but large. It needed to be,
for it was very full. For one thing, the desk was enormous. It
was laden with two lit candles in tall holders (the day was
cloudy) and at the user's right were an inkstand and a pile of
fresh paper, while at his left, the desk top held a jar of unused
quills along with a tray containing sealing wax, a quill sharp-
ener, a sander and a little silver bell. There were shelves round
the walls, full of books and folders and piled maps, and in
addition, there were several stools and a settle. Cecil sat
down at the desk, told us to take off our cloaks and sit down
as well and then said: 'You must have urgent business, Ursula.
But first present your friends.'

I did so and he nodded. 'I know who you all are now that
I have both your names and your faces. You have been abroad,
have you not, Ursula? And this is Mistress Atbrigge, your
present gentlewoman companion. We haven't met before but
I had heard, Mistress Atbrigge, that you intended to make a
new marriage though as Ursula has introduced you as Mistress
Atbrigge, you presumably haven't done so.'

Laurence Miller had been busy with his reports, I thought.
Cecil was continuing. 'Master Spelton, of course, I know. You
are a Queen's Messenger and also one of Sir Francis
Walsingham's agents. So, who will begin?'

Christopher took the lead, describing his encounter with
Berend Gomez when both of them were on their way to the
court. At that point, Cecil interrupted him, seeing that Mildred
wanted to take up the tale. She told him of her lightning
romance with Berend, their alarming journey to Brussels, and
then the story of Berend's determination to find the battle plan

and send it to England. And then, with embarrassment and an anger that it was clear she still felt keenly, the way he had used her to make sure that it would get there.

'I pursued her,' I said, as Mildred fell silent. 'I was just behind her when I got to Brussels. There we saw the duke and he gave us a letter for my sister the queen. He would have given it to Berend, I think, except that Berend was no longer trusted. We have it here. We have come to deliver it.'

There was no need to recount the ghastly scene in the inn at Neustad or its aftermath when Nicolas Alvaro, who was a human being after all, even though he was an unpleasant one, was buried in a marsh with only an impromptu prayer to fill his sails as he departed from this world.

Christopher looked at me and I took the scroll out of my hidden pouch and handed it to Cecil.

'This had better go to Her Majesty at once,' Cecil said. 'I will take it to St James' myself. Now, the battle plan. Can I hope to take that too? You have it, Mistress Atbrigge?'

'Here,' said Mildred, taking the hood out of the bag she was carrying. 'My hus . . . Berend stitched it into the lining of this. We have looked at it but put it back and I sewed it up again. There's something else with it, too, about a man who was murdered here in England some while ago.'

She used the word *murdered* quite calmly, as though to her it had become an everyday matter. I listened and was sorry. I had often wanted Mildred to mature but not in that way, not the callous way of the seasoned secret agent.

She had produced her shears and was cutting the stitches inside the hood lining. She drew the papers out and handed them across the desk to Cecil. He studied the battle plan intently for a few moments.

'Defensive,' he said, echoing Christopher. 'Yes, the information we've been getting through other channels is right. Philip doesn't want to fight at sea. He wants to descend on our coasts like a sudden storm, land soldiers and despatch them to seize the city of London and the queen. If he's unlucky and he is challenged at sea, he's ordered his captains to lead our ships into a dangerous position, close the trap and then proceed as he originally intended. So now we know for sure. Good. Now, what is this extra letter . . .?' He turned his attention to Berend's confession. And then turned pale.

Cecil's complexion was naturally pale. His hair and his forked beard were fair, now fading into white, and his eyes were light blue.

Now, before my eyes, I saw him turn from merely pale to chalk-white and the worry line between his brows, which had always been there as far as I could recall, deepened even as I looked at him.

'But this . . .!' he said. 'A man has been condemned for killing Juan Smith! The farmhand who found him. Watkin, his name is. He hasn't any other. He owns a crossbow; crossbows are welcome at his local butts on Sunday afternoons and he is one of the champions; he has won contests. It was enough to condemn him. He is supposed to have killed the man for the purpose of robbery – thinking that a lone man on a good horse was likely to have money on him and might be easy meat. The body wasn't robbed but it's assumed that he heard his workmates, Will and Thomas Thomson, father and son, calling for him and panicked, thinking he hadn't time to search for valuables after all. It was assumed, in fact, that because he is poor, and maybe not so very bright, but good with a crossbow, that he must be guilty.'

He paused, collecting his thoughts. 'I've never been happy about Watkin as the man, nor has Walsingham. It was the inquest jury, all local men, who pointed the finger at him. So he was taken up and tried and condemned. I would have liked to take it further; one of Philip's agents, getting rid of a traitor, was a much more likely perpetrator. Smith was a double agent, one of our own. But once you start exposing agents publicly, you never know where it might lead. We don't like having agents revealed and named in open court. Better leave sleeping dogs alone, Walsingham said. We kept track of events, though; the death of an agent is important. We asked for details of the trial and so forth. We didn't like the verdict but there was no evidence to the contrary. We didn't know Gomez was in the area and if we had, well, he's one of ours just as Smith was. He had no motive. Or so we would have thought. And so it was a private feud and the perpetrator is out of our reach in Parma's dungeons by now. Only . . .'

He raised his head, looking into our faces, one after another. He said: 'If only we had had this information sooner. Poor Watkin is to hang at eight of the clock tomorrow morning!'

'Where?' said Christopher sharply.

'Lincoln.'

Christopher stood up. 'I am a Queen's Messenger and I have the right to use the royal remount service. My horse is tired but if you can start me off on a fresh horse with a reputation for stamina, I can reach Lincoln before morning.'

Cecil was rubbing his head, full of anxiety. 'The confession hasn't been seen by the county sheriff for Lincolnshire, or read by any other council members . . .'

'It will bring the execution to a halt if there's a reprieve with your seal on it, Sir William, and if I have the confession in my hand as well.'

'I'll write the reprieve for you now.' Cecil snatched a sheet of paper from the waiting pile with one hand and with the other, reached for the little bell. He rang it furiously and the butler came at a run.

'I want Hampton Sorrel saddled and waiting in five minutes. Master Spelton will need him. And then a second horse – I am going to St James'. See to it!'

The butler vanished, once more at a run. We heard his receding footsteps. Cecil was writing rapidly. He sanded the document, rolled it and the confession together into a scroll, used one of the candles to melt a blob of wax, sealed it with the ring that was always on his right hand and gave it to Christopher. 'Will you take a mouthful of wine and a meat pasty before you go? You've a long hard road ahead. Are you sure you can find the way?'

'I've ridden it in the past, Sir William. I will have the pasty and wine, though. It might be wise.'

The food and the wine were forthcoming at speed after another fusillade with the bell and we all partook. Christopher, however, gulped the wine and all but swallowed his pasty whole. Then he was on his feet, taking up his cloak and brushing crumbs off his doublet.

'Can you really do it?' Cecil asked. 'Do you really think you can get there in time?'

'It's still only six of the clock. I'll be there by seven tomorrow morning if there aren't any delays at the remount stables. They are always supposed to have a man on duty at night. If any of them haven't, I'll wake them up with a will.'

We all went to see Christopher off. A good-looking chestnut horse was waiting. He swung himself into the saddle, reached down to pull the girth up a notch, made us laugh by burping (the result of gobbling the pasty), and was gone, breaking into a gallop the moment he was out of the gate. We could only call *Godspeed* after him and pray for his success.

Cecil said: 'You had better both stay here tonight. Where's your gear?'

'We left it at the inn where we stabled our horses,' I said.

'I'll send a couple of men to fetch it and your horses as well. Come inside. I must get my riding boots on and set off to St James', but my wife will look after you.'

TWENTY
The Summons

'I got there,' Christopher said. 'Barely in time, but I got there. It was past seven in the morning and the execution was to be at eight! The gibbet was set up and there was a lot of bustle round it already, putting the rope in place, harnessing the horse that was to pull the cart from under the poor fellow, and a crowd was gathering to watch . . . I had a hard time getting anyone to look at what I'd brought, either the confession or the reprieve. I grabbed one of the most earnest organizers by his jacket collar and pushed the papers under his nose and then he said he couldn't read! So I shook him and bawled at him to find someone in authority who could and eventually a constable was fetched and he sent for a magistrate, and I told the magistrate that if he wouldn't attend to the documents I'd brought, I'd get up on the cart with my sword out and defend Watkin to the death. Well, in the end, I got the documents inspected and someone told the executioner not to go any further and somebody else was sent to release Watkin and there were murmurs from the crowd because they were being cheated of their show . . . I was so tired, after riding all night, and it all took so long . . .'

Here, Christopher sat down heavily on to the settle in my little parlour. 'I brought Watkin back with me,' he said. 'Bouncing unhappily in the saddle of the horse I hired for him. Watkin has ridden before but only bareback on farm horses. He didn't want to go back to Master Harman, said there'd be a lot of talk and people nudging each other and looking at him as if they were still wondering about him. Wasn't even sure that Master Harman would take him back, for the same reasons. His own family don't want him back, apparently.

'That's why I brought him home with me. He can be useful

at West Leys. Joan Janes has found him a bed in her cottage.
You've seen her cottage, I expect. If you can call it a cottage.
Extraordinary place – built three generations ago as a two-
room hovel, then the family got bigger, so someone built a
couple of extra rooms on, and then someone else took the roof
off and built another storey and put the roof on again – now
it's that sprawling place out on the northern edge of my six-
acre meadow. It used to make Kate laugh . . .'

He stopped and I saw that he really was utterly worn out.
After that wild ride through the night and the frustrating
struggle to get the unfortunate farmhand released, he had only
rested a day at Lincoln. The next morning, he and Watkin had
started out on what turned out to be a journey of three days,
because it had to be adjusted to Watkin's abilities as a
horseman. He hadn't been fed well in prison and had hardly
slept at all, because he was in such a state of terror. As a
result, he was no longer the strong lad that he used to be.
They had to go to Whitehall first. They had arrived at the end
of the third afternoon, and Christopher had deposited Watkin
at an inn while he made his report to Cecil. Walsingham was
still in his sickbed, apparently. Next morning, he had taken
Watkin to West Leys and handed him over to Joan Janes. Now,
the very next day, he had considerately come to Hawkswood
to tell me what had passed and also to bring Mildred home.

'It was kind of you,' he said, 'to send Mildred over to West
Leys to help out until I could get back from Lincoln.'

'It was best for her to have something to do,' I told him.
'She has been through a bad time and also, I am still so cross
with her . . . well, you can imagine. She was best out of my
sight. Running off like that with a man she hardly knew,
talking nonsense about falling in love – again! – tangling us
all up with secret correspondence and confessions and battle
plans . . .'

'Without Mildred, Berend might never have got either the
plan or the confession to England,' Christopher said. 'Mistress
Atbrigge did well by us and by Watkin. I'm glad my children
have had Mildred during these difficult times. She likes children and she's gentle with them. Joan Janes means well and
I can trust her to feed them and keep them clean and she

knows what to do if they get chicken pox or measles but she's not . . . not quite what Kate would have wanted as her deputy.'

I agreed wholeheartedly with that. I hardly needed to say so. Instead, since because of Christopher's standing as a negotiator as well as an agent, Cecil might have talked to him with some freedom, I said: 'Did you learn anything about the letter from Parma?'

'I waited until the queen had seen the letter, and after that, Sir William Cecil saw me again. I understand that I shall probably have to go back to the Netherlands with the queen's reply and as her representative, to do what we hope will be the final talking. And yes, he did tell me about the contents of the letter. The final talks between me and Parma will be based on it.'

Wilder came in with some Malmsey wine and sliced cheesecake. Christopher rapidly consumed three slices, sank his nose thankfully into his wineglass and then said: 'Parma doesn't want to go to war with us. He knows quite well that the English Catholics have little appetite for a Spanish invasion, for all Pope Pius' encouragement and threats. Given that his terms are met, he will avoid conflict with us.'

He grinned suddenly. 'Cecil told me that Parma has made it clear that he realizes, as perhaps Philip does not, that we, an island nation, are so impervious to outside influences, in fact, so intransigent that even if the queen and all her council were seized by the Spanish, the people of England would remain unmanageable. The idea of turning England Catholic by degrees, as Parma is trying to do with his Netherlanders, wouldn't be likely to work. According to Cecil, the letter actually *says* that. Thank the good Lord that Alvaro didn't get his hands on it.'

His grin widened. 'As for the terms that Parma wants, they include no more intervention in the Netherlands and various favourable trade arrangements, which he has described, and one down-payment – Cecil said that the precise amount still has to be negotiated. The amount that Parma wants is high but Cecil said the trade agreement might perhaps be adjusted if Parma lowers his demands for gold. In the future, the English may have to pay higher prices for blue and white earthenware. When I go back to the Netherlands I'll be carrying Elizabeth's final proposals about all that. But Cecil hopes that her majesty won't haggle too much about the gold. She has an economical turn of mind, but this is too important for cheeseparing.'

I looked at him gratefully. I had missed Brockley during my adventure into the Netherlands, but Christopher was a man of authority and he was permitted to know things that would never be told to Brockley.

'Will you be away often now?' I asked. 'I mean, will you go on acting as a Queen's Messenger – or an agent – now that Kate is gone?'

Christopher ran a pensive finger round the rim of his glass. 'No. I want to give that up,' he said. 'I will make this last journey to Brussels and then stop. I gave it up when I first married Kate, if you remember, but then we had that disastrous harvest and we needed money. So I went back to carrying messages and spying, because it's well paid. But the crops are promising well this year. Unless, God forbid, the Spanish land. Then I must volunteer to fight. I am handy with a sword.'

'I know,' I said, with feeling. 'I have seen a demonstration.'

He dined with us, and then, though still obviously tired, got himself into Jet's saddle and returned to West Leys. He had collected his own horse from Cecil's stable before leaving Whitehall. I decided to be pleasant to Mildred. Christopher had mollified me somewhat by pointing out that her behaviour had led to a good result in the end.

For a while, in fact for a month or so, we had peace. A nervous peace, during which we saw beacons being built on hillsides to the south, and took to watching them anxiously, but peace all the same.

I had of late been worried about Brockley's health, because of the recurring fever he had contracted a couple of years ago. Now, I was relieved to learn that there had been no sign of it while I was away and therefore no sign of it for nearly a year. With luck, he had at last recovered.

On a warm, clear afternoon late in July, Captain Thomas Fleming of the *Golden Hind* saw the approaching sails of the

Armada and sent hurried word to the queen. Two days later, the escort came to fetch me to her.

I was taken to St James' Palace, where the queen was waiting, and we rode fast. Brockley was with us while Dale, who couldn't cope with such fast riding, followed in my small carriage, along with the baggage. It was a clear day, though the sky was hazy with the smoke of the beacons that burned on the hilltops, their flames flickering pallidly in the daylight. England had been warned, from coast to coast and all the way to the Scottish border. The enemy was coming. The captain of our escort remarked that the sky would be clear at sea and Thomas Fleming had been lucky to have such fine weather for sighting the oncoming sails. 'Please God, let our luck hold,' said the captain piously.

Later that day, I was safely delivered to the queen ('like a package of goods, ma'am,' Dale remarked to me when she caught up and we were in my room, unpacking). After that we had nothing to do but wait, the Brockleys at hand, and me, most of the time, beside the queen. Usually, when I attended her, I was a lady of the bedchamber and was private with her only rarely. This time there was no such pretence. I was her sister and with her nearly all the time except that at night we separated and her usual ladies shared her room.

The twelve days following my arrival at St James' were among the longest I have ever known. What they were like for Elizabeth, I hardly like to imagine. I sometimes think that the only thing that kept her heart up during those interminable nights and days was the obliging attitude of our temperamental English weather.

Reports were constantly coming in. Sir Francis Drake was back, and taking charge of things. Before I had arrived at St James', the English ships had moved out to intercept and attack, and as had been clear from the battle plan, the Armada had taken up a defensive position. Our own ships had manoeuvred cautiously; aware that to approach too close might let the Spanish formation close its jaws on them.

That same evening had brought further good news. In fact, when I arrived, I found the queen in reasonable spirits. There had been an explosion on board one of the Spanish vessels, crippling her but not sinking her. English sailors had managed to board her. She was carrying foodstuffs and the sailors had seized as many barrels as possible, including casks of wine, salt beef and beans. More viands for our men and less for the Spanish, a matter for rejoicing.

But after that, for many days the reports were simply of fighting. They arrived regularly, brought by a stream of messengers. The English had been ready, much readier than Philip had expected, and had completely put a stop to any notion of landing Spanish soldiers in a sudden swoop to set them marching on London before our defences could be mustered.

Nor, said one of the messengers gleefully, had there been any sign of a fleet laden with the Duke of Parma's soldiers crossing the North Sea from the Low Countries to descend on East Anglia and sail up the Thames. Philip's commanders had depended on him, and his help wasn't forthcoming.

'He keeps his word!' Elizabeth said. Christopher had made his visit to the duke, and returned to say that terms had finally been settled. Parma would stay out of the invasion. The dragged-out decoy talks in Ostend were over. Our delegates were already home.

Meanwhile, the weather turned wet and often stormy, with fitful, gusty winds, although there were occasional breaks. Once or twice the queen took advantage of clear skies and took us all hunting in the handiest piece of forest: Epping Forest, a lengthy ride to the north-east but a good day in the fresh air. The Armada was reported as trying to approach Portsmouth and the Isle of Wight but failing to do so because a powerful south-west gale had set in and driven them off course. The next news was that they were heading for Calais.

'For France?' Elizabeth said uneasily. It was possible that in Catholic France, they might find a friendly reception.

'They won't land there,' the messenger said reassuringly. 'Our ships have surrounded them. Our fleet can manoeuvre more quickly than theirs. We have better vessels! And now, so I understand, Sir Francis Drake has recommended fireships.'

The fireships were tried. Eight of them were launched at

midnight on Sunday the seventh of August. When we heard the details, Elizabeth was grimly pleased; I saw her father in her then. King Henry the Eighth would, I think, have been pleased in the same savage fashion. The fireships scattered the Armada well and truly and for that I too was thankful and yet, to my own surprise, I had a twinge of pity for the Spaniards. I didn't speak of it to anyone, least of all the queen, but those towering vessels, all aflame, advancing through the darkness, would have terrified the bravest of men, and the moment when a fireship reached a galleon must have been unbelievably horrible.

The sails of the Spanish vessels would be down presumably, but in my imagination I felt how a vessel would judder from the impact, how the fireship, which by contrast would have sails up and all ablaze, would loom over the men on deck, how the heat would scorch them, how the flames would lean in the wind and set the masts burning. Then fire would race over the deck . . . there would be oarsmen, slaves, probably chained to their benches, God help them! Thinking about it made my stomach turn to water.

We heard that after the fireship attack, the wind veered about and during a swing to the south-west, forced the Spanish vessels to run before it, northwards through the North Sea. We heard that some of them, perhaps trying to keep in sight of the coast, followed the Norfolk coast round into the Wash and then, as the erratic wind veered to the north, were trapped by what the latest messenger called standing waves.

'What the devil are standing waves?' Elizabeth demanded.

'Why, Majesty, they happen when the tide is running one way and a strong wind is blowing against it. The waves get trapped between them and they seem to stand, like walls of water. If the Spanish had any notion of trying to land there, they would have been blocked as completely as if the walls of water were walls of stone. Some of their vessels were already badly damaged by the fireships. Being driven on to standing waves could have sent some of them to the bottom and very likely did.'

The wind changed again, back to the south-west, and the remainder of Philip's grand Armada was reported to be racing before it, still further to the north. But report also said that despite the fireships and the unfriendly winds, at least a hundred of the Armada vessels had survived, and were apparently under the command of highly skilled captains. England was still in peril. The army that had been raised to defend our shores in the south might now have to race north to challenge a Spanish attack there. It was currently gathered at Tilbury, a deep-water port on the Thames, under the command of the Earl of Leicester, awaiting further orders.

When the news was brought to her, Elizabeth sat in her study to examine it. I stood behind her, watching her hands, those long-fingered, white hands of which she was so proud, as she read the scroll. I saw her back straighten. Her head came up.

'This is the crucial moment. Our navy and God's good winds have repelled the enemy from Portsmouth and London. But now the danger is racing north, in some disarray, but if the Armada is a wounded hornet, it still has its sting. If they try to land in the north, we must be ready. But before our men march or embark for the north, we must show them that their queen is no timid creature cowering behind City walls, but a strong leader who is with them in deed as well as in words. We must go to Tilbury.'

TWENTY-ONE
The Heart of a King

'Certainly I had something to do with it,' said the Master of the Revels, Sir Edmund Tylney, as the barge slipped downstream along the Thames towards Tilbury. 'Who else would be consulted? I arrange masques, provide costumes and properties when Her Majesty's players put on a performance. I organize processions. I searched the storehouse where I keep my properties and found that silver cuirass that the queen is wearing, and when we get to Tilbury, I understand – I *hope* – that the horse that will be waiting there for her, is something quiet, that won't mind trumpeters. The trumpeters were my idea.'

'They're certainly loud,' I said. We were in the second barge of the procession that was gliding down the Thames towards Tilbury. The queen was in the first, which had Tylney's trumpeters stationed in the bows. Every now and then they sounded a mighty fanfare.

'Did you choose the horse, sir?' I asked. If Brockley had been with us, he might well have asked first as he was interested in all things equine. But I had no attendant. There would be local people at Tilbury to watch but the queen wished her personal contingent to be as small as possible. 'If you want a protective escort, Ursula, which I seriously doubt,' said my royal sister, 'you can have the Master of the Revels on one side of you and Lord Burghley on the other. Walsingham is still too unwell to attend. I would have allowed Christopher Spelton to be present because he has given such admirable service lately, but he wishes to stay at home. He has motherless children to look after.'

He had indeed, and for the moment, Mildred was in no case to help him. He had returned from his final trip to the Netherlands not only with Parma's final agreement to stay out of the conflict but also with the news that Berend Gomez had been found guilty of heresy and would have died at the stake except that at the moment when sentence was passed, he had snatched a phial of poison from his underclothing and swallowed the contents. He had died within hours despite all that the physicians could do. He was brought to trial still in the garments he was wearing when he was arrested. No one had searched him.

Mildred went to West Leys while Christopher was away on that final journey, and on his return, she at once asked for word of Berend. When he told her what had happened, she had been completely overset, weeping with thankfulness that Berend had not been made to die by fire, weeping with relief because she knew she was a free woman now, whether or not her marriage to Berend was legal and also weeping in simple grief for him.

I was still at Hawkswood when Christopher brought her back, and she at once took to her room and stayed in it for nearly a week. I let her have meals taken to her, let her get it all out of her system. She had eventually emerged, and after that, the first storm over, she became very quiet and thoughtful. I was thankful for that. She would have to be the mistress of the house while I was with Elizabeth.

Tylney was answering my question about the queen's horse. 'It was up to the Earl of Essex to decide what the queen should ride. He's the present Master of Horse! I heard that he was thinking of something that would catch the eye, something that would impress the troops – typical of him!'

Sir Edmund raised a well-manicured hand to push an errant lock of white hair back beneath his red velvet cap. 'Leicester was an excellent Master of Horse,' he said, 'but Essex is all magnificent ideas and not much sense of reality. I had a word with him. A fine prancing stallion, all fire and trampling hooves, may be a goodly spectacle, I said, but if the queen were to be thrown, that would be a spectacle of a different sort. He listened to me, God be thanked, and what I expect to find awaiting Her Majesty when we get to Tilbury is a sixteen-year-old white gelding with a nice broad back and all the excitability of a suet pudding. Leicester told me about it, grinning.'

From my other side, Sir William Cecil said: 'We're nearly there.'

We were not part of the official procession, just part of the queen's entourage, following her about or watching from a distance. She was to make an overnight stay so most of her ladies-in-waiting were with her, together with council members and some other dignitaries. We were all to spend the night in a nearby manor house and the queen's ladies would have to maid each other.

When we disembarked from the barges, the next thing was a two-mile walk to West Tilbury, where the soldiers were quartered. Only the queen was mounted. Elizabeth was an impressive spectacle, of course. The promised white gelding had been waiting for her and if the horse itself was a stolid animal that wouldn't have caught anyone's eye on its own, its trappings made it splendid. It needed to be placid, because the trumpeters, marching ahead of her, continued with their fanfare all the way.

It was a windy day with scudding clouds and bursts of sunshine. Once at Tilbury, we were met by a crowd of folk from the nearby village and its manor, although they were being kept back by some slightly harassed guards who didn't want to keep people too far away from the queen they regarded as their own property, but knew they must also insist on a distance that was respectful.

We also found, stretching far across an open space, the encampment where the soldiers were for the moment being accommodated. Some of them had brought womenfolk. Elizabeth at once began to ride about among the tents, leaning down to talk to people, to a woman tending a fire, a soldier cleaning his sword, and to a blushing and anxious new recruit who had to be nudged into his bow by an equally anxious sergeant. Elizabeth laughed, and then they laughed with her.

Her escort for this part of her visit was simple, four gentlemen and two young boys. They were ordinary folk, chosen to represent her people. But they were still an escort, and they took their task seriously. They smiled and bent courteous heads to the people they passed, but all the men were armed.

I think everyone had aching feet by the time that first day was over. The accommodation we had been promised in a local manor house was ready for us (I never did find out whose house it actually was) and there we were given a late dinner and beds. The council members dined with the queen, but the rest of us ate separately and only her bedchamber ladies saw her that evening, although we were all under the same roof.

Next day, the formal part of the excursion took place. It began with a march past and an exhibition of cavalry manoeuvres. The final part of the proceedings, when she was to address her troops, came in the afternoon. Before that, came dinner. The queen and the earls in her retinue dined in a general's tent while everyone else had soup and bread and cheese in the manor house.

That sounds uninspiring but was not. The soup, made of meat and vegetables, was a dinner in itself, and there were two kinds of bread, white manchet and dark rye, and we had a choice of cheeses, including Dutch cheese, in firm golden slices, with a red rind. Its price was probably about to go up. There was wine to go with it, or water if preferred.

Later, we were taken to the place where Elizabeth was to make her speech, to find that the soldiers had been gathered in readiness, rank on rank of them, with their officers trying to keep them in their tidy rows despite their evident desire to press forward for a better view. They were not all professional soldiers; many were men and youths who had left their farms and trades to take up arms against the Armada. Some of them had makeshift weapons like billhooks and pitchforks and from the look of their untidy lines, they had hardly ever been drilled, if at all.

Suddenly and unpleasantly, I recalled witnessing Parma's troops being drilled, being moved about like counters in a game of chess, and charging their targets with drawn swords as though they were going into battle. I could only hope that Parma would go on keeping his word to us.

Elizabeth approached her men in all state. The leader of the procession was the Earl of Ormonde. He was Lord Treasurer of Ireland and had spent much time there, which explained why I had never seen him before. A tall, lean figure of a man, walking proudly, head held high, he was in full armour and he bore the Sword of State, unsheathed, holding it upright before him.

Behind him, came a man leading a charger, a powerful bay stallion, high-stepping and caparisoned in white leather and silver buckles.

'She has to have a warhorse present, even if she isn't sitting on it,' Tylney explained. Elizabeth herself rode behind the charger on her placid white gelding, and if the horse wasn't a striking figure, its rider made up for that. She was magnificent.

Tylney had chosen to present her as the virgin queen, Diana reincarnated. Her gowns were of white velvet and her jewels were pearls and diamonds. 'White jewels only. I insisted,' Tylney remarked to me now. 'I am particular about details.'

She had been spectacular enough on the first day, but this time, the gown was longer, with glittering cloth of silver slash-ings on the sleeves. As on the day before, she wore the silver cuirass rooted out from Sir Edmund Tylney's warehouse. But now she also wore a silver helmet although some of her hair was showing and in it were jewelled clasps, bigger ones than on the day before, and her big drop earrings, also much larger than on the day before, were set with pearls. There were diamonds in her pristine ruff. Whenever the sun came out, she sparkled.

As before, she had her escort of four men and two boys, walking close beside her, but today the Earls of Leicester and Essex, who was actually Leicester's stepson, rode on either side. And her dignity was palpable. No one could have mistaken her for anything other than a queen of a great nation.

Tylney and I followed the procession and found ourselves a good place to stand, not too far from the queen and if only the wind would drop a little, we thought we would be able to hear something of what she said. The front ranks of the soldiers would probably be able to hear as well. The ones behind them would have to be content with looking at her and hearing her voice in the distance.

I know what she said because afterwards, Cecil let me see a copy of the speech she had prepared and had studied for hours during the preparation for the Tilbury visit, so that she would be able to deliver it, if not quite word for word, then nearly.

Ormonde stepped aside as they came close to the soldiers, and the charger too was led aside. Leicester and Essex withdrew a little as well. Elizabeth rode forward to face her troops alone.

I thought how lonely she seemed. She was the queen and therefore the leader of the army awaiting her words. Because of them, she must appear wonderful, gallant, full of optimism and power; the kind of power that can even defeat a Spanish Armada, the kind of power that armies will follow and fight for.

I had not been born to one of King Henry's lawful wives, but I was still his daughter. Just a little change in circumstances and it could have been me, alone out there except for a placid white gelding, looking at what was most of my land army, knowing that even now, there might still be enough soldiers on the surviving Armada vessels to wipe this modest force out completely. Trying to put heart into them while the heart within me quailed and trembled. I have never been more thankful for my bastard origin.

Elizabeth began to speak and the wind, spitefully, grew stronger. She had a carrying voice but I could make out only snatches. I heard her begin, however. She was declaring her trust in them.

My loving people . . . some have warned us against committing ourselves to armed multitudes in case of treachery . . . I will not distrust my . . . faithful people . . . I lost most of the next passage but then she moved the horse a little, probably wanting to give the men a better chance to hear and for a few moments most of her words did reach me . . . *I have resolved to live or die amongst you . . . to lay down for God, for my realm of England and for my people, my honour and my blood . . . I may have the body of . . . feeble woman but I have the heart and stomach of a . . . king of England . . . think it foul scorn . . . any prince of Europe should dare to invade . . . my realm. I myself will take up arms . . .*

The horse moved again and the wind gusted and all the rest was lost but I had heard enough to make me wonder at her, and love her for her courage, the courage that I well knew had needed all her strength. When the soldiers cheered, I cheered too. I longed to be close to her, to offer her company and comfort for that loneliness, except that I wouldn't dare to offer either to that solitary, valiant figure with the silver breastplate. I saw now that she was holding a truncheon; she had used it to gesticulate, to let it be seen that their queen was armed.

She finished, and that was when the cheering broke out. Standing beside me, Tylney said: 'I am told that here we have most, though one hopes not quite all, of England's army. I have heard that Parma's is much bigger and very well trained. If he doesn't keep his word, and his forces succeed in landing, God help England. As for the Armada, its vessels are rumoured to be stuffed full of fighting men. If they once come ashore, then once again, heaven help us. Elizabeth has done all she can. If anything could put heart into an outnumbered force, that speech could. But now we're at the mercy of fate, or the weather.'

TWENTY-TWO
End and Beginning

W e returned soberly to St James' Palace. The sober mood seemed to embrace everyone, for as the exhilaration of that heroic speech and that glittering white and silver figure faded, England remained in deadly peril, and we could do nothing but wait helplessly for news.

St James' was full of a waiting silence. It was as though the very air were listening. For the arrival of messengers? Or for the tramping feet of a Spanish army? No one talked about it. No one talked much at all. I wished I could have stayed at home, in Hawkswood with my own people around me and everyday tasks to perform. There were so many things that I would have liked to see to. Sometimes I recited them in my head.

I really must look for a future steward and a future chief cook; a couple more maids would be a good thing; I hadn't checked the accounts for I couldn't remember how long; and there was Mildred too. I would have to think of a way to counter her propensity for falling in love at five minutes' notice. I couldn't be sure that her recent experiences had cured her of it. A part of me itched to be at home, dealing with all these things, and I had a ridiculous feeling that if I really could go back to them, they would be like a magic spell that would dissolve the Armada out of existence.

Which was of course absurd. If the Spanish landed, then I would be whisked north, taking a route that wasn't likely to encounter any of them and thrown on to the hospitality of young King James of Scotland. If the Spanish prevailed, it would be a long time before I saw Hawkswood again. Perhaps I never would. Sometimes, secretly, at night, I cried. I also kept my saddlebags packed. What must be, must be. Like

Elizabeth herself, I could only await events, and the decision of fate, or God, however one wanted to put it.

News continued to trickle in, not all of it accurate. A rumour that the Armada had made a landing somewhere and that Spanish soldiers were marching on London turned out to be false, but kept us terrified, unable to sleep and hardly able to eat, for three days. Elizabeth practised sitting on a throne in the Presence Chamber, dressed in the same white velvet gown she had worn at Tilbury, with a crown on her head and the Sword of State across her knees, making a speech of dignified greeting to her conquerors. When she recited that speech, everyone around her trembled for she made it sound so real.

But the next news was better. The Armada still existed but the capricious wind had now settled down to the business of chasing the ships north. There had been a landing in Scotland but not a dangerous one. A ship had been wrecked there and the men on board were now marooned on the shore, at the mercy of the inhabitants.

'They'll be massacred for sure,' Sir William Cecil said. He wasn't staying at the palace, but visited us often and was there when the messenger rode in with the news.

It turned out eventually that the Scottish inhabitants had indeed cut down a few Spanish sailors but that others, because they were wet, frightened and unable to understand anything that was said to them (even the ones who knew some English couldn't make sense of the Scottish speech), had inspired pity. They'd been taken in and looked after by compassionate families. We never knew what finally happened to them. For all I know there are now Scottish households where the father is a Spaniard and the children have dark hair and olive complexions.

We heard next that what had become a remnant of the Armada had rounded Scotland and was making its way south. It was limping from damage caused by our cannon and by the fireships earlier on. News came in of further wrecks, along the western coast of England, and on Irish shores as well. Some of the ships had taken a course round the west of Ireland. The remnant fleet showed no sign of trying to resume any kind of formation; no indication that it intended to round

Cornwall and once more try to attack Portsmouth. Nor would the obliging wind have helped them. It had now made another useful swing and was blowing them south and west; to get to Portsmouth they would have had to fight it and they were not doing so.

Nor was there the slightest sign of Parma.

'I think,' said Elizabeth at last, holding up the latest scroll of news, 'that it's over. The survivors are making for home. God has declared for us. The death of Mary Stuart will not be avenged by Philip of Spain. In the eyes of the Almighty, it was lawful.'

That time, Cecil was not there when the scroll arrived, but he came to St James' later that day. He rejoiced with the rest of us and came with us to the chapel that adjoins the palace, where the queen had commanded a service of thanksgiving to be held immediately. I chanced to be side by side with him as the service began and he said to me that when the euphoria was over the queen's treasury would be a sorry sight. We had beaten down Parma's desire for gold to some extent but there was still a mighty gift of sovereigns to be sent to the duke without delay. 'The price of England, more or less,' Cecil said ruefully.

'It kept us out of Philip's hands,' I said. 'Let us not complain of that.'

'The queen has an economical turn of mind,' said Cecil. 'She'll mourn for those sovereigns.'

When the service was over and along with the Brockleys I had returned to my apartment, Dale said: 'Is it really finished, ma'am? Will we go home soon?'

'As soon as I can possibly arrange it,' I told her.

It took time, though. The queen was reluctant to release me. 'You have been beside me all this time,' she said, 'and you have been ready to give up everything for me, your home, all your life in England. Now, I would like you to share in the rejoicing.'

I therefore attended a succession of fine dinners, church services, dramatic performances, displays of dancing and acrobatics from players, tumblers and musicians somehow collected from all over the realm. The series seemed unending. I enjoyed them, naturally. But Hawkswood was calling to me, troubling my dreams. Then, at last, on the first day of September, I was granted my wish. I was private with the queen just before I left and for one short moment she let herself be my sister, like any other sister, and embraced me.

When the Brockleys and I arrived at Hawkswood, we were welcomed as though we had personally routed the Armada. There was laughter and some tears too, of joy and relief at our escape. The good news had of course reached Hawkswood, a good fortnight ago. Ben Flood had gone to Guildford, to collect our regular order of candles and buy fresh supplies of flour, and came back saying that a crier had been walking the streets to announce that what was left of the defeated Armada was making its way back to Spain. 'We all wept with relief,' Wilder said to me.

Next day I had to eat yet another fine dinner. My cook John Hawthorn always seized a chance to create one, and Ben Flood had a real gift for thinking up unusual dishes.

After that, I settled down to work. The accounts came first, but there was nothing amiss. Throughout all the political storms, Hawkswood had gone quietly on, rearing its sheep and cattle and growing its crops. There were plenty of fish in the lake that my late husband Hugh had created and stocked and we had a good crop of wheat that would soon be ready for harvesting. Laurence Miller had sold four young, trained trotters at a satisfactory price. All was well.

Then, after all that, I had to consider Mildred. She no longer visited West Leys now that Christopher was home. During my absence, she had helped Wilder to run my household and now that I had returned, she continued to be helpful. She also continued to be very quiet, and I had no idea what she was thinking. Sometimes, though, she talked about the children at West Leys.

'I often wonder how they are getting on. I taught Susanna and Christina the alphabet but they need to practise reading regularly. They really ought to have a governess – and a tutor later on. I hope that's going to happen.

'I hope there hasn't been any more trouble over feeding

the baby Elizabeth. Mary Bright's milk dried up and we couldn't find another wet-nurse and cows' milk was no use, even if we watered it down. She just threw it up. Then somebody thought of goats' milk. I had to go to four different farms looking for a goat and in the end I was directed to Brentvale village and to a widow there who keeps hens and goats and makes her living from eggs and goat's cheese and what produce she can raise from her vegetable patch and her redcurrant bushes and an apple tree. Poor soul, I gathered that in autumn she harvests the apples herself, climbing a ladder and getting into the branches, only she's beginning to be afraid that she won't be able to go on doing it and her apples will go to waste unless a neighbour helps her. She rears goats for sale, and she was quite willing to sell this one. It had had a kid which died, but its milk was still there. I rode home leading the goat and believe me,' said Mildred with feeling, *'it didn't want to leave its flock. I didn't so much lead it as tow it all the way back to West Leys. But the milk suited the baby so it was worth it.*

'I do hope that Master Spelton is keeping that woman Joan Janes in order. She slaps the children sometimes and Susanna is afraid of her. Susanna's a timid child. None of Joan's children are timid! There are two of her daughters at West Leys, as maidservants. Joan slaps them too but they don't seem to care and when she shouts at them, they shout back.'

Mildred wasn't drawing a very agreeable picture of life at West Leys. I remembered the days when Kate was there, running an orderly household, with a big, friendly kitchen at its heart, where anyone who called was instantly welcomed and offered wine or cider and Kate's latest savoury pies or slices of honey-cake, topped with marchpane.

Towards the end of September, I told Brockley to saddle Jaunty and I rode over to West Leys on my own. Jaunty was taken off by the groom Jimmy, doing his job efficiently as before. But the moment I stepped inside the house, I sensed trouble. The baby was crying loudly somewhere and from the kitchen came sounds of a loud altercation. The maidservant who let me in noticed my disapproving expression and said brightly that that were her sister Cat getting what for from our Ma. 'Let summat burn, I expect. Cat's that careless; it's forever happening.'

'Where is Master Spelton?' I asked, raising my voice to overtop Joan Janes. If she had given that speech at Tilbury, everyone would have heard it, right to the back of the ranks.

'He be out in the fields.'

'I need to see him. Go and fetch him, or send someone.'

'I'll have to ask Ma . . .'

'I'll ask her,' I said, and marched into the kitchen, causing the wrangling to stop. Joan Janes I recognized at once. Cat, who I had not seen before, was a sturdy lass in a temper and with the scarlet sign of a slap on one cheek. While the two of them stared at me, I repeated my request for someone to find Christopher. Fortunately, however, he came in while I was still talking. He was dressed for farm work, in a sleeveless jerkin over an old shirt, well-worn breeches and stout boots caked with mud. He started to welcome me and to ask after everyone at Hawkswood but I cut him short. 'I need to talk to you privately,' I said. 'Can we use your parlour?'

'I hardly ever use it. It probably hasn't been dusted today . . .'

'That I can believe,' I said. 'The parlour will do.'

It certainly hadn't been dusted but I ignored Christopher's apologies and sat down uninvited. He then sat down as well. 'Ursula, what is it?'

'We know each other well enough to get to the point without polite ditherings,' I said. 'This suggestion may startle you but I would like you to think about it, at least. Christopher, do you think that you could consider marrying again, even though it's so soon? I mean for the sake of the children, and with the hope of more children in due time.'

He showed no sign of being startled. Instead, he said: 'I am ahead of you, I think. Mildred?'

'Mildred,' I agreed.

'I'm not in love with her,' said Christopher frankly. 'Nor she with me.'

'If Mildred falls in love again, I shall drown myself in the Hawkswood lake! I think . . .'

This time, I had startled him. 'That's one of the saltiest remarks I ever heard a lady make!' he said.

'Harry's father nicknamed me Saltspoon,' I said. 'I dare say I haven't changed much.' It occurred to me, secretly, that it was a good thing I hadn't married Christopher. He was as likeable a man as I had ever met, but as partners for life, we were not really suited. However, there was no need to say so. 'I was going to say that Mildred is good with children and I think she is missing yours.'

'You want to make someone else be responsible for her?'

'Frankly, yes, I do.'

'I've thought about this already, you know. She was very good with my little girls and I think she ought to have some children of her own. It's a shame she lost that one. And,' said Christopher thoughtfully, 'I think she needs stability. Neither of her marriages exactly gave her that, did they? Yet I think it's precisely what she wants. She may not know it herself, but I am fairly sure it's true.' He ruminated. Then he said: 'Have you told her you were coming here to talk matchmaking with me?'

'No. I'll leave you to do your own courting. But when I first came into the house, I mean just now, there was a mighty uproar in the kitchen, with Joan Janes bellowing and that girl Cat bellowing back and Joan had obviously hit her. And the baby was crying somewhere – she's stopped now but when I arrived, no one seemed to be doing anything about it. This house needs a competent mistress.'

'And Mildred would be that?'

'She ran a home when she was a vicar's wife. She takes my place at Hawkswood when I'm away. And think how she helped to look after things when Kate . . . when poor Kate died. Mildred knows the work of a household, as long as you take your time over showing her how to deal with the accounts, and don't ask her to help with the lambing. She's nervous of account books and lambing would terrify her.'

'I can do my own accounts. I would probably show her how they work but I wouldn't let them worry her. Nor will I ask her to help with the lambing. I have an excellent shepherd, with two young sons who are both now old enough to be useful assistants. And,' said Christopher thoughtfully, 'she is good at cooking the solid, simple food I like best.'

'Oh yes, when her parents tried to marry her off to the man she refused, he said he wanted her to learn new recipes and that scared her as well. She was brought up in a Puritan house where the food was always plain.'

'That will suit me perfectly.' Christopher's nice brown eyes were smiling. 'I think,' he said, 'that I should change these working clothes for something more elegant and come back to Hawkswood with you now.'

I agreed, smiling, and wondering what Gladys would have to say about it. If Mildred were to marry Christopher, then Gladys would assuredly claim that *that* was the wedding ring the scrying bowl had foreseen for her. And oh, how she would cackle.